famine

ALSO BY TODD KOMARNICKI

FREE

famine

TODD KOMARNICKI

ARCADE PUBLISHING O NEW YORK

FIRST EDITION

This novel is a work of fiction. Any references to real people, events, establishments, organizations, or locales are intended only to give the fiction a sense of reality and authenticity. All names, characters, places, and incidents are either the product of the author's imagination or are used fictitiously.

Library of Congress Cataloging-in-Publication Data

Komarnicki, Todd
    Famine / by Todd Komarnicki. —1st ed.
        p.   cm.
    ISBN 1-55970-365-2 (hardcover)
    I. Title
    PS3561.O4523F36 1997
    813'.54—dc21   96-44313

Published in the United States by Arcade Publishing, Inc.
Distributed by Little, Brown and Company

10 9 8 7 6 5 4 3 2 1

BP

PRINTED IN THE UNITED STATES OF AMERICA

For my precious sisters,
Robyn Lynn Hubbard & Kristyn Anna Komarnicki,
with endless gratitude

ACKNOWLEDGMENTS

Ruth Gruber and Michael Brunn, for giving me a place to hide away and write.

J. Marshall Cobe, for having such a generous spirit, and being the F. Scott Fitzgerald of friends.

Sean McDonald, my editor, for his insights and courage.

To my agents: Ginger Barber for her faithful support; Alyson Becker, my passport to the world; Jay Mandel, the king of hip-hop; and especially Jennifer Rudolph Walsh, for the kind of friendship and dedication authors dream about.

And to my parents, Marigrace & George Komarnicki, my deepest thanks. There are no words.

T. A. K.

famine

1. Things that we need. Milk. Salt. Bread. Corpse holding the list is early thirties. Rigor mortis, the devil's arthritis, has subject nearly in motion. Arching for something just out of reach.

No stench. Detective appreciates this. Corpse has been waiting for him three days, patiently, body preserved from within. Twenty-two empty bottles of Bushmill's Irish whiskey provide the proof.

Detective moves to corpse shyly, as if a beautiful woman has asked him to dance. Places two fingers tenderly on the carotid, the back of his hand hot against forehead. Stiff is in a double bed, elbows hard into mattress, back bowed ten inches. Detective eyes the third-world circumference of the dead white man, the belly swollen with the granite of hunger. Bubble begins below the breastbone, swallowing everything down to the loins. Ribs hidden, belly button inside out. No exit wound, no damage. All the blood drying behind the skin.

Call came in this morning, shy of ten. Detective found it connected to a string of go-sees, dead bodies like relatives in need of a visit. This is the last. Then home to wife and the son he's afraid of.

But this is not a homicide. File and forget. Time to go home, eat what this sonofabitch neglected to. Make a joke about a Macy's Thanksgiving Day float to the Coroner. Steal a few books to take home to wife. Stop for a bottle of Bushmill's to scratch the itch that keeps moving.

Detective is forty-four, quiet, lips thin from lack of use. Chin weighted, pulling his gaze down. Eyes colorless save bloodshot static and vacant black pupils. His hair is boy-thick, embarrasses him. He wishes for baldness, an oblivion, and he has the gait of twenty years in bad shoes. Detective is sorry, but not really, and he relies on days where nothing makes sense.

Mothers murder children. Priests rob banks. Wrists slit. Bombs shred. This comforts him. The chaos. He needs it. Keeps him above the believers, the ones who call 911, seeking answers. A tourniquet. Someone to stop the blood. And he comes by, whispers to widows, takes down statements like recipes, all the time calmed by new evidence of the random. He is a satisfied man.

"Malnutrition." Coroner whistles in Detective's ear. "Acute starvation."

"No," Detective disbelieves. "Food poisoning."

"I can slice this fish from nape to nails we won't find a taste. Discoloration at the neck and jawline. This body hasn't chewed for weeks. Months."

The murder groupies gather. Low rank, the ones who bully onlookers and wrap crime scenes in yellow ribbon, as if the dead might return. Cameras, notepads, shameless eyes take notice of the exquisite corpse. Beautiful in the arc of his pain. Detective will wait. Hide in the bathroom. He still has something to say.

Late. Closer to eleven than ten and no call home. Detective opens the door, finds a lamp blindly, knocking things over. Things of no use. Corpse is still, waiting. Detective opens his hunting knife, a gift for trips not yet taken with his son. The knife is friendly and heavy, and from ten feet away, the dead man begs for an attack. A lunge, a plunge to wake it up, shake it alive. Detective moves to it, the thrill of the hunt a flavor on his tongue, and he knows why he has stayed.

A young man has starved to death in his own apartment in New York City. Not Harlem or Washington Heights, but a brownstone, windows onto Gramercy Park. And this corpse has been waiting. Patiently. For Detective to arrive. To make the Coroner's cut. To find the morsel, the poison, the chaos that stretched young skin so tight. It will bring Detective comfort to pop the balloon, set all the vapors dancing. Intoxicate him, send him home woozy, convinced. Something killed here. There was a murder. This is not an accident, and he is here to report that fact. It is Detective's only chance.

But before the dagger, a greeting. From the doorway a form, more outline than identity. "I knew you'd come."

2. Snow. I was newly fourteen, and there was an early November snow. Wet, like rain only not. On any similar day, had it been rain, I would have stayed inside, watched cartoons, snacked, napped. I wouldn't have pulled on my new boots, flipped off the TV at the last possible second, and corralled my four-year-old brother to play. In the snow.

Warren had been born ten years and seven days too late to be my twin, but he remained pinned to my side from the moment he could walk, eavesdropping on my life, trying to keep up. I was his teacher, coach, and confidant. When nightmares or thunder robbed his sleep, it was my bed he tunneled into, not Mom and Dad's. Our tiniest soldier, he needed someone close to the ground to count on. And my parents seemed somehow relieved to pass his raising on to me.

My two eldest sisters were far from home that wet-snow November afternoon. One married. One being schooled. Nina, my final sibling, was in her room sewing her senior-prom dress so a boy from Harvard would have something to help her out of on the momentous night. She was silent but for the pianissimo of the Singer pedal and her unconscious humming of "The Wedding March." My father was in the city, cursing his way through traffic after having let himself out early again. Most days he stopped at

P. J. Clark's before he hit the bridge but not that afternoon. The rain and snow had joined. A black ice formed beneath all our feet.

My mother was in the kitchen, rushing Warren and me out the door. There was the white smell of potatoes and soap. Though we lived in a too big house with yard enough to hide in, as I nudged my little brother out into the stinging hour before dark I felt that we were poor. Desperately poor. That no meal was safe. Even dinner felt threatened. Mother shut us out, shivering, then locked the door.

Warren and I were set adrift. The house and everything inside its protective walls were sucked into a hungry past. Spikes of snow closed my eyes, and I knew, out there in the yard, on the driveway, survival was slippery. I wanted to cry out. For Mom to let us back in. To be four and as overdressed as Warren, knocking on the back door. Please. It's too cold. Let us in. I didn't. I was raising Warren. I had to protect him from my fear.

In the yard we assembled a sloppy snowman, soaking our fingers. I rolled Warren down a small hill at his repeated request until his face was white with whiskers and his green eyes shone, new marbles. The day gave in, finding us numb and far from home. I hoisted him onto my shoulders, the house receding before my eyes. "We should go in," I said, not moving.

"No."

"You always say no."

"Sometimes I say yes." Warren's stuffed nose stealing his vowels.

"One skate around?" I asked, and the cheer came through, joined by several celebratory blows to my head.

"Told you I said yes," he gloated.

"One skate around, then in."

"I love you," Warren announced from his perch.

"I love you so much more."

The basketball court on our driveway was next to the garage and hadn't been salted since the cold snap. It was slick enough to skid around on the way socks worked on the hardwood floor inside the house. For a skate around I would take Warren by the hand and simply drag him behind me as I zipped in circles as fast as I could. This, of course, left him in hysterics. It was a consistent way to make him laugh, get him to go to bed, eat his vegetables, whatever. Skate arounds were a guarantee.

"Don't put me down," he ordered, locking his hands under my chin.

"How can I pull you if . . ."

"Too cold. From up here." His nails dug in.

"Okay, but this won't be as fun," I warned. "And hang on." He knocked on my head to acknowledge, and off we pushed. At first I skated carefully, my new boots extra nervous on the ice, the snow pouncing down harder.

"Faster." I picked up a little speed, our house now almost invisible on the far coast of the first fourteen years of my life. I leaned into it and could hear Warren yelp with delight. Faster, then faster, hoping that wherever I was headed would appear and make losing home not so unbearable. Hang on, I said to myself. You're almost there. Hang on. "Hang on, Warren, here we go."

But he didn't. He threw his arms up to say yes, to say thank you, to howl at the beauty of being four with wind and snow and fresh tears all at once, and for his gratitude gravity threw him to earth.

For a second I imagined covering his body up with snow right there on the frozen court. He had been mine to raise. No one loved him more. But as a line of blood interrupted his perfect face, I could not move. And we waited for Dad to come home.

3. He sets down the knife. Lays it on the spherical stomach of the corpse. The outline in the door is of a woman, not thirty, lovely as she closes the gap, a sleeping baby in her arms. "You found him. You finally found him." Her voice is the sound Detective hears when the volume is off. He asks her to repeat, though he heard every word. "I've been waiting for you." The baby kicks.

"I'm investigating," Detective tries, ashamed of the knife. Of his presence.

"He is dead."

Detective takes this badly, hidden things crossing his face. "I was going to wake him."

"Too late," she hums.

"I should go home," he says, a caught schoolboy. But he wants to stay, hold the woman, the child, anything warm. He takes off his jacket and covers the corpse, his knife. "I am sorry."

Woman turns, her back a seal on all that he has known. "We've been waiting so long." An infant joy, and they are gone.

Detective finds a blanket and pillow, calls his wife. He is alone in an odorless room. He will not be home tonight. Neither will his son. Outside the snow rains. He pockets his knife, afraid of the blade, puts his hands on the chill cool of a belly unfed. Waits.

He is alone. With a corpse. In an odorless room.

4. Nina stayed by the nurses' station, pretending to be with other people. Dad barked instructions at a succession of cheery doctors. They'd enter Warren's ICU room three at a time, giftless Magi, and adore the babe, lying there, wrapped in bandages. Their voices fluttered high against the walls, drowning the beeps of the heart and brain monitors. Each doctor determined to be more hopeful, fly higher, till all any of us could see was open sky. No walls, no curtains. No borders. Only hope for us. For Mom and her blood-bitten lip. Hope for Nina, who'd be able to finish that prom dress. For Dad, because he demanded there be hope, expected to be billed for it. For my two eldest sisters, who'd been spared the ordeal, and of course hope for me. Because I was the youngest child. Again.

Warren's eyes rested in the hammock of his skull. His minia-ture body pinned and separated by tubes shooting him full of not enough. Mom grabbed my hair from behind, her fingertips prickly cold against my scalp. She gripped tight, so she wouldn't fall over. Nina came in, and, with the doctors banished, the four of us said good-bye to Warren, without anyone opening their mouth.

I didn't feel guilty. Guilt would have been bliss. If I had been guilty, I could have paid. But, now I owed nothing, could offer nothing. I was as unnecessary as Warren's heart once his brain banged off. We drove home, waited for my sisters. The phone rang. People visited. Nina sewed Warren a suit. He could have grown into it. Everyone kept very busy, and forgot about me. I had been excised, a tumor in the story of this little boy's death. The standard answer became "He was playing in the yard." They took him from my shoulders. They stole my dizzy circles, the clotting snow, Warren's hands raised in praise. They plucked him from the air and left him dead, alone, on the earth. He was mine to raise. He was theirs to bury.

Two days after Warren's death, I was sent back to school. "You're missing Friday for the funeral," my mother said, as if it were all vacation time. The day was a haze, kids bumping past me, crashing me into lockers and opened doors. I sleepwalked through a series of lectures and quizzes, finding myself at the chalkboard during Algebra.

The teacher came up to me after all the other kids had sat down. My problem remained, what does X equal? "Are you all right?" she asked, my mouth open, chalk dry.

"Yes."

"Did you do the homework?"

"I know the answer."

"Then go ahead. We don't have all day."

"No, we don't," I agreed, and started writing as she backed away. It wasn't until I returned to my seat that the classroom murmurs drew the teacher's attention back to the board. There were nine problems in various states of completion, but mine certainly had the strongest answer. I KILLED MY LITTLE BROTHER, it said after X equals. It was a relief to tell people, though no one seemed to understand. Students near me stopped their nervous laughter and moved closer to the door. The teacher thought it was sick teenage-boy humor until I handed her Warren's wrinkled obituary. "I'm fourteen," I told her as she led me to the Principal's office. "What's fourteen minus four?"

They held me for an hour in the Principal's office because there was no one to pick me up. Nina was with Mom at the funeral home, Dad was at work, and the two eldest were slow to arrive back in Rye. I finally convinced them I was calm enough to go home, promising to visit the school psychologist the following week. I was excused again, no one willing to give me the blame.

On my way home I bought three cans of spray paint from a hardware store. "Fixing my brother's wagon," I reported, unable to laugh at my own joke. It was less than a mile to Midland Elementary School, and I walked around back, children's heads visible through classroom windows. A gym class finished up, gathering their equipment and fleeing the wet November afternoon. Some snow announced itself and I shivered into my work.

The paint was stubborn in the cold and my arms grew tired after the first word. DANIEL. It was my name, but it looked funny in dripping black letters on the schoolhouse brick. Not like a name at all, but a word I'd never seen before, would have to learn to pronounce. The rest came easier, the sentence finished just before the tykes raced to their buses and parents' cars, oblivious. DANIEL KNOWS WHO DID IT, my message dried. If they wouldn't let me confess, they would at least have to honor my memory. They would not steal this death from me. It was all of Warren I had left.

At home no one was surprised at my paint-stained entrance. The wind had blown blue and black back onto my white oxford, and my hands were dark from where I'd fingered in my initials. Nina and Mother were excitedly discussing coffins. They talked of the bargain they'd gotten, how pleased Dad would be. "Not a lot of children die in Rye," I said from the kitchen door, temporarily noticed. "Those little coffins are hard to sell."

"What happened to you?" Nina sniped.

"Got kicked out of school."

"For what?"

"Figuring out what X equals." They shooed me away, a fly at

their picnic, and left me alone to ponder. I considered spray painting the entire living room with my decree, but I knew there would be painters there by morning, and I was tired of strangers. Instead I went to my room and asked Joe Namath. With black streaks under his eyes, his Jet arm poised to toss another perfect spiral, Broadway Joe seemed full of wisdom. I talked to him almost until dinner, discussing where Warren had flown to, and the best strategy for avoiding the blitz. His focus never strayed. Two hours we spoke, and he didn't look away. I thanked him for his attention, and headed downstairs.

Dad was home, grimly determined to be pleasant, calm, funny. All the things he was not. There was a blur of potatoes, beans, beef. Water spilled from their hurried hands and clinking glasses. Thirty minutes later, I was alone at the table, plate still full. Dad turned the television up to block his thoughts. Nina hummed along with her Singer. Mom washed dishes till the squeak hurt. "Cut that out," my father yelled, scooting closer to the set.

I crushed a potato with my hand, stored the vegetables in my pants pocket, and threw my dried-out chunk of roast beef at the television. Dad picked it up and held it till a commercial, refusing to look my way. "I'm not hungry," I decided. "Ever again."

They made me look. The open casket, the little red head trapped in Nina's oversized funeral suit, and the coffin a suitcase, ready for travel. "I did that," I told the minister as I walked by my former brother. Mom pinched me till the skin broke.

The eulogy discussed the death as pure accident. Strange spirits had stolen Warren from his bed. An unnamed disease that claimed one child a century had snuck into our precious town. He had been struck by lightning, trapped beneath an avalanche. He had reached the far edge of his life and there was nothing any of us could do. I stood up to correct the misinformed pastor, but got yanked into place by several adult hands. "He's wrong," I offered.

"Shhh."

Outside, the chill was a relief. I hit a car with a snowball. It was ours. Occasionally a strong hand would squeeze my shoulder, or muss my hair. I was consoled in this rough fashion till the parking lot was empty, a party atmosphere promised back at the house. Turning to get in for the ride home, there was a flash of yellow. A wave. It was the only color I saw all day, but my parents stole me, slamming every door.

"What was his name?" I said into the back of my father's neck. Mom turned up the radio.

"Who?" came exhausted.

"The one at the church. The boy they're burying."

"Warren," Dad answered automatically, then turned on me, his face black with grief and rage.

"Not him," I challenged. "The other one. The brother." The brakes screamed. We were at the head of a caravan, and the followers screeched and spun to a halt. My mother turned red, her ears aflame. Nina muttered something against me, and Dad was silent, his hands strong enough to break a neck. He waited. Waited for me to get out and walk across someone else's manicured lawn, enter their house, and leave him in peace. My hand was on the lock when he pinned the accelerator. My possible escape receded over dull suburban hills, and this strange new family, one without room for sons, took me home.

5. Detective is home. Park Slope, Brooklyn. Morning. In their bedroom, wife sleeps somehow. Son's room is void. The cat. "I thought we had a cat," Detective says, waking his wife, the cat appearing, as cats do.

He doesn't want to talk, sorry he woke her. Doesn't recognize her until after she showers anyway. This scares him, living with a stranger who exits the bathroom disguised as his wife. He wonders when the disarray began. Wife digs her way back to sleep. Detective bathes and shaves in the dark.

The house is new. He bought after a five-grand bump and his wife whining about all the screaming Italians in Carroll Gardens. It is quieter here. Less tension. Less pride. People live nearby, but it is an island. A man could die and not be discovered for days.

The fridge: baking soda, onions, salsa, Pepto-Bismol. He needs a list. "I'm going shopping," wife says from the doorway, but he isn't hungry. "I'm concerned about the boy." Her hair is kindling, he wants a match.

"I'm on a case. Doing interviews all day," Detective announces. A tingling nausea maneuvers in, and then he wants to say, I love you. He doesn't.

His wife's face slowly finds its shape. Flat brow, pretty nose, bruises for lips. "The boy."

"Benjamin," Detective bites off his son's name, spits it out, "thinks he still lives in Carroll Gardens."

"He's fourteen."

"Give him time. It's not like he's on the street." Detective doesn't miss having his son around, is afraid of his angles, his wordless demands.

"I'm scared with the boys over on Hoyt, and the talk. Isn't right for a cop's son . . ."

Detective erases the space between them in three strides. Then a kiss, a push. He brushes her sticks of hair with the back of his hand. Has no idea who she is.

Back at corpse's house, Detective can unwind. Body's gone, elbow imprints its final autograph. Bed looks comfortable. Detective tries it. No photo albums, diaries, signs of life. No records. No ID. A visit to the woman who put in the call. Landlady. Apartment in back.

"Not noisy, no. But such that if there was no activity, I call." She is a sturdy woman, old New York, with pewter hair. "Ellen," she introduces herself.

"Not important." Detective takes notes, his thrice-broken right hand slowing the pace.

"You need a right-hand man," Ellen quips. Cold air comes from her mouth. She could change the weather. "I've lived here thirty-two years, come January, never saw a nicer boy."

"Said he was noisy."

"Active." Ellen chooses her words precisely. "He brought over the unfortunates."

"Unfortunates?"

"He kept it all well . . . contained. Hell of a tuna casserole. Paid in cash. Which is nice."

"Cash? Are you referring to some type of crimi—"

"Heavens, no, Detective. Detective . . . ?" She stands on tiptoes to get personal.

"Go on," he says.

"He fed the hungry." A well opens in Detective's stomach. His waistband tightens. Breath sneaks in and out. "Let them clean up. Stay. Some stayed awhile."

Detective wants to ask Ellen more questions. Whether corpse has any enemies. Strange behavior. If family ever drops by, the usuals, but a staggering hunger takes his balance. He wants to lie down. "One last question," he manages.

"Are you all right?" Ellen's face stretches into a sliver of moon. Her mouth drops to the floor. Detective is afraid.

"A woman" are his words. "Woman with child."

"Do come in." Ellen tugs on Detective's sleeve. Needing her for equilibrium, he follows. Pinks and greens swirl from wallpaper and carpet. She runs her fingers through his hair. A beret of wet snow circles his crown. Her touch calms him. Her lap is a cradle. He need only lie back. "You look familiar." Such tenderness. New.

"Was he married?" he sputters, still vertical.

"Do you like Verdi? What kind of tea?"

"There is a homicide. No time for tea and ballet."

"Opera," she corrects.

"Please!" His outbreak steadies him. He senses his surroundings. Plastic upholstery, garish decorations, fake African sculptures. "Ellen. Tell me." He needs her on his side so he can leave and quell this miserable desire. As if he hasn't eaten in weeks. His body is eager, nothing to digest but itself.

"No. Not married," she surrenders.

"Children?"

"I don't know."

"Next of kin?"

"Couldn't say."

"Ellen, why did you call the police?"

"I had to. He needed . . ."

Detective stands by the door, a harpoon of hunger sunk thick into his belly. "There was a woman with a child in his apartment last night," and as he says it, the oddity strikes him. How had she gotten in?

"There were women. And children." Ellen paws for cigarettes she no longer smokes. "He took care, you see. It's what he did."

Detective's legs wobble. Vision flickers. He cannot find a chair.

6. There was always a seat in the cafeteria. My Algebra stunt had brought a specific infamy and I walked the halls alone. I had entered Rye Public High School as a freshman after having attended Catholic school through the eighth grade. Most of my friends continued on to Sacred Heart, but my parents wanted us exposed to God for only so many years. Otherwise we might start expecting something from him. So after just two months at the public school, I had dubbed myself dangerous, and my new classmates had no intention of discovering otherwise. Once, a fat boy approached, his friends in the background, and said, "For real?"

"Boo!" I puffed, eyes wide, sending him jiggling for cover. Not eating and my decision to match my parents' attempts to make me invisible had me appearing a bit scary. By spring, I was too sickly to participate in gym, watching from the bleachers as my peers ran and kicked and fought. They were on the other side of the glass, one of us stuck in the zoo.

Sometimes Nina would try to introduce me to her least cool friends, but my pallor always left an instant impression on their face. They backed away from my thinness as if it were contagious, took chocolate bars with them to class. "Dying won't do it," Nina confronted me near the end of my freshman year. "It's like you're already gone."

"I know who did it."

"Stop it, Daniel."

"Okay." I was too weak to argue. Nina was right. My starvation plan was getting constant gawks at school, but not a stir in the house. Dad hadn't looked at me since the day of the funeral. And Mother's gaze was most commonly fixed on the bottom of a glass.

The summer before my fifteenth birthday I decided to eat. Mom noticed mostly that there was less in the house, the need to shop oddly increased. She would shake empty cereal boxes, flummoxed, and write long lists in hopes of catching up.

With breadth came height. I stretched to equal my hunger, hitting five feet ten and 160 pounds by the start of my sophomore year. I returned to Rye High School, a stranger to my classmates. Strong, taller, not so afraid to smile. People wondered who the new sophomore was. A few girls asked me to the Halloween dance, not believing I was the same boy.

Nina had gotten into Harvard, and I began paying attention in class. A year of pathetic grades had put me in a hole, and I took an extra class over lunch hour, eating sandwiches I made myself while boning up on Biology. I quickly learned what I had done to my body, what I'd denied it, and marveled at its resiliency. I was hungry for knowledge, proof. Things I could write down and explain. I was putting edges on all my empty space, filling everything up to the borders, hoping it would make a life.

I stopped visiting Warren's grave. Pretending seemed to be working for everybody else, so I decided to give it a try. I rolled up my Joe Namath poster and hid it under the bed.

At home I planned on being the good son. I announced every entrance and exit. Shared remarkable report cards with my parents. Called Nina, who was never in and never called back. I prowled the catwalk of my improvement, displaying hard arms, a honed intellect. I was something to be proud of. All they had to do was look.

"Hey, Dad."

"Hmmm? Ask your mother."

"A Christmas tree," I said, jacket already on. "I thought we could go pick one out. Together."

He had just come home, the day dark on his brow. He looked at me for a second. Who is this strange boy? flashing across his face. "No."

"Are you too tired? It's just that it's already the twentieth, and we usually . . ."

"No one's here," he said, eyeing his shining shoes, hoping his next line would reflect up to him. "Nina's going to Vermont with some goddamn graduate student. And your sisters . . ." He tailed off.

"There's still the three of us, Dad," my face ripe with a fragile joy. "You, Mom, and me."

"No one's here," as he shrugged off his coat and shouted after my mother in the kitchen. He'd left my report card unread. Never mentioned the shine of my face, the strength of my grip. He couldn't see me.

Mom ended her happy hour grimly, spitting ice cubes into the sink. She spoke to him about Nina, his work, how the groceries kept getting used up. "Not me," he swore, patting his nerve-thin belly.

"I'm going for a Christmas tree," I announced. They looked at me as if I'd threatened to burn down the house.

I took my time, spying for the thickest and tallest tree our house had ever seen. Something to represent me, confirm my existence. The choice was blue with promise, and with the help of a worker, I had it tied to the roof. It wasn't until I heard the siren that I remembered that I was only fifteen. I traded the keys for handcuffs, and was driven away, my beautiful tree rootless and forgotten.

Dad gifted me with a night in jail, a little lesson. Mom bailed me out in the morning, after eleven, her face drawn like shades.

"You are only fifteen," she reminded herself. We drove home slowly, stopping for groceries I no longer had the hunger to eat.

Inside, I didn't need to look in the living room to know there wasn't a tree. I waited till I was halfway up the steps before turning to announce, "There is no one here." Mother stared at me, the tiniest tremble in her chin. Then she turned and poured herself a drink.

It wasn't difficult to hide. I heard the janitor kill the mosquito buzz of the last fluorescent light just before six. From the end of a darkened hall, I watched him lock me in. It was the night before Easter vacation, and I had been planning the event for weeks. There were no PTA meetings to dodge. No team practices to avoid. The building was mine.

I entered the art room first because it had the most toys. Paint, clay, brushes, glue. I took my time laying out all my materials, careful not to ransack the cupboards, gathering all I needed on one long table. I chose acrylics for their quick drying, grabbed enough brushes, and headed for the gym.

The basketball court was easy, lines marking what was out of bounds and what was free. Though alone, it seemed hundreds were cheering as I spelled out my message over and over. My sneakers squeaked with hurry. I wasn't afraid of getting caught. Just of getting caught before I was done. I needed a ladder to paint the backboards, strokes of color filling up the Plexiglas, blocking the light.

I refilled to do the locker rooms, showers dripping, percussion to my silent symphony. In the girls' lockers my heart tapped more insistently, forbidden shapes and aromas sneaking up on me. I sat on a bench wondering what strange country I'd stumbled into.

For fun, I turned the halls into rinks of paint, sliding headfirst from one end of the school to the other. The sweet colors mixed on my body and tongue, satisfying a hunger long forgotten.

In Biology, I freed frogs from formaldehyde swimming pools and unpinned butterflies, crushed chalk underfoot and tore up ungraded tests.

The library had its own lock, so literature was spared my anxious hands. I filled the Social Studies chalkboards with the same message I'd left in the gym. It seemed more specific, so small and white. Easier to read, but also easier to erase.

In the nurse's office I spelled it out with cotton balls and tongue depressors. In the typing room, I banged it once onto every ribbon. With a small brush, I painted it into corners and on glass doors. With a roller, I spread it across the principal's window. It was nearly eleven when I jumped in the pool to get clean, and then opened a fire door, setting off the alarm.

I could hear the sirens as I walked home. The night was gentle, blossoms dabbing the air. I inhaled, sensing the exact shape of my lungs, weighing the oxygen, tasting it.

I entered the house and my bedroom, Mom throwing me a goodnight like a punch. I closed my eyes, convinced of my victory, my presence. Relieved that my message would be read.

It took two days for the local paper to catch up. There was a photograph of a fireman, a smear of paint across his back, where he had fallen. VANDALS MAR EASTER. That was it. No article, no details, no credit. And the plural, when they knew there had only been one. My message had been obvious, every nook and cranny bearing my signature. Personal graffiti. Daniel, I had painted, written, sung. Daniel. And still.

"Mom."

Nothing.

"Mom. Mom. Mom. Mom." I called her quietly up from the kitchen with my chain of sound. Eventually it would reach her. "Mom."

"Stop it." She opened my door to find me sitting cross-legged on the bed. She was liquor dull, leaning on the jamb for balance, unable to look at me.

"Mom."

"Leave me alone."

"I do," I said, seeing her rotate and walk away. "Mom." She stopped against her will, ice protesting in the glass. "I have to go away."

She kept her back to me, refusing to see the rise of my bones, the quilt of my flesh. I was made of balsa wood and thin glue. I would need help getting in the car. "I'll call your sister."

The grass was too green. And in the hallways, no one looked at me. Those administering care spoke in hurried tones, but their movements were calm, their bodies not fooled by their voices. They dug holes in my skin to put air back in my balloon. I felt tiny as Warren, people buzzing above me, flies unwilling to land. They stung me on each arm and on my hand, escaping before I could swat them.

"I bet you're hungry," one said from the doorway, a clipboard blocking his identity. "You just rest now. We're going to do the work."

"My sister." My throat buckled, crushing the last syllable.

"Everybody went home."

1983. My peers were graduating from high school while I was resting. Everyone else seemed to have so much extra energy. Rolling over was a chore in the ward. The fatigue could put me to sleep with my eyes open. So tired I didn't know I was tired. The nurses would find me this way, wake me, then put me back to bed.

The daily cavalcade of pharmaceuticals went a long way in providing the state of dysphoria. Elavil at 8 A.M., Sinequan at noon. Librium by 3:30, back to easy E around 7. Ten P.M., and a nightcap of Amoxapine to flatten my dreams.

Emma was in the hospital with me. She was seventeen, too, and didn't mind if I didn't talk. Emma was homemade: beautiful to those who knew her, invisible to the rest of the world. She had a way to saturate her surroundings, disappearing, leaving only an outline. I had to convince myself of her voice, it was so quiet. Her eyes were chalked over, a tiny nose, and the mouth always open.

"Why are you here?" I asked two weeks after I'd been moved to her ward. I needed her to stay. To not get well. "How long will you stay?"

"I'm tired," I barely heard.

"You're here because you're tired, or you're tired because . . ."

"Tired," she said, padding down her corridor, soundlessly.

I began to follow her. Not to pester or even to speak with her. Just to be near. She was a half-revealed secret, a wise man's final words. Necessary, and I couldn't help but chase her down.

"You follow," she told me one lazy morning.

"Sorry."

"I don't mind." She made her way to breakfast, her pace an invitation.

"My name is . . ."

"I know who you are. You must know my name." I leaned to test the delicacy of her language.

"Yes. Emma."

"Hold my hand." We shuffled to breakfast, a prematurely old couple. I couldn't believe we were touching. I took her scent in and hid it away for future intoxication. "You should eat today."

"Okay," I relented, a small hunger nicking my sunken frame. I was a soldier awaiting further instructions.

"Don't follow me anymore," Emma explained. "Stay close."

❦ ❦ ❦

There was a narcotic fade to our hours together. We would meet after therapy or group, making a picnic out of stolen food and fresh bed sheets. We didn't need words, and we kept our borders sacred. It was enough to share space. To listen to her oval breathing, watch her hands quiver when the dosage gave way.

"Emma."

"Daniel," just to remind each other that we were still alive. She was my only good news, and it kept my belly full.

After three months, I asked Nina to sew her a dress, guessing at Emma's size. It was too small.

"For my daughter," Emma thanked me.

"You have a little girl?"

"I will. And she will wear this dress." There was no guile in her. I understood these things would happen. She took my hand, turned soft by exhaustion and regret, and squeezed the blood out. It turned white, nearly bone, the color of her face. "At night I hang my wrist over the edge of the bed and pretend I can fill the room with whatever's inside. And when I float to the top, with my cheek cool against the ceiling, I swallow what I've given and sink back to sleep."

"I know," I said. "I can hear you."

Everyone in the world had forgotten us, so we made our gestures grand, our predictions epic. Her mouth found my neck and opened.

"Whatever comes, you have to promise me." This was the closest I'd ever been to a girl. Her damage. Her impossibility. My skin memorized. "You will take care of me. And Sophie."

"Your little girl."

"Promise?"

There seemed in her tone a chance that I could say no. But I didn't remember how, so I dedicated my life to saving two, to make up for one. "I do."

After my vow, I built us a fort in an abandoned supply room, made of towels, stretchers, gauze and medical tape. We had a place to rest together. Once we kissed, but we were so tired all we wanted was somewhere warm to lay our heads. She let me trace on her stomach where Sophie would grow. Told me the games we would play, how much laughter would be born. In all the strange whiteness of that place and our blank hideaway, the words came out in great strands of color, rising and spilling at our feet. Crazy alphabets of indigo and sunflower, hunter and gold. It was all hope in our forgotten temple deep in the heart of fatigue and lonely. We were going to keep each other awake long enough to find a way out of the white.

7. The police station is no place for a child. When Sophie cries, officers, lawyers, criminals remind Emma what the police station is no place for. After a bit, the noise lulls Sophie somewhere between whimpering and sleep. She dangles there, peeps of sadness sneaking out every few minutes.

Emma will recognize him, the asphalt stare, heavy, trembling chin. The bold arm he nearly used to puncture the corpse. She'll recall the aroma of a man in the wrong place. Nervous. Like garlic. And the flat-paint scent of wondering. She is also certain Detective will remember. The baby girl. The voltage of getting caught. Those things stay with a man.

"I've been looking for you," Detective enters saying, trying to turn the tables, failing. This woman, with the silent voice and sleeping daughter, has him. They both know this. The charade won't play. "It would help if I had your name. For your friend." Another cop lie. Emma rises.

"I don't think you're ready."

"Wait, wait, okay," he fidgets, searches. "I don't know the . . . there seems to be a different vocabulary at work here." She takes his effort as hospitality, and stays. "Maybe you think I'm some . . ."

"You don't know what I think," Emma tells him. Sophie is humming in rhythm with the phones.

"Facts." Like a schoolboy with a dictionary, Detective pulls out his notebook to cheat his way through. "A Caucasian male. Dead in his bed. For days. Unorthodox final pose, forgive the poetic license, reaching, calling out. . . . I mean I'm running a homicide investigation."

"You spent the night," Emma reminds him, Sophie like a sleeping owl on her shoulder. "Now there's work to be done."

Shivers, a cramp. He wants to pace, but cannot. He is riveted to the spot. "Help me."

"You want his name. His friends' names. Addresses, résumés, school records, family histories."

"Yes."

"You're looking in the wrong direction. It's not about him, Detective. It's about you."

She's at the door too soon. He asks, "Can you . . . will you help me?"

"Who are you?" is her response, but he pretends he didn't hear the whispered question.

He pulls his sore ear and wishes he were bald. He is afraid of his son and that if he stands too close to his wife he will burst into flames. Emma turns the knob as he rushes, "Where can I find you?"

Emma laughs. Sophie laughs. Great rainbow laughs that stripe the room and light their way out. "There are others" is the thought she leaves behind. "When you're ready, we'll be around." Detective sees Emma and child eclipsed by the daily mayhem of the precinct. For a moment he is comforted. "There are others," he hears again. Outside, it can't quite snow.

Detective stops at Sloan's. Wife is at home unloading groceries. Their son helping. Son has a six-inch gash stitched closed he refuses to discuss, but he is home. This feels good. Wife will surprise husband with dinner and son and conditioned hair, familiar face. Nothing is different. Except the Detective stopping at Sloan's.

"Do you have gift wrapping?"

"Sir?" the stock boy answers.

"Gift wrapping," Detective repeats. "I'd like to buy a gift for a woman. And a child."

"Sir, this is Sloan's you're in. Grocery store." Detective knows this, knew it when he came in. Knew it when he asked.

Ninety minutes. Twenty-one bags. The stockboys are still carrying it up Detective's stairs into his house, where his wife and son have finished dinner and have nowhere to go.

"Put the rest down there, really, thanks." Detective hands over an exact tip and closes his family in. There are bags keeping watch in the hallway, living room, on the TV, at the foot of the bed.

"Hope you didn't buy ice cream," son says, changing rooms.

"I promised to do the shopping." Her washed hair can't steal his focus.

"What's with the eye?" Detective barks, chasing son through the house, then out the back door, a French salute his good-bye, leaving Detective stranded with wife and twenty-one bags. "I just wanted. To see his eye."

He explains while they're stacking the seventy cans of soup and twenty-five bottles of olive oil that you can never have enough. What with snowstorms and blackouts and thought he'd save her some time and seeing as how he was there . . . and he talks this way to her, like a shop-class teacher explaining car ignition, for all twenty-one bags, until his mouth is hinged with dry saliva and his wife is afraid and weary. It's early, but they go to bed because there's nothing left to say. She expects him to be gone by morning. She is right. Detective falls asleep, a foolish bliss on his face. His mania has kept him safe through this part of the tremor. Tomorrow the famine begins.

8. "Hungry?"

"Good morning, Mom."

"Nina sent some goodies. I escaped with a few left." Mom handed me a plastic bag of oatmeal-raisin cookies. They showed the strain of the long postal trip from Boston. Crushed raisins and crumbs filled one corner of the bag. My appetite shut down. "You look good," she said with sudden surprise. She did too. Clever makeup hid her birthday, and two sticks of gum gave her an air of sobriety.

"I've been eating."

"Dr. Kleiner says you're making a move." It was true. I had reached the point where the drugs had diminished and my desire had raised its feeble head. I felt ready to go. Not home, but somewhere. I just couldn't bear to leave Emma behind. "We discussed a release date."

"Don't," I complained, "discuss me."

"Don't you want to come home?" then shifting quickly, "Start over. Maybe school."

I tiptoed across the wire of crazy, trying to play both sides. "That thing at the high school. I did it."

"I know."

"But . . ."

"They called the next morning," she explained. "There were paint footprints on the front steps. Your father paid."

"Does he know," I asked, amazed at being caught, "that he has another son?"

Mom reached for the cookies, as if I deserved to be punished for my impudence. I opened the bag and ate one, the sugar electric on my tongue. "Come home," she said, standing. "There's room."

"Can I bring someone along?"

"She must have a family," she countered, knowing I was dreaming of Emma. "She'll be fine." But it wasn't Emma I was worried about.

"Soon, Mom." We bumped into a good-bye, and I snuck the cookies back into her pocketbook.

They discovered our mini-hotel one week before my discharge. Actually, I tipped them off. I didn't want Emma to rendezvous with anyone else, so I took away the nest. I hoped it would be my last selfish act toward her.

When I told her my release date she said, "Oh, yes. They're asking for me now, too." As if we'd evaded the draft board and finally would be shuffled into the crossfire. "I hope you have a dreadful time," and "You mustn't forget Sophie and me. You are bound by sacred laws."

"I'll visit."

"No," she decreed. "I won't be here."

"I mean your house. Out there."

"No."

"They're making me go." I was willing to build another fort, dig a tunnel beneath the hospital, shape an underground castle with my bare hands.

"This is only the beginning. You won't get away." She kissed my forehead, sending curious light deep within. She was setting up house and had just claimed the land. I left her, knowing what boomerangs always do.

My mother picked me up eleven months to the day since I'd been put to sleep. I was eighteen, knowing I'd been gone, but expecting everything to be the same. The car smelled of visits, little jaunts from here to there. I'd forgotten how big the world was. The drive home was like the crossing of the Alps. I kept quiet at all my wonder for fear she'd think me crazier than before. "Wow, look at that fat lady." "I've never seen that color car before." "Pull over, there's a Burger King!" All these exclamations of unbridled enthusiasm I rolled into one-word answers to Mom's timid questions. Even then, I sounded too happy.

"Are you tired?" Mom asked.

"No!" I couldn't believe it. Not tired!

"Dad's coming home in time for supper."

"Great!"

"Tuna casserole." Her eyes on the road, she was desperate to check the map of my face for directions. "Caught the tuna myself," she added gracefully.

"Perfect. I trapped a wild casserole by the North Gate." My joke was fine, but it was immediately apparent that any mention of the hospital was against the rules. I would be allowed no happy anecdotes, no petty complaints. It was a fever the whole family had survived and it was not to be roused. As far as they were concerned, it had never happened.

"I met a girl."

"You say this every time," Mom clipped.

"Do you remember her name?"

"Don't be ridiculous." The one visible vein in her neck tripped and stuttered. The car felt heavy. Slow.

"Emma," I mumbled, "and I'm sorry. For being ridiculous."

"Starting this thing off right," she told herself, and me and any passing stranger. It was a proclamation. A voodoo sentence to ward off the past, order the future, and somehow help us through the present. She was a different woman than the one who'd visited me in the hospital. Meaner. She had me on her turf again, and the rules were new. Gone was the antiseptic timidity, replaced by a bawdy courage, a foolish strength. She was trying her hand at being brave.

We ate dinner without Dad. I knew he was late on purpose, hoping to find me asleep when he finally trudged in well past ten. I was in the kitchen, digging at leftovers, not quite ready to go to the confines of my room. Mom kept switching records every few songs. Tony Bennett. Doris Day. Rod McKuen. "A Man Alone." That one came off with a fresh scratch in the vinyl.

Dad grumbled his greeting like a threat, and went straight upstairs. I found him in his T-shirt and suit pants, shuffling papers madly, looking for a winning hand.

"Hey, Dad."

"Hey, there," he answered, not looking up. "Goddamnit if I can't find that report. Good to have you home."

"Camp was great," I said. "Thanks for all the postcards."

"You're welcome," obliviously. But I wasn't welcome. I'd broken into his life. When he picked up the phone, I expected him to dial 911. "Be with you in a minute. I can't believe I . . . Alison? It's me. Shitty to bother you at home like this." I left him nervous on the phone, amazed at how successfully he had ignored me. I sneaked to my room, slightly in awe.

At midnight, unable to sleep, I slid into the den. Dad was watching programs flip by, testing his hand-eye coordination. "I learned that the eye processes information a thousand times faster than the brain. That's why you can keep flipping. Your brain eventually catches up. Tells you what you missed."

"Yeah," Dad said. He'd gotten uglier. Weight and pallor leaning him to the wrong side of the spectrum. Too much green and yellow. Not enough blood. "Well, it sure is good to have you home."

"I met a girl," I rescued him.

"No," he decided.

"Emma."

"Never liked that name. Sounds like a grandmother." He had a punishing grin.

"She is. Eighty-five. I like them mature."

Slowly, "Huh-oh, there you go. Keep on my toes with this one around," he explained to himself.

"Emma. She's getting out soon. I think you'll like her. I know you'll like her." I wanted him to hold my face to feel how good it felt to talk about her.

"Getting out. What is she, in prison?" Laugh. Stupid and mean.

"The hospital."

He sat up and glared at me, his compassion undressed. "I think we've got to have a moratorium on that kind of talk. Your mother's upset as it is."

"Her name is Emma."

"You're home now, and I know you're strong. Let's keep it that way. I believe in . . . Who's the one who didn't visit? Because I knew you'd come home. Hungry?" He left the room to escape himself, handing me the remote. I looked at the television, flipping channels, always watching and waiting. Waiting for my brain to catch up.

On the day that I'd checked out of River Glen, Dr. Kleiner had said he had great hope for me. But then he kept it all with him. He kept Emma. I was having trouble navigating the rugged terrain of our house. I devised a flawed system of avoidance, kept a schedule of my father's expected arrivals. Listened for sounds, warnings, taking all precaution to escape hallway meetings, or dinnertime gatherings.

Dad worked later and later, doing his part to sustain our truce. Mom continued buying Wrigley's in a vain attempt to veil her ferment.

As an outpatient, I was encouraged to gain employment, but my lack of experience and my former address conspired to leave me jobless. As I exited a pharmacy after being told they weren't hiring, a teenage clerk warned the owner, "That's the guy that killed his little brother."

"I heard it was an accident."

"So?" I closed the door, grinning, ecstatic to have been recognized, relieved to have been blamed at last.

I visited the high school to apologize for my former re-decorating job. Familiar faces pushed past me, anxious to arrive in their futures. My former schoolmates were graduating, leaving things behind. I envied their clarity. In the principal's office, secretaries received my name like sour medicine and clutched their purses.

"I'm over that," I offered. "Don't be afraid."

"Come on in," the principal invited. "I'm really under the gun, though, Daniel. What can I do you for?" His toupee matched the color of his suit perfectly. He looked like a slice of chocolate cake.

"I'm sorry," I said.

"Pardon?"

"That's all. Just wanted to apologize."

"For what?" He pressed his thumb to the bridge of his nose, adjusting glasses he wasn't wearing.

"Making such a mess. The paint and all."

"Oh, that," he mused, as if I'd shot a spitball in class. "All forgotten. All in the past."

"Oh."

"No need to apologize. Things happen. Got to move on." The principal stood too quickly, banging a shin, his face blooming red, but still smiling. "Hate to do this, Sport, but I'm about a year and a half late for a staff meeting." He didn't wait, but bumped past me out into the hall. "Hang in there," he said, a cat on his bulletin board advising the same.

"Sorry," I told the tense squad of secretaries. They grinned badly. "Thanks for remembering. Can I have a pencil?" Two of them jabbed new ones my direction. I took the one with the Rye High School Garnet mascot emblazoned. "Proof," I explained, and left them embarrassed and afraid.

At Warren's grave, I used the eraser end to carve my name in the dirt. There were fresh violets and lilies strewn across the base of the stone. It wasn't clear whether they'd been left for my brother or blown from another site. I collected them into one bouquet and propped them up, covering our last name. "I remember," I managed, the words strange in my mouth. "I remember, Warren." I swallowed, everything crooked in my throat. "I miss you," waiting, as if for a response. The sound of my name. "I love you."

"I love you so much more." I heard it, the voice more familiar than my own. But I didn't need to turn around to know I was alone.

Four weeks, then a shout from the stairs. "Emma." Not, "Telephone call, son," or "Hey, phone for you, pal!" Just the name. Emma. It hadn't been spoken in the house since the first night. Emma.

It was early afternoon, a blue-white sky that tricked the eye. I stretched the phone cord so I could sit out on the back porch. My stockinged feet were no match for the cold wood and I did a slow Indian dance to keep warm. "Emma?"

"You sound tired." Her voice was the vapor coming out of my own mouth. The words smoked and swirled and disappeared.

"I was napping," I confessed. My daily maintenance doses of

Elavil plus the alternatives of television and dodging room to room to avoid conversations made me a sleepy boy. "Are you free?"

"I'm at the train station. Waiting for you. Say good-bye. Our train leaves in . . ." I was already in the house, phone hung up before I heard our departure time. Upstairs, I jammed random clothes into the nearest bag. My pulse sliced beneath the skin. How amazing it felt to be in a hurry. From my father's drawers, some boxers, socks, things he should have given me for Christmas. And a tie from the closet. Brown, with golden noodles of color. It seemed like directions home. Just in case.

Keys in my hand, standing at the door, I remembered I couldn't take the car. That would be crazy. "Mom, I need a ride."

"Not now, honey. I'm watching."

I palmed my refilled medication and tried to sound sleepy again. "It's just that my prescription ran out, and I'm feeling sort of, you know."

"Damn it," as she huffed in from the other room. "You're all flushed. Red as a rose." She put her cheek to my fever, her perfume like booze.

"Could we go?" I handed her the keys. "I'll tell you in the car."

"What's with the bag?" We stopped. Adjusted to the sound of each other's voices.

"I'm sorry."

"It's okay. What's with the bag?" We were stuck there, Emma on the train conductor's lap, pulling away with only a beauty-pageant wave.

"In the car." She gave in. She had an idea by now, and was trying it on.

In the car, talk radio blaring, and we drove. "Where are we actually going?" she requested.

"The train station."

"Tell me about Emma." Less contempt.

"I don't need drugs, so we can drive straight there, and Emma is great. You'd really like her."

"Is she pretty? Not that it matters." Mom's shoulders fell an inch, a white flag.

"Yes, yes. Very. And the way she talks . . ."

"You're going to her parents' house? She's not some gray-haired nut, seduced my son?" The question ticker-taped out of her slack mouth, running in long rail lines down her front, crashing at her shoes.

"I know how to get home, Mom. And I know the number. I'm eighteen. You don't have to look out for me."

"Never did." We were near, and the train into the city was pulling in, loading up. We were near enough to see it pull away. "You were the one with the invisible leash. It always pulled you back in safe, so we just stopped watching." Her eyes were stones, but there were tears swelling up her knuckles, bumping in her wrists, banging down her throat. She was stuffed with tears, sick with them.

"I'm sorry about Warren."

She squared to me, hands still on the wheel, and finally said my name.

9. Detective gets an apartment. A portrait of a pig decorates the building on First and First. Inside, it is cell small, but clean. One long room, like an ironing board, with twelve-foot ceilings, excellent for stacking. He brings no pictures, music, books, memories. He is new, mole blind, but seeing. He moves with purpose, measuring, calculating. Outside: traffic, trucks, sirens, his colleagues in a rush, trapped, hemmed in. But not Detective. He is liquid, filling in corners, splashing on the walls. Baptizing this place for what will come. He goes shopping.

Nothing from the Polish bakery. No fresh vegetables. He seeks nonperishables. Canned goods. Food with a future. At Key Food on A, he backs his unmarked into the loading area, his badge excusing his behavior. He is throwing his weight around. He has a bunker to fill.

Lentils. Chickpeas. Carrots. The cans stack precisely. Living room, floor to ceiling, wall to wall in the bedroom. He will sleep on his NYPD bedroll. More room for turnips, pineapples in their own juice, baked beans. Distilled water. Four to a crate, each on the other's shoulders up to where the paint peels from the landlord-controlled heat.

It is 1 P.M. Delicate, dangerous snow. He has three murder

scenes waiting, and a woman and child to find. He showers, shaves, sleeps for twenty minutes. Now he is ready to devour.

First scene: bullets, blood, old news. There's nothing left here but clues to the past. Detective needs clues to the future. Leaves. Underlings call after him. His hair is thick today. Proud. He smooths it as he walks past the horror.

Second go-see is similar. Knives maybe. Listens long enough to hear heroin and Hispanic. Exit. Senses a widening behind his eyes, can see sideways. Nothing will sneak up on him today. He didn't choose this, but it is liberating. He wants to tell someone.

She is waiting by the crisscross of police tape at the third site. "Don't go in," she tells him. He obeys. She is carrying the child in a papoose, and the baby plays with her mother's beads.

"Like before?" he asks, knowing.

"Yes." The baby rattles.

"What is your name?" She tells him. "Emma," he repeats. It is a name to be hummed, savored. It has a flavor he remembers.

"And Sophie." Sophie turns and gurgles. The flash of white and gold shuts Detective's eyes.

"You were waiting for me," he hopes.

"Everyone is."

10. Emma tapped on the window. She was holding a stuffed toy bunny with long ears covering its eyes. It was new, the price tag still hanging on like a scarf around the rabbit's neck.

"That's Emma."

Mom looked at her an instant then back at me. "You missed your train."

"There's another."

"She is pretty."

We parked and took Emma and rabbit into a teashop on Purchase Street. "Are you in love?" Mom asked between sips. I banged my teeth on my cup.

"No," Emma stated.

"It's all a little Romeo and Juliet, isn't it? The train, the call from the hospital grounds." She was trying to sound casually mean, but Emma was so calm she needed no defense.

"I've been out for weeks."

"You said you'd call," I hurried.

"I had to wait for the right time." Emma handed me the stuffed rabbit, and with a tiny gesture spun the price tag around to reveal three words: "I love you." I stared at her, my face transparent, bright blue with gratitude and relief. But she knew. And she knew she'd see that face again, so she never took her eyes off my mother and never stopped sipping her tea.

"I didn't mean to be snippy," Mom deadpanned.

"It's okay," Emma said. "It doesn't matter."

From the train window, Mom looked one-dimensional, like the design patterns Nina cut out for her dresses. Maybe one day she might make a good mother. The hour ride into the city I only smiled. Emma parceled out information about the apartment she'd found for us and how it was small, but so were we really. How the rabbit was a sign and that the minute she'd seen it she knew she loved me. I never needed a rabbit. I knew the first time I heard her voice without needing my ears, but now she'd gotten inside where nothing belonged. She was slipping past gates and wires, digging trenches, nailing up scaffolds, swinging from pipes. She was swimming my canals till I was drunk with the perfume of her. Addicted.

Our apartment was in the East Village. On the corner of First Avenue and First Street, long, and narrow as a doctor's mind, with a pig on the outside of the building. Traffic rattled the windows. There was no bed, so we fashioned a fort as of old. Towels, sweatshirts, enough to cushion our new fatigue. It wasn't the sterile exhaustion of prescriptions under our tongues. We were tired from feeling good, using muscles long atrophied.

We made love slowly, Emma talking the whole time, but not words. I could hear her ancient, endless sentence wrap around my neck and back and legs to rock me into place. Naked, she was tiny, without the strength to stand. She stretched full out upon me, drawing mercury and light, draining me. Sated, she lit up from within, her heart beating aqua, lungs sulfur, skin invisible. She was a woman in reverse, all senses to the world. She would need protection.

"It doesn't matter," I said.

"Of course." She was beside me, still humming, glowing. She looked like dusk.

"I mean right now. Nothing matters."

"Daniel," she called. "I will need you. We will need you."

"Emma," I said, knowing I'd never learned how to hang on.

11. Inside everyone is. Waiting for Detective. There is a path cleared, plowed for his arrival. They see a different man. A ravenous man. He forgets to keep an eye on the woman and child. He knows he needs them, but this new attention is charming. He eases into it, testing it against every set of eyes. Colleagues defer. Strangers seek counsel. He is in demand. His hair, thick. Shoes fit. There is a leanness, a hunger about him. He looks put together. Flap A, slot B. He is the only one in motion. His chin, lighter, nods on its own, signaling his arrival, acknowledging the respect.

In the pink-bubble-gum bathroom, face covered, belly swollen, waits another body. "What do you think?" Detective asks a Sergeant, luring him in.

"Pretty fucking weird." The Sarge has gray hairs spackling his twenty-six-year-old hair. He keeps trying to back out. Detective maneuvers in the doorway.

"Not exactly Murray Hill," Detective says. "More like an Alphabet City corpse."

"He's all swelled up."

"That's what happens. When you forget to eat." Detective pulls out his hunting knife, clears the room, save the Sarge. "I'm going to show you something." Detective's knife pops into the dead man just below the sternum.

"Shouldn't we wait for the coroner?!" Sarge puts one hand on cool tile, one on his own throat.

"Just a little science experiment, Officer." Detective yanks down on the knife like a slot-machine arm, splitting a seam through the globed abdominal wall, stopping at the belly button. Exclamation point. "Give me a hand." The Sergeant doesn't move. Detective grabs the Sergeant's hand and pins it to the corpse. "Hold him down," he barks. "I'm not sure what's going to jump out of here." Detective peels the belly wide. Nothing. Certainly fluid. Pink, gray, black blood, and the malodorous complaint of torn tissue. Sergeant leaves the Detective with his knuckles deep into death, kneading clues.

"Go on home, Detective," Coroner grumbles, not upset, more sad. No answer. "You're leaving me a hell of a mess to explain." Coroner's whiskers itch. He wants to be at the movies. He's getting ready to call in some help. Embarrass Detective. "Hey. You've got your hands in my pie."

"Clues, Doc," Detective says, still fingering ribs, tickling the pancreas. "Connecting two, at least two murders. Police work."

Coroner kneels onto the mean tile. His knee burns. "Suspension. Arrest. Jail." Detective's hands stop moving inside the treasure chest. "Now wash up, Detective. Go home and do your police work tomorrow. And get your hand off my fucking heart." Two smiles and the sound of hands escaping wet sand. "Hair looks good. You cut it?" Coroner examines as Detective washes viscera from under his nails.

"There is a connection. I have a toe tag with matching p.d. Stomachs like medicine balls. Like the kids on the news. In Somalia and Africa." He reaches for a towel, then dries them on his pants. "I have a witness. Or a suspect. Something."

"Check with the officer in charge because this call came in straight eight MI. No monkey business. Just a busted valve." Detective lifts the towel off the corpse's face. It belongs to a seventy-year-old Bernard, call him Bernie, with a diamond-shaped age spot below his bewildered eye. "The Mrs. is going to punish us this time. This is Murray Hill, Detective. They don't believe in scars."

Detective goes to Milano's. It is 4 P.M. A row of disciplined drinkers. He orders a Dewar's and quarters for the jukebox. "Takes dollars," the paddy bartender lilts. "I see you're a man of the cloth."

"No," Detective returns. He wants to wash his hands again. He can smell Bernie's last supper.

"From your badge, Officer," paddy explains, acknowledging it on the bar, by the wallet. "You're from the finer pasture of Ire as well. Detective . . ."

"Bell," Detective finishes. "Detective Bell."

"Got a first name?"

"Only if I owe you money."

"That you do. Four for the Dewar's. And shame on you for drinking Scotland's piss."

"Shame on you for selling it." Detective Bell inhales his spirits and slides the glass. "Bushmill's. And I'll need a clean glass."

In the single sink, Bell wrings his hands of Bernie and his weak heart. "She lied," he mentions, then turns to fill the afternoon with Frank and Nat and Glen. "She lied."

Bushmill's on a treadmill and he's drunk before five.

"Off duty," barkeep teases.

"Now I am." He's not Irish, and his blood knows it, absorbing the whiskey poorly. His mother's third husband was a Bell. It was short. He stole it.

He is alone in this downtown bar, but even empty it is cramped. The room a vein, splintered with stools and bow-legged tables in the back. Walls glossy with snapshots of legendary drunks, moonlighters, lost tourists. Above the liquor a Sinatra shrine, crowded with cracking bumper stickers. Ethnic pride. Alcoholic boasts. It is just past five. Laughing people are entering. His last song fades to hiss. He's intoxicated. Wears the cologne of another man's journey between his fingers. His wife is packing, his son fighting, stitches torn like wrapping paper. Yet all that matters to Detective Bell is that Emma lied.

He is terribly hungry. There is a vintage poster tacked to the wall he is leaning on, yellow and torn at the nearest edge. The picture is a woman grinning hard. A wartime widow canning food at home. "I'm fighting famine," she exclaims. Detective Bell tears off a strand of poster. Chews, swallows it. Then another strand. Halfway up the poster, still devouring, thinking, "This is when I eat paper." It quiets a pang he's had for days.

On his way home he takes the D train by mistake, remembering he's moved to Manhattan only with Lady Liberty in view from the Brooklyn Bridge. The hell. He'll go home. Just a visit. It hasn't been long. They'll remember me. The whiskey haze rises into a tight knot in his temple.

On the streets of Park Slope, his son sneaks up from behind. "You look like shit."

"How's your eye?" Detective Bell asks his scarred son.

"Your leaving doesn't mean we get skanked on insurance?" He is afraid of his son, angrily fourteen. "Your mother?"

"Wigged. Packed everything. My stuff. Her stuff. Yours. Then called UPS."

"I didn't mean to hurt . . ." Detective fails.

"Beauty, Dad. Needs a little rehearsal, though. I'm going into the city."

"Wait." Detective believes he's holding a rope here. Either around his waist or neck. He's tugging gently for direction.

"No, thanks," son yanks away. "Go to the house if you don't want all your stuff mailed to Alaska or some shit."

Bell follows his shoes home. Outside he hears locks clicking, tape tearing. Grunts, kicks, the unfamiliar curse. Upstairs, wife is sweating. He can't remember seeing this. She stops. "Are we going to talk?" Yard-work gloves have her prepared to throw a hook. He wants a blow to the skull to break the knot into a thousand little mice, lost inside him.

"I'm hungry."

"Everything's packed," though her eyes scan for anything to feed him. "It's a she, isn't it? Please, God, no one from Carroll Gardens. I'll scratch your eyes out, you poisoned it back there for me." She's gotten closer. They trade aromas, booze and bother.

"No."

"I don't want to know. Who?"

"A body."

"You're cruel."

"A dead body. A murder." He looks at his empty house. Likes it empty.

"So what? New York City. Every day you have this fun. Why, this time, do you have to disappear?"

"Because I'm hungry. And there's nothing here." She tries to answer, but she understands so well that her tongue quits. She shakes her hands at him. Go away. Oh, well. They sit on boxes and stare at nothing. "He won't make it," speaking of their son.

"That's why I packed his things. I'm sending them far away and hope he goes looking."

"He's not going to make it."

"Detective Bell. It's been a long time since we talked." He nods, her hand reaching for his face, falling short.

12. She rose at dawn undone, her hair splayed out like a headdress. She made no sound but I always knew when the bed was empty. The covers grew heavy, a thin chill descending. Into the bathroom, where she laid out her medication like tiny darts, aimed and swallowed. She let the water run uninterrupted and flushed the toilet twice before sliding back to bed. She would curl to frame my position, but never touched me, her heat bridging the gap. It took me a month to stop noticing her ritual. I still couldn't believe she was mine.

We lived in medicated peace like ancient lovers. Even new discoveries seemed familiar. We were following a map neither of us needed to read. The way was simple, destination guaranteed. I gladly disappeared into Emma, family wounds healing in her salt. She enclosed me, fed me. I needed nothing else.

We were friendly with neighbors. Shopkeepers and the postman knew our faces if not names. Yet we never invited anyone in. Not enough room, we'd say, but even in a mansion there wouldn't have been enough space. We filled each other in.

"Let's run away together," Emma said.

"We already did."

"I know. Just pretend," Emma scolded, her voice as serious as a child at play.

"Where to?"

"Gramercy Park."

"I'll pick you up at midnight. Don't be late."

Granted, Gramercy Park was only twenty blocks away, but with Emma, any adventure would do. I packed a late-night supper picnic, some candles, and we set out for a neighborhood that was more than a little stiff. Young couples with Park Avenue aspirations often made Gramercy their first stop on the ladder. And the apartments that directly faced the lovely park were filled with dowager queens and rich men who coughed a lot. Also, it was only if your building faced the park that you'd receive the downtown symbol of nobility, a key to the iron gate surrounding. This rule made for an extremely pristine setting, ringed with azalea bushes and great green walkways, from April to Thanksgiving.

It was just cool as Emma and I approached our iron-clad picnic grounds. I was up and over the fence first, nimble as a burglar. Emma handed over the basket to a chorus of coughs. Then she clambered to the top and I caught her feathery fall. "Don't giggle," I warned too late. Grass crunched beneath our shoes, nature's alarm. I tried to guide Emma to an obscure section but she stopped dead.

"Out in the open or not at all."

"People will see us. There's a ninety-year-old woman on twenty-four-hour sentry."

"She's welcome to join. If she can get over the fence." I laughed and yielded, spreading out our blanket, unwrapping sandwiches, opening wine. "Candles."

"You really want to get caught," I said.

"It's not a picnic without candles," she intoned. I took it for logic and lit three candles. The breeze sent shadows boxing across Emma's face and I could see who she would become. Picture her at eighty, eyes perfect, skin relaxed, mouth in an almost smile. One candle blew out and she was back again. "Wine tastes better here."

"Everything does." We leaned into a kiss and took it as another flavor.

"Thanks for doing this with me."

"Anytime, Emma. I'm your getaway."

"Really." Another candle blew out, darkening her glow. She kissed me again, a quiver to her lips. We stayed close until it quit. "It's getting cold."

"No, it's not," I willed. I wrapped her in my arms and legs, hoping some octogenarian was watching and remembering what love was.

"We can go home," Emma allowed.

"Not yet."

In the beginning Emma worked several jobs at a time, staying long enough to swing a good schedule and quitting when she was in the mood. She loved to quit. She said it proved she was right.

I didn't work, collecting a minuscule monthly check from my parents and selling my prescription drugs to the kids at the Palladium on weekend nights. When I felt the undertow grow, Emma shared her pills, but I was too glad to be awake to let the narcotic nap lay me down again.

In October of our second year together, Emma got pregnant. Not by design, but not by accident either. "Sophie's coming," she said in the waiting room at Saint Vincent's. I shuffled for the proper response. It didn't matter that I was glad. Only what my face and posture betrayed. Emma eased it, saying, "I know you're happy, too." She kissed my forehead, mussed my hair. I was going to have a child. Someone to raise. I was two weeks shy of twenty.

Emma's body started storing nuts for the winter. She put herself on a strict diet of everything she wanted. I painted the ceiling of our apartment tangerine and traded a hundred Elavil for some soundproof windows. It took us a week to fall asleep in all the quiet.

Emma cut her hair off so Sophie would have nothing to pull. I sanded all the sharp edges, including my nails, laid down a Crayola array of carpet swatches to plush Sophie's footing, and made every household item that I could completely baby-safe. The apartment was ready. All we had to do was wait. Seven and a half more months.

Emma cut back to two jobs, and I took one tending day-bar at Milano's, an Irish pub on Houston by Mott. Long and drain-pipe narrow, it was a haven for rummies to spend their unemployment checks and be home in time for dinner. The decor was a patchwork of forgettable memorabilia and timeless Sinatra kitsch. Bumper stickers and antique posters covered every cranny, Gaelic boasts shoulder to shoulder with classic beer slogans. It was a pleasant enough place to work, considering the jukebox played the Rat Pack and the daylight drunks were too old to fight. The only drawback was that the boozehound regulars had never been introduced to tipping. I gave up hinting after a month, and just started taking it out of their change. I had a family to support.

"Do you ever wonder," I asked Emma, my chin gentle on her stomach, "how we'll be?"

"Perfect."

"I mean as parents, considering the examples we got."

She sat up, straightened things. "I'm the only mother Sophie will ever have. I have to be perfect."

"You will be." I didn't ask her many questions. I always chased her away with them. "I guess I meant me."

"Because of your brother." Her face was gray, but not cold. "I wouldn't have met you if it weren't for Warren."

"I don't understand."

"Just that things come together for a reason." Pause. "And if it leads to Sophie . . ." But if it cost Warren, I wanted to say. We were running over sacred earth. We needed tiptoes.

"I just met you. That's all." We usually agreed. This was a blind spot.

"I don't, I wouldn't turn in my . . . what I went through. You were my answer. And Sophie." Her color returned. She was satisfied.

"But nobody died."

She walked quickly to me. "No."

"I don't mean it's worse, like a measurement."

"But you'd turn it back if you could." She was fierce.

"Yes. In a minute. Every day. Every day I'd stay inside, not pull on my boots, ignore my Mom. Every day I'd take him in before it got dark. I'd hold him when we skated the way you'll hold Sophie. Every day I'd . . ." Tears circled my eyes but wouldn't drop.

Her thin hand on my back. "Even if it meant never meeting me?"

I jolted. Her hand stinging me. I was in a panic. Pills. Pills. Pills. "Don't ever say that!" I commanded her. "I don't have to trade you. I can't trade you."

"But if you could." Stranger.

"We're making this up. It doesn't have to be. I love you. I love Sophie. I love us. There is nothing that could get in the way of that." But she didn't believe me. She saw something in the way. A suffering she'd never known. And for all that we had shared, we had never shared a death.

"I trust you with Sophie. Only you." It was not a compliment. It was a decree. She held a candy bar in each hand, both opened, neither bitten.

It was a small apartment with nowhere to go but out after such a conversation. "I can't even start to tell you . . . ," I stumbled. I put on my coat against my own silent protest. "This was stupid," I spat. Emma stood there, angry, hungry, wanting a death in her past in order to have all of me in the future. She would get her wish.

"Eighteen percent. Sounds high, I know, but that is the figure for first-time pregnancies that don't make it to term." The obstetrician had bird eyes and feathered hair, and he was telling us that Sophie had gone down the slide.

On the cab ride home, I wanted to lie in every pothole to absorb the rattling of Emma's tender loss. It was nine days after the argument, and of course, I felt responsible. Emma took it well. We were even. I hated myself for imagining she'd somehow done it herself. Not physically, but willed it. "That wasn't Sophie," she announced just inside the apartment.

"Emma."

"No. When Sophie comes, she'll stay. That's how we'll know her. Remember that, Daniel."

"I will." I made her tea, brushed her lovely short hair, and tucked her in, leaving her to her strange dreams.

"Sophie's coming," she prophesied, and I closed my eyes, seeing Warren holding Sophie in his alabaster arms.

13. Bodies in a row, like wax figures. Detective breathes deeply of the chemicals keeping all the corpses in line. It is morning and he is the first live body around. Soon staff members will groan into lab coats, blinking their eyes, hoping for a different view. Detective Bell follows the wrinkling of plastic, the sound of dead leaves, into an examining room. Three young black men lie at attention, the insult of bullets hidden by their stillness.

"Here to watch," Coroner hopes. He's a show-off, still proving he's not afraid of the dead. Detective Bell presses his thumb into a deceased shoulder. "Stays crunchy," Coroner bellows. "Even in milk."

"Any come in with bloated, like?" Bell plays charades badly. Coroner gets bored and digs into his first helping. "Big bellies," he explains, "but not fat."

"Just skinny people bought it last night, Detective. Thin, healthy, washboard. The Young and the Breathless."

"Ever find anything?" Bell is over the doctor's shoulder, a conscience.

"Found a Florida license plate in a spook once. Still valid." He chomped down on the bitter root of his joke. "The hell you think this is, *Jaws*? These assholes are dead. They come in like cords of wood. I play the xylophone, check for bombs, and have lunch. What the hell do you do?"

"Same thing." Bell backs away, worried he might stick an instrument in the Coroner.

"You breaking a case? You donut eaters only visit the haunted house when you're hungry."

"Do you have a drink?"

"Bottom drawer. Next to the fingers. Just kidding." Coroner giggles and digs. Bell pours Old Granddad into a beaker and erases it.

"You ever afraid," Detective tests, "that you'll find something?"

"What, like a soul? Or the devil?" Coroner's glasses have slid down the slope of his nose; he pushes them up with a mottled hand. "By the time I get them, the only thing left inside is a lot of bad machinery. Whatever happened, somebody stole the motor. They left all the parts but . . ."

"What about you?" Bell says, back near his shoulder. Something buzzes.

"It's eight in the morning, I've got my thumb on a thorax. Don't go getting morbid on me." Bell can't seem to leave. A vulture afraid to land. "Look, take a few home, get some drinks in them, see if they'll tell you about the other side. Otherwise get out of my light." Coroner stabs his scalpel somewhere hard and glares Detective out of the room. In the hallway, Bell can hear happy singing.

Records office, a secretary, plump from the waist down, finishes a secret fruit pie. Bell catches her with a cherry smear on her lip. He hands her his paperwork, request forms, they don't speak. Her fingers touch hundreds of folders, divining their contents, pulling out two. "Again. The address?"

He is hungry enough to kiss the pie off her face. "Gramercy. Twentieth, near Irving."

"Wrong," and she tucks one away. "Here. Caucasian male, five feet ten, a little of this, a little of . . . starvation?" She looks at Bell for the first time. "Detective Bell?"

"Yes."

"People don't starve. Do they?" Her frame withers before him. She stares out at him from black onion eyes, her dough skin drawn back, suitcase tight over the skeleton. "Not in New York."

"You have something wrong with your face," he warns her, taking the file, leaving her scrambling for a compact.

Downstairs, a supervisor checks body temperatures, pulling out tray after tray of human disguises. An Asian man, white teenager, Puerto Rican grandmother, all the same color, dipped in death's turpentine. "Looking for a big belly," Bell shouts, flipping through the report. "Name of . . . here it is."

"Family took him this morning."

"This guy?" Detective show and tell.

"Yeah." Supervisor is a mosaic of pinks and grays. His body does not sleep all at once.

"This is a homicide. Family has to get in line."

"Somebody signed the papers. There. A woman. Everything seemed in order. Nobody said anything about a homicide. Body was unmarked."

"Where's the ME's report?" Detective asks himself, yanking it out, tearing the corner.

"See, no homicide," Supervisor jabs his finger. "Toxicology, blood work. Clean. Guy was healthy. So to speak."

"I need that body." Bell sees the torn paper. Eats it.

"Steady, Detective."

"The address. To send the final report."

"I have it inside," he answers, eager to end the argument. "It's in the 'burbs. They're having a funeral."

"Not yet," Bell growls, and leaves for the hunt.

Detective likes the drive over the Fifty-ninth Street Bridge. It is a fluid day, easy travel. He leaves the radio off to listen to the *om* of the tires and grates. He relaxes into the rhythm, wants to wave at passersby. Does.

The driving, the needle percolating at sixty-five, remind him of weekend trips to Vermont. Day visits to D.C. he never took, but always planned to. With his wife and frightening son. Never managed to get them into the car. He once sat for hours in the driveway, wishing any minute they'd notice him missing, his bags gone. That they'd race or trip into the driveway. Where have you been? Where are you going? Nowhere.

Detective is feeling almost the idea of happy as he trundles into Rye, another Westchester County town where houses grow like bacteria and children run from their parents' arms. There are curbs and walls. Gates and garages. Architecture with mean lines and hunched shoulders. It is the thousandth day in a ten-thousand-day cycle where everything remains the same. Where people believe, hang on, shut eyes, grit teeth. The perfect day. The greatest day.

Detective enters the private enclave of houses just off Route One and parks his car. He wishes for cigarettes, though he doesn't smoke. He wants that rolled-up paper in his mouth. The house he surveys doesn't stand out. It is dull and beautiful, an advertisement for a certain life. There are moderately expensive cars in the driveway. Figures pirouette behind the windows. He isn't sure how the boy who grew up here found his way to Gramercy and such a hunger, but Detective will trace it back. Using mirrors, tall tales, ghosts, he'll fit that empty belly back into this house, fill it with jelly beans and candy corn. Shut the boy up with calories and attention. Spoon-feed him, careful not to drop any flavor, massaging each bite down his brittle throat. Nurse him back to size.

"Excuse me," comes with a tapping on his window. A woman in her mid-thirties, magenta hair, hard knuckles. Her knock sounds more urgent than she means. Bell rolls down the window. Some of her hair sneaks in and grazes his face. "I didn't mean to scare you."

"You didn't," he pretends.

"You're here for the reception," she tells him. "You were a friend of Daniel's. You're early." It is an invitation and an identity.

"I am."

"You're blocking my way." Detective sees he's parked directly in front of the driveway. He is embarrassed, flustered, too close.

"It's okay. You can give me a ride," the woman explains, crashing into the passenger seat. "I'm Nina. And we're out of ginger ale."

On the way to the store, Detective makes up a name and a job for himself. They give him a shortcut through the woods of the family. Nina is thirty-three, punched by insomnia, with gracefully crooked fingers. She speaks of her drive down from Massachusetts and the Common, what works about Boston and doesn't about New York. Detective nods, terrified of what he'll do inside the grocery store.

She is far too pretty to be in his car. She mentions his hair. He compliments hers, hopes it trespasses his way again. They speak in familiar tones, she especially, leaving her hand on his knee too long, smiling, highlighting her charms. He could kiss her in aisle four as she hands him the two-liter Canada Drys and makes an unfunny joke. He begins to distrust her lack of sorrow, hoping it's overcompensation. He wants to like her. She is his camouflage. "Do you know a woman?" he inquires, failing to mention the child. He puts his hands in his pockets to keep from filling their cart with canned goods.

"Is this a trick question?" Nina bows and swoops before him, a magician's assistant, drawing the eye.

"Not if you know her. A woman. A certain woman."

"Emma," she concedes.

"Yes." He feels safer now, part of something. The ground settles.

"You know Emma?"

"Yes," he proudly shares. How does he know her? "Will she be there? At the reception?"

Nina hands the cashier two balled-up fives before Detective's protests can be lodged. "I should pay. It's my brother's . . ." Nina takes the change like keys to a cell and breaks out. She's playing piano on the car roof when Detective catches up. "Emma is not a family favorite. I'm sorry if you like her."

Bell guides her in, holding her hand. "I don't really. I've only met her. I just wondered."

Nina slips into a berm of sorrow, and quickly tries to scramble out. Her footing won't hold. "Drive around the block, will you? It's not time to cry yet."

"Nina," Detective soothes, "it's good to finally meet you. Daniel always said . . ."

"Did he?" she beams, cutting him off, unable to receive even the comfort of a lie. "Welcome home," she says, as they pull up to the house. "I'm glad you're here."

14. Rain. Almost snow. It fell as slush from the sky, not waiting for the taxis to do the mixing. We were almost twenty-one, celebrating our birthday a few days early. They came two days apart. It was Halloween, too warm to snow but the weather was anxious. Meanwhile Emma and I had nearly come to a standstill. One drink at a time.

I was still employed. It was the occupational hazards that were tapping on my liver. Between Sinatra singles, I was shooting back Bushmill's doubles, getting into drinking contests with the regulars, losing and watching them steal back their tip money. I was a freshman tippler, but I savored every flavor. I liked to drink, and I was getting good at it.

I'd clock out at 8 P.M., come home and sleep until 1 or 2, when Emma got off shift, and we'd go to the bar on the ground floor of our building, to eat fries and down pints of Guinness, Emma as thirsty as I. We'd pull each other upstairs and spin into bed, grateful not to talk, to ignore the newborn space between us. Alcohol had become the coda to every day, and it had us sleeping too deeply again. Each sip carried a hospital malaise. Comforting and frighteningly familiar. We had stopped moving forward. It was getting harder to feel Emma's kiss, her voice had trickled below audible. I'd find her hand on my knee and wonder when it had reached me.

So on our birthday we decided no booze. Maybe that would speed things up. We both got the night off and ventured to the Greenwich Village Halloween Parade. The rain clung to us as we barged crosstown, telling strangers to sing us happy birthday. Emma seemed to know many people I'd never seen before. I felt like a little brother, tagging along. We weren't wearing costumes, but the event was vibrant enough to make me feel dressed up. The drag queens and the Wig party limboed up Sixth Avenue to the wailing of drunk Wall Streeters. Packs of executives in a frenzy of adulation. "I don't like these people," I griped, enclosed by a triangle of umbrellas.

"Because you're sober," said Emma.

"I'm not like that. Slapping. Drooling."

"Because you're sober."

"I'm not like that," I said, looking for a bar. "Can we sit somewhere?"

"Everyone's having fun but us," she accused.

"So?"

"It's our birthday. And it's Halloween. Make it fun." She said this into the back of the neck of the twelve-year-old girl in front of her. We were caught in the gutter flux, and there was no stopping.

"Make it fun," I repeated.

"Yes. Pretend. Or something."

I pulled Emma by the wrist, and banged us toward the barricades. A cop with thick hair whose hat had been stolen stopped us with his crooked hand. In the middle of the street, the parade was making space for a twenty-five-foot-tall witch. She was made of black and orange parachute cloth, with a Styrofoam hat big as a tent. She skated over the street, her long black dress covering the mechanics. In her right hand was a broom, and in her left, a black cat she held by the tail. It was enough to awe the drunks silent. She was magnificent, with a genuine witch scowl, moving ominously uptown, purring with dark power.

A circle of human witches surrounded her, stirring cauldrons, casting spells, and keeping the fringes jittery. Our cop's hand quivered. He pocketed it. As the tremendous sorceress passed our way, a wet gust lifted her hem to reveal the motorcycle and cart that gave her such fluid motion.

"Do I know how to drive a motorcycle?"

"No," she answered, unsurprised.

"I mean, is it really hard? Would anyone get hurt?"

"Oh, Daniel."

With Emma locked on, I weaved us under the sawhorses and onto the street. The cop hollered, and I turned to face him. He had empty eyes, and was afraid. The circle of witches covered us up, and we snuck under the dress. Walking slowly, we kept up with her forward motion and could see the precise apparatus of her stature.

"Hey, who is it?" The voice came from the motorcycle up front, and Emma and I introduced ourselves.

"This is Emma," I told the rider, who blushed at Emma's face. "And I'm Daniel. Great umbrella."

"Parade sucks. Too slow. Too wet," the driver said. "Had this up in Massachusetts last year. Place went bananas."

"Probably thought she was real."

"No doubt." He was our age, a long-hair with tie-dye jeans and Birkenstocks. "Dude, mind keeping her wicked while I score a couple slices of Ray's?" Before I could answer we had our opportunity. I was on the bike, the dude was on his way for pizza. Emma got on behind me, her fingers my safety belt.

"We should wait for him," I countered coyly, knowing she was hoping to take off and start our own parade, and knowing we would.

"One more minute."

"She's insured, right. She's gotta be insured."

"I love you, Daniel." I gunned it. Through my sight holes, I could see the Village People float weaving out of the way.

Onlookers cheered wildly as our witch made her move. Past the *Les Liaisons Dangereuses* float and the Solid Gold Dancers until Fourteenth Street gave us a left turn. Down into the meat-packing district we went, the Wicked Witch of the West Village. Transvestites and butchers saluted us. I circled around, waiting for a siren to make things interesting, but we were on our own. Up Eighth Avenue through Chelsea, where people lined the streets like the Pope had arrived. I cut over to Midtown, giving our lady of the evil brew a chance to window-shop. "What if she wants something?" Emma asked.

"They'll never have her size."

I took a couple of spins around the Plaza Hotel entrance just to spook the valets. They told us we wanted the Helmsley. "Witch way?" I asked, sending the reserved Emma into back-pounding hysterics. We kept hearing sirens, but none of them were interested in us. By the time I rolled us to Central Park, we were feeling slightly jilted. "I know this is a dangerous city, but you figure a thirty-foot witch is good for something."

"Staying out of the rain." Emma kissed me wet under our witch umbrella. "See what happens when you take a little chance?"

"Every time I look at you."

"I wasn't a risk. God put us together."

"Then he has a dangerous sense of humor," I joked.

"Of course."

"Maybe we should find that guy." It made me nervous when she got mystical. I suspected there was a Daniel doll somewhere, with pins, or a potion brewing.

"Stay with me."

"I'm right here." Her embrace had more strength than she had to give. She passed through my skin as mist, hardening on my insides. Digging in. "I can stay like this," she warned.

15. Detective is the only one at the dessert table. His fingers find cookies easy to palm and lift in one motion. He eats fifteen this way, looking like a toy in a store window. He wants to chat casually, squeeze a shoulder, sink unseen into a chair. Swap memories over the simmering soup. Feel less naked. He's grateful it's years since he filled out the sticky chafe of his sergeant's blues, riding herd on parades, game sevens, afraid of the nightstick in his hand. Dressed up like a blue ghoul he never could have sidled into a stranger's house, a lovely at his side. Here he's treated like an in-law, a date. Sisters check on the fullness of his stomach, the mother forgets his name, as he does, because it's a fraud.

He is led to believe the whole family is here. Scattered nieces and nephews run into things, shout, take over. They look at Detective and decide he's a good man for throwing long passes between tree branches and telephone wires. "I toss to my boy every Sunday," he lies, delivering another perfect spiral, forgetting where he learned to aim.

He had come to the house to take back the body. The police weren't finished with their son. Ongoing investigation. But he's become a party guest, eating yet not full, drinking, maybe tipsy. He falls into a chair, and Nina takes it for a joke. Everyone is on his side. He changes his story for each questioner. He sets land mines all along his escape route.

"How well did you know him?" one of the older sisters asks.

"How well did any of us?" and she is nodding at his sad wisdom already.

"The kids seem to love you."

"Yeah. Me and kids."

"Will you stay for the service?"

"It's why I came," he lies. "I don't have to be back for a couple of days."

"Where did you say you were from, again? Scarsdale?" He eludes her with upstate. Binghamton he tries this time. Car dealership. "Right," she exhales, cracking a pretzel.

Nina kisses him on the cheek, smoothing by. Mother takes his hand. "I'm glad you're here." She can't let go of his hand, testing it. "You've broken this."

"Three times," telling the truth.

"At work?"

"And at play. It always seems to get in the way."

"You still have it," she reminds him, placing it at his side, tenderly.

It is clear they did not know their son. They have invited their friends. Neighbors who knew Daniel before. Before anything. They are strangers, mourning the loss of something so long gone they aren't able to be sad. They eat in his name, drink, joke, lie in his name, but the boy who grew up to starve to death is unrepresented.

On the basketball court, Detective sinks ten shots in a row, impressing youngsters whose faces fade even as he looks at them. They bounce and jump where things have broken, kicking hard on a shallow grave. The father comes home, eager for a one-on-one game he's been denied for decades. He is fifty-eight and no sweaty match for Detective, who is on his home court, surrounded by cheerleaders, sinking jumpers for Daniel's sake. The ball is smooth and belly round, one with Detective Bell's hand and hunger. He is part of an unbreakable straight line to the basket. He finishes the father off, is greeted by Nina, a towel, and a request to shower quickly before the memorial.

The father stops short, the ball in his stubby hands. "Who the hell is he?"

Nina chats Detective Bell up until the minister enters. He is a bottled man, drawn at the waist, bowed at the feet. His voice whistles up out of him, creating a narrow draft. He relies on the inherent sorrow of a young death, mentioning the age thirty-one seven times, though Daniel was thirty. Detective sheds his impostor fears, taking Nina's hand during a poignant recollection. He is deeply sorry, tears appearing faster than he can blink them away. The relatives want to cry like Detective Bell, but they are dry. They are burying a stranger. He is burying family.

"Well, I don't think we'll ever really know the effect . . . ," a sister eulogizes.

"He was our special boy. Our first baby boy," from the mother. Nina stands up, but can't form the words. Detective's shoulder receives the grief instead.

They scatter in the parking lot, promising to meet back at the house. Nina piles in with her parents. Other than Detective, only two remain.

"What did they say?" this late arrival, a woman, asks Detective in a voice that sneaks through the snow. "Did they tell the truth?"

"I don't know." His hand aches and he is bitterly alone. "Would you and your baby like a ride?"

16. I started walking. Something we never did in the suburbs. From porch to car was the longest trail we'd blaze. Then at the hospital, the sedated steps, too exhausted to pull one foot into the lead. So Manhattan was an invitation, a dare. Off hours and days between, I began going in any direction just to feel the push of boot against pavement.

From the broken glass and old soul food outside Princess Pamela's, west on Houston to Milano's to whisper to Emma. Down Mulberry into Little Italy, where crime was a rumor that never spread. Have a Bud at Mare Chiaro to be regaled by Tony's tales of the Chairman's visit. A cannoli on any corner. Attitude and accent. And on my two feet I could go anywhere, taste anything. Freedom.

Occasionally I'd steal Emma and we'd walk uptown to Madison, spy the fur coats and face-lifts. Eavesdrop on conversations about tiaras and college funds going bust. Enter stores as if we belonged, Emma's face getting away with everything. We'd put down bids on garish paintings, keeping straight faces until we were a block clear.

It didn't matter the temperature, the crowds, traffic, breathing always felt good when I walked. I tasted a different oxygen, better than the rest, because my pace got me there first. And the city felt like only open space. Skyscrapers were short enough to leap. Bridges and tunnels maintained the flow. Pedestrians bumped by, missing the joy of the air. I was a man in love. In love with motion.

"Don't go out," Emma nearly warned.

"I was just going to take a walk."

"Come to bed." Emma took off her clothes so slowly she appeared to be dressing.

"All right."

Under the covers we pawed and paused for new treasure. Her body coiled and sprang with such tenderness she didn't seem to be moving. Yet she spun herself around my center, webbing me in, catching me there. She made me wait, hand over my mouth, promises blooming below, until I finally surrendered the flash. Still on top, she refused to climb off. "Emma."

"Shhh. I want you there." I waited as long as I could, a strange weakness claiming my legs.

"Please."

"Almost," she decided.

"What?" I barked, sorry at once. She clung a few more seconds, then pulled apart. "I'm sorry."

"It wasn't to hurt you," she whispered.

"That's not it. I'm sorry. I don't know why I got weird."

She faced me, her thumb dusting my lips, smoothing below my eyes. "You can go for your walk now."

"I love you so much!" I blurted, smashing my lips into hers, smearing her mouth. I pulled close enough to suffocate. She didn't protest, just waited for me to finish. I laid her back down gently, as if she'd crack open. "I love you."

"I love you, Daniel."

"I get scared. It's so good I get scared." I knuckled tears away, gritted my teeth. "I don't know why I get you. Why I'm here."

"You're here for me and for Sophie."

"And what about you?"

"To make sure you don't leave us." I looked at Emma and her simple view.

"You know I won't."

"I know," she bubbled. "Had to give myself something to do in your little dilemma."

I sat up, our narrow apartment thinning. "What if I did?"

"What?" Boredom.

"Left you."

"And Sophie?"

"Before Sophie."

"Leave me, you leave Sophie. Never mind. Wouldn't happen." She smoothed the sheets, pressing out the doubts.

"But if I did?"

"I wouldn't let you," her voice louder. Too loud.

"How?"

"I just wouldn't."

"I'll have to wait and see?"

"Take your chances," she closed.

"Do you want me to be afraid of you?"

"Are you?" she untangled individual hairs.

"When I don't know you."

"Like when I talk like that. I know," she admitted. "I don't really get it, either. It's just that you can't leave me."

"Simple."

"Exactly."

"How did I find you?" asked with a curious kiss to her chin.

"You didn't. I was waiting. Very patiently I waited and then you were brought to me." She was giving a news flash. Her eyes static but her mouth clear. "You were my gift. What I deserved."

"I don't understand."

"Either do I, Daniel. It's just talk. Being goofy." We laughed it off, but we both knew she was serious. Somehow she had earned me. "I get scared. That's all. So I talk weird."

"To scare me, too."

"It's easier when we're both something."

Under the covers, I brushed her skin, a lullaby of touch. Her eyes drooped, the conversation faded. "Please, don't try and scare me, Emma. I'm no good when . . . I don't ever want to be afraid around you."

She brought her knees to my chest. "That's up to you. I'll never say another word." She hung the wordless threat around my neck and pushed off to sleep.

"You're not allowed to leave either," I challenged.

In the bathroom I checked to see if anything was gone. If she had started to store away little parts I wouldn't miss. We were young, but growing older together, doubling our decay, and I wanted to be able to recognize what we were about to become.

17. Weary, his foot weak against the accelerator. "They're waiting for me back at the house."

"You won't be missed," Emma assures him. He disagrees, yet is too sleepy to do anything but drive on. Sophie is awake, her tiny hand making shell shapes against the windshield. He can see her more clearly with the headlights of trailing cars. Her face is a bubble of surprise. Her profile catches a shock of high beam, shutting her eye, blacking the other side of her face. Detective sees her as the moon. All in front of him, so much in shadow. He wishes she could speak, tell him in a child's phrases what he was doing in his car, where he was headed. He is so exhausted the only things open are his eyes. His lungs are closing, his heart, his mouth.

"We have to pull over," he pleads.

"Keep going." He does. "I'm going to tell you a story," Emma says without words. "It will keep you awake. Do not close your eyes."

"I must."

"Listen." She tells a story of colors. A painter's cadmium, auto metallic, the purple of violence. Mixes them together, stretches them apart, hiding the windshield, erasing the steering wheel, she takes Detective up and out of the car. He is gauzed with first blue, egg blue that breaks into yellow, and lava that oranges everything to ash. Puckered pink, blind white, the red of a lie. She leaves him bars of color, wedges and chunks, heavy browns to shoulder, backbreaking beige, sand-weighted, mud in his eye. Teal, amber, sunflower gold, boxes and stripes, Emma's own plaid.

"Are we running away?" Detective asks, rainbows in his way.

"This feels like running away."

"From what? To what?" Sophie is asleep on her mother's palette.

"I thought I'd arrived somewhere."

"Daniel's house? A mirage." She is insisting.

"Or this," Detective guesses.

He is standing in the lot. The church parking lot. The key is in the car door as Nina yells from a passing car, "Hurry home."

He does.

The house in Park Slope is empty. No sign of anything having taken place here. No ghosts.

Real-estate footsteps surprise him out a window and onto the roof. There are churches, buildings with decayed faces. Immigrants on the street, hustling toward something. He is tired of spinning, thinking of the leap.

"Mr. Bell? Detective Bell?" Detective sees a blazer in his periphery. It flashes toward him. "What a lucky stroke," the Realtor belts. Her gold jacket and brass-bed hair making her like foil in the dying light. They all blink and bow. "This is the proud owner and now seller of 171 President. One of New York City's Finest."

A hand appears, squeezing Detective's shy offer. "Pleasure." It is a woman from Staten Island. Bell can smell her husband's career on her. "Beautiful home. Gorgeous home."

"Divorce," Detective informs them all, explaining the sale.

"Oh," Realtor feigns surprise.

"I wouldn't have it any other way," the lady from Staten Island punctuates.

Detective is ready to push them off the roof into a waiting cab and out of his house. Instead, he drops fifteen thousand off the asking price and leaves them all handshakes and smiles at the corner. It is just dark now, snowing. Or not. He thinks of people he knows, and where they might be. He imagines lamps in windows, fireplaces, ballgames, his old life. Poker, hobnobbing, fitting in. He has nowhere to go.

The Irish keeper at Milano's remembers him, leaving a Bushmill's at the end of the bar. Detective meets it halfway, ready for revival. A foreign couple dances to "Summer Wind" and Bell pretends he is the words that they speak.

18. We stopped going out. Getting Sophie back became the unspoken priority. We both worked and occasionally saw a movie, but only as a pretext for making love. We had to comprise new ways of tricking ourselves into the act. Emma often found herself naked, looking for something, sometimes for an hour, or until I wore down, or the neighbors applauded. There was nothing scientific about it, based on ovulation or even the horoscope. It was sheer determination, and we felt we owed it to Sophie to give our last effort to hurry her to her rightful place in the world.

There were three false alarms, the third of which was followed by Emma's sworn statement to bring whoever manufactured EPT to their knees. It was terribly unfair that these blues and pinks and yellows could hold so much sway over our lives. I began seeing random things turn blue before my eyes. A girl's sweater. A dog's fur, even bubble gum went in pink and came out cerulean.

We tried incense, tea leaves, tarot, fasting, lights on, lights off, water running, Vivaldi playing, everything except halftime at a Knick's game.

I couldn't tell whom Emma was blaming. She was so convinced of her place in this world, and of mine in hers, that she kept the patience to push on. But I was running out of energy. There were times I was afraid to see her, the ever more clinical first kiss, the tired bump and skirmish. It became a bother to excite one another. We were worn out.

"Maybe we're doing it wrong," she guessed from our familiar position, counting cobwebs.

"Emma, it's not us."

"Who else, then? Have I been missing something?"

"We did it once before. We've just got to let it happen naturally. I think our bodies are all tied up and they're forgetting what to do."

"Forgetting?" she doubted.

"Like when you have a test, and you know all the answers, but your mind goes blank."

"We're doing it wrong. Something is wrong."

"Emma."

"We didn't, obviously, get it right before." She shut up. Her hands investigated her belly. "I'm too tiny," she documented. "There's got to be more space." She rolled out of bed, eager to adopt new theories. "Will you love me fat, for Sophie's sake?"

"That will make less room," I argued. "She needs space to grow."

"You're right," as she set down the M&Ms. "We're having too much sex!" No kidding, I thought, grateful for the breakthrough. "We're crowding her, not letting her settle." She dove onto the bed, arms and legs around me. "I knew there was a reason."

"Nobody's fault."

"Less sex. Maybe once a week," she offered.

It didn't sound like much, but at the time, even that seemed daunting. "Okay."

"Except for now," she nuzzled, her spirit roaming. "Once more to commemorate." Her relief unwound my tension and we fell together in glorious disarray.

❢   ❢   ❢

The pills were gone. Emma washed a final Impramine down with a warm glass of Coke, and threw the orange prescription bottle away. "Merry Christmas," she said, wrapping me up.

It was Christmas Eve and we took a cab uptown to look at the trees on Park Avenue and watch the skaters at Rockefeller Center. The streets were full and friendly with revelers, an odd humility in the air. Everything felt safe, windows open, temperature near fifty.

"How far. Which corner?" the cabbie asked, his hair ink black and sticking out all around his fez. His photo didn't capture the happy in his voice.

"Just drive, Mahmed," I read. "We may never get out."

He laughed as Emma touched hands with a teenage girl skipping through the traffic. "I am glad for this job. Tonight I am glad." Mahmed turned to face us after nearly rear-ending a limo. "Six years," he said, holding up the proper fingers.

"You're so young," Emma consoled.

"Twenty-six."

"Like us," I volunteered. "We're twenty-four."

"Brother and sister?" he asked.

"Almost," I said, then Emma with "Husband and wife."

"Congratulations. You look very happy."

"You'll have to meet our daughter." Emma was shimmering, her loveliness an inch outside her frame.

Cars honked us forward. We zipped onto Park at Forty-fourth, joining the parking lot of celebrants. Trees dressed only in white lights streaked the avenue. Old men drove convertibles. Children let go of balloons. "Do you celebrate Christmas?"

"Wrong holiday for me. Nice holiday, but not for me."

"Could you imagine the lines?" I stumped Emma. "I mean if all the Muslims and Hindus and Buddhists went shopping, too."

"I work today. Tomorrow. Every day."

"Every day?"

"I love to work, every day."

Emma leaned in between the seats. She wanted him to pull over so that we could get him something. "You must take Sundays off. Mondays?"

"Six years. Every day."

I wasn't buying it. "And you sleep in the cab."

"Twenty hours a day, seven days a week," Mahmed bragged.

"I don't believe you."

"Believe me, you," his smile a block of teeth. "For three hundred and fifty dollars a night you stay awake, my friend."

We were driving with a rich man. "Can we borrow some money?"

"How much longer," Emma pressed, "before you disintegrate?"

Mahmed turned solemn. "One year. One year more." We relaxed, traffic thudded forward. "I have saved enough to feed all those who will come."

"Come where?"

"When the hungry come. In the time of the Famine." Mahmed cut off a police car and shot west on Fifty-first.

"Mahmed," I tapped on the Plexiglas. "What country is . . . where will you return to?"

"I work hard for seven years to prepare, to feed the people. You don't understand."

"No," we said.

"You will. You are lucky to meet me. You still have one year left."

"But what country?" I pressed him.

"We live here," from Emma. "We have a little girl."

"No country," he said, not smiling, dropping us off in a mad swirl of tourists. "Merry Christmas." He didn't take our money, just left us there with a year to go, and no idea what to do.

"Did you get the cab number?" Emma said, hand in my pocket. "I liked him. He could be our friend."

"When? He works all the time. And then he's leaving."

"He didn't say he was leaving," she corrected.

"Strange, you wanting a friend."

"It's Christmas, Daniel. Everyone wants a friend at Christmas." Coats bumping into us, we pinballed toward a popular spot.

"Not getting bored, are you?"

"Of what?"

"Of, you know." I meant us, but I also meant even more. We had both eased through six years without so much as a hunger pang.

"It's not the pills, is it? Are you worried about me off the pills?"

I wasn't, although it was the first time of our acquaintance when she didn't have anti-somethings fiddling with her personality. I didn't know who she was at the bottom of the bottle. "No, I know you."

"Wouldn't kill us to have a friend." She had unstuck herself. She was free-floating. "In fact, I bet we could find ourselves a friend in this crowd. At least one."

"And do what?"

"Whatever friends do. What do we do?"

"We're not friends," I explained. "We're us."

"Well, we'll just ask them, our new friend. They'll know what to do. Won't they?"

We began sifting through people, going by touch, smell, using our hidden senses. We got a mixture of bellows, stares, and grins, but nothing lit the meter. "Should they be young?" Emma shouted, twenty feet away, surrounded by unwitting auditioners.

"Can they be pretty?"

"Do names matter?"

"This one's too tall!" We probed and peeked our way through an hour of wanderers, winding up in hysterics outside a Japanese bookstore. Emma hadn't found us a friend, but she did wind up with two scarves, a hat, and a map of Staten Island. "I think this is a sign. We should move to Staten . . ." I kissed her quiet, knowing she was at least half serious. We didn't need any friends. I didn't know what to do with them. "Have we given up?"

"I hope so, Emma." We decided not to skate and started walking up Fifth Avenue, waving at people.

"This counts. Sort of."

"If you earn a wave back, you've got a friend for life," I said, as if quoting a dead grandfather. We waved more frantically.

"I like that." By our rough tabulations, we had more than two hundred lifetime friends by the time we sat with our coffee on the steps of Saint Thomas.

"I think he's right," Emma mentioned. She held her coffee under her chin, steam veiling her expression.

"I think he's crazy. Drive around nonstop for five years, you're bound to spill some sauce."

"Six."

"It's Christmas. I don't want to talk about getting skinny. I just want to get fat." I hugged her awkwardly, causing her to stand.

"Then you've got one more year." She dumped her coffee on the church steps, hailed a cab, and we hurried home. My stomach curdled. A strange hunger dug in.

19. Back at work things are fine. Detective fits in his chair. Doesn't panic. He sits behind his desk and waits for a murder. Shuffles papers, looks comfortable. He can see everything coming at him through his glass window. He is very, very calm.

Phone rings. Some of the boys wanting his takeout order. Beans and carrots, canned, he requests. The usual, they laugh back and hang up. He is very, very calm.

"Harlow case is closed," someone yells in his door. "Mind sending the paperwork downstairs? Thanks, Detective." Something to do. Simple behavior. Orders. Bell likes this. He attacks it with a fervor, but calm. He checks his breathing, feels his carotid pulse. Knows where he is, the ache of this chair, the ringing, slamming, shouting. He rests into his job.

"Da fuck, Bell," his Captain fires, slamming the door.

"Harlow case," Bell offers. "Closed."

"You cut open a corpse and had a greenhorn hold him down, Detective." The Captain's neck is throbbing. "I've got the wife screaming for the body, an ME who wants to cover for you, and we're calling, calling, calling."

"I moved."

"And you moved! Who the hell told you you could move!?" They're closer than angry men should be. "Explain yourself,"

Captain holsters. "Been a good cop, a quiet cop for me. Why the scalpel act?"

Outside, children from P.S. 121 scream in one sustained pitch. Scream to alert someone or to change the direction of the wind. Detective dries the back of his neck with a paper towel and checks for blood. He seems to be tearing at the seams. "Did you order?" he asks the Captain, concerned at the thin sleeplessness under his eyes. He rises and offers his chair.

"Am I talking to myself?" Captain sputters. "Did you cut that fat bastard open on Thirty-first and Third?"

"Yes."

"Why?" It is a simple question, and Detective has an answer, he just doesn't know if it's the right answer. The one that will make the Captain go away and give him his calm back.

"Wrong body."

"No shit, Bell. And even if he was the right one, whatever that screwy sentiment might mean, you don't get to ventilate him. You've got to earn that right, with years in the basement, an ugly wife, and formaldehyde on your breath." Breath. "And don't tell me your wife's ugly, 'cause she ain't, I've seen her at the Benevolence dances, and it still won't float." The Captain is highly skilled at blowing up. He has reached his denouement. He expects his audience to learn something, waits for evidence.

"Captain," Detective says, grateful for the passing of the gale. "I am sorry." Captain nods. "The other one got away."

"The other one."

"The one with . . ." Bell doesn't know what to call it. Clues? Secrets? Something hidden. "From Gramercy. The young man."

"The white Ethiopian," Captain jokes. "All puffed up? That poor creature?"

"Yes. The family got him."

"I signed him out myself. Beautiful wife. Little girl. Tragic, but it wasn't a homicide."

"He wasn't married," Detective reports, taking the Captain's hand. They freeze like little brothers outside a haunted house. Their watches click and shine. "They buried a kill."

The Captain forgets the turkey carving, lets Detective reopen the case. Someone will have to contact the family, exhume the body. Detective will need an assistant. He is still a family friend.

They bring him a Rookie with a vowel-deprived ethnic name. He has short legs and a long torso, taller sitting down than standing up. He looks soft, but he runs faster than a car in traffic.

They have never seen each other before, their greeting awkward, knuckles bang. "I am Detective . . ."

"Bell. They briefed me."

"Good," Detective warns.

In Detective's car, they siren to Gramercy Park. It is noon and the snow melts before it hits. "The canvass is for homeless individuals, grocery-store owners, clergy, if need be. And a woman. With a little girl."

"What does she look like?" Rookie asks.

"Like nothing else."

They scan produce sections, newsstands, coffee shops from Irving and the park to Fourteenth and Second. The homeless don't remember or don't feel like conversation. It's too cold to help a cop. Without a picture of the victim, Bell's left describing the final condition instead of what friends would recognize. He is shaking the skin to find the snake.

"We in the wrong town?" Rookie bites into a gratis apple. "You know that chick won't show."

"She does sometimes. Just appears."

"How come you haven't questioned her?"

"She was about to spill. And when I asked, she took off."

"Do we have enough on her?"

"We do now," Bell realizes. "Falsification of city records. Claiming a body."

"But she didn't claim it, just signed for it."

"That's all we need." Snow gets aggressive, sticks. They move to the car, stepping on toes, still not comfortable.

"Think she did him? What, with poison?" Rookie's mind is clicking, blood in his ears. He remembers graduating the academy. He finishes his apple, seeds, stem, and all.

"Rookie," Detective chastises. "Just want to talk to her."

"I'm only saying . . ."

"The more face you give her, the quicker you are hers. Believe me. We're the ones who should watch out."

Rookie rocks in his seat, touches dials. "What?"

Detective blocks Rookie's question with a raised finger. He hears something between the silence of the snow. "She's close."

20.

"Bullshit!" Smashing things was new. She broke a pitcher we found at the Grand Street flea market. It was blue, the color of held breath, and she exhaled it against the door. "They are such fucking liars." And the cursing. It came with the smashing. The pills were gone, and that was good, but they left us exposed in a few circumstances. I didn't have the courage to ask if she'd broken things before the hospital. I didn't want her thinking she'd fallen back somehow. As long as they didn't last more than half an hour (only once), and included my least-favorite breakables, I decided to ride them out.

This one, as others before, involved my parents. "You don't even like them," I said. "I don't get why it's such a big deal."

"They shouldn't lie. Parents should never."

"No." She was right. "And it's my fault, too. For thinking people change."

"But they do, Daniel." She grabbed my shirt, would have broken it if possible. "We changed. Other people change. They must. But your fucking parents . . ." She scanned for a new victim. An ashtray stolen from the Waldorf lobby, off the back wall, a thousand diamonds on the bed.

My parents had made the mistake of offering Emma and me a night on the town. They'd done a remarkable job of ignoring us for over six years. They saw the hospital at each mention of Emma, and the hospital was an undulled reminder of the death of one son and the collapse of another, so they did their best to limit their potential for grief. Warren's ghost was fourteen by then, with strength to travel and a voice of his own, and we never knew where he would raise his red head.

For three weeks, we'd swapped phone calls, Mom and I discussing shows, talking restaurants, and Emma and Mother actually chatting on the phone for a few moments.

I weaseled a bottle of Black Bush from Milano's distributor, and Emma sewed lace curtains that hung like winter surprise over the windows. They'd sent us cash for great seats to see *Fences*, reservations were set at Le Zinc, and Mom and Dad were due at 5:30. The call came at 5:45 to meet at the restaurant. Then another at 5:49, to go on without them. Dad's work or Mom's arthritis. Car's brakes or the roof gave way. The reason squeaked through the receiver, and before I'd hung up there was whiskey on the wall.

"For fun," Emma suspected. "They're home eating meatloaf and laughing."

"We still have the tickets." I paused. "Paid for with Dad's money." She didn't want to admit it, but it was a consolation prize.

"Scalp and eat?"

"Absolutely."

"What about the mess?" she said, the first push of regret nudging in.

"That's why they invented tomorrow."

We got our money back plus fifty outside the theater and snuck off Upper East for hamburgers and frozen hot chocolates at Serendipity's. We ate till we bulged, and I let Emma trash my parents to assist her digestion. "I'm glad they bagged," I half lied.

"I'm glad they don't know what a wonderful son they have." Emma fed me ice cream. She was being corny. Very unusual.

"Em, what about your parents?"

"Off limits," she said, not looking up.

"Forever?"

She showed me her face as a reminder more than a warning. It was concrete. Forehead, cheekbones, jaw. All the mass her voice had to travel through to be heard. The fortress she was escaping, one sentence at a time. I'd seen it twice when we were young, but she was tired, and the ugliness seemed a flicker. This was an offering. To protect me and help me wait for her, as she turned to vapor to trick the stone.

"I love you, Emma," feeling small and helpless. Miles away.

"We're coming, Daniel. Hang on."

21. "Tell me everything. Everything you know."

"Everything?" The Rookie's tired of sitting on his ass. Wants to canvass, ask questions, not answer them.

"About being a cop."

"Why?"

"As if you're going to get out of this." Detective feels assertive. Greater than. He's just warming up.

"I mean why are you doing this?" from Rookie.

"Because everything's new now."

"What is?"

"The case."

"Captain told me all cases are the same."

"What did he tell you about me?"

"That you slit some DOA neck to nads and went panning for gold."

"Think that's normal?"

"Not especially."

"Typical procedure for detectives in this precinct?"

"No, sir."

"And I'm telling you this case everything is new." Rookie retreats, wants his vest, wants air. "Roll down your window." Rookie does, and snow knuckles in. "I'm not scary," Detective says. "Right hand is lame. Can't shoot fast and I go home alone. I put in twenty years of nothing new, just like the Captain, so I recognize. This is new."

Impatiently, "So what are we sitting here for? Let's catch the bad guy. Get on the news."

"This is so you don't flip on me, kid. Or die. Not a pep talk."

"Yeah, okay," Rookie grumbles. Thinks he's gotten stuck with a loose wire. Time for an early pension.

Something lands on the roof. Rookie bangs his head he sits straight so fast. Again. Rookie pulls his weapon, hand on door. "Snowball," Detective says. Another one plasters the windshield. Rookie, embarrassed, gets out, gun in view, yelling. Kids run, laugh away, Detective drilling one in the elbow with a perfect toss. "Okay, Rook?"

"Yeah."

"Good thing you had your piece."

Rookie shakes it like a burning match. "Nice throw, Detective."

"I always could aim." They brush off flakes, return to the cocoon, sit a little closer, a little cooler.

"Thanks," Rookie says. And they wait.

22. The drugs. They left us alone. Emma had been unmedicated for four months, laughing more, speaking louder, she was more overt, yet somehow less apparent. She didn't mention missing them. There were no nervous calls to the Doctor, no midnight pharmaceutical runs. She even drank less, working more hours to dull the jags. She worked in a coffeehouse days, collecting middling tips, and started on at Milano's nights. She took over for me and served suds alongside Paul, John, or Maggie till past 4 A.M. The only time I saw her was when she skidded into bed near five. I'd pretend to be asleep, then watch her play elaborate games to fool insomnia. She made saliva bubbles, tapped out songs on her eyelids, held her breath for minutes at a time. Nothing worked. I never stayed awake long enough to see her nod off. She didn't show frustration, patiently attempting the next ritual, prepared to be let down, willing to fail.

In the morning, just before ten, I'd crack the shade to give me guiding light. Emma would signal from a distant kingdom of sleep, then fall off again. I had a beer for breakfast, usually with a raw egg, sparing Emma the banging pots and simmering yolk. Protein, I told myself. Medicine.

I shaved in the dark, cutting myself, blood and cream leaving maroon stains on my robe. I hummed music in my head to stem the loneliness. Emma slept on. Our apartment had grown narrower, purchases cluttering the walls and floors. Tables, lamps, items bought for color and shape. Things in the way.

Everything reeked of alcohol. We bore the sterile sting of our combined twenty-four hours a day in a bar. I smelled like the ancient drunks with whiskey blood and floating eyes. A hard, wooden scent they passed on through handshakes and secrets shared. Rotten teeth, sugared grins, and the thick lacquer of fermented grief.

Emma came home bright with the aroma of spilled Guinness, loud youth, and thirsty artists. Ten fingers of tequila, ringed with lime; fast scotches and popped bottle caps. She had nicks and hangnails from the hurry of the night. My wrists were strong from slow pouring, exact doses. Emma moved in a blur, filling glasses like a survivor bailing a sinking boat.

Occasionally, I would sneak back and watch her from the jukebox, hiding behind lusty NYU boys with their eyes on my Emma. "Such a fox," they'd say. "I'd take her in a wet suit." "And out." They'd slap hands, seals trained for such ogling. "Ask her out, man," they'd encourage, but the suitor would always return with the same crestfallen posture.

"Married, dude. So young. What a waste."

"Where's the ring? I don't see any fucking ring." This excited the seals. Splashing. Confusion.

"She doesn't wear it working. Said she's been married since she was eighteen."

Groans. "Probably some old Persian bastard, supporting her."

"And she's working here?"

"To be around people her own age, man. Guy probably has her chained up at home."

"God, that's so sad." They'd console her from afar. Lift a glass, still stunned by their loss. "She is a babe."

I wasn't spying on her, I just never got to see her in motion anymore. I was there to appreciate the line her body cut through the air. How her eyebrows waited for orders, the flight of her small hands over all that glass.

Once she caught me, bringing relief instead of guilt. "You're watching me again."

"Again?" I said.

"You think I don't see you, clever boy. I don't have to." She took more shouted orders, holding me there. "I know when you're in the room."

"I can't help it," I told her. "I want to be where you are."

"She's married," a frat boy confided in me, acknowledging he knew my pain as he took three Harps away.

"Maggie called in sick, why don't you come back and work? At least we can bump into each other." And though I'd already worked eight hours that day in the sticky well of the bar, the offer was irresistible. We were slow that night, our tips low. But the sweet brush of a hip, a hand, a knee were our focus. We were doing our work under the table, paying off old debts to our bodies.

Last call. John cleaned up and Emma and I played "Crazy," dancing old style. "You work too much," I complained.

"I'm not as good in between."

"The pills."

"It's just easier when I'm busy." Her forehead rocked across my chest.

"Don't forget me, Emma."

"Just for a while. I'll adjust." Locking eyes, "I want to do it straight. For Sophie." We held our arms out to our sides, hands clasped, forming a star, a cross, a union.

"Think you'll be able to sleep tonight?"

"No," she confessed. "I have something else in mind."

23. Detective Bell is back in the suburbs. It is two days since the funeral, cookies drying on party plates, behind flowers, on top of the piano. "No one ever learned to play," the mother tells Detective, cleaning up. Detective is here as a friend. Rookie will be by soon to request the exhuming and won't recognize Bell, will play-act like in the third grade when he was a tree onstage, only better this time. And Detective will be there to calm their fears, make it seem routine. He will be a car salesman from Binghamton, but he will know just enough to soften the blow. Rookie will be fair, has been instructed as such.

"Where's Nina?" Detective asks, planning a trip to Boston.

"She'll be down," Mom mumbles. "She leaves today. Strange that you've come," meaning strange nice, unexpected, but this is not how Detective hears it.

"I just left after," he stumbles, "and it was all so . . ."

"I know." Then her hand in his broken one. "You can help me clean up." She offers him a dull smile, but not unkind. He grabs soda cans and cracker bits.

Nina comes down unprepared, hair in barrettes, make-up neglected. "I don't believe it," she says, hand on her collarbone, forgetting her appearance, genuinely glad. Detective had forgotten how lovely, the rawness of her. They embrace. "I thought you had to, must've headed back. Mom. Look who's here."

"I know, honey. Don't steal him till we're done cleaning up."

In the living room, Detective waits for the collected Nina to return. He flips through photo albums left nearby. There are shots of a young Daniel, though Detective doesn't recognize all that lank and lean. There are sisters in skirts, bikinis, graduation gowns, tackled on beaches, kissed on boardwalks. Sisters with both eyes looking away from the frame, the family. Sisters en route. He sees Nina climb the tree of adolescence, scraping herself badly, pulling up and out into full leaf. Detective takes on the memories, stores them, slides in a carousel in his mind.

There is a small boy who appears briefly. He looks borrowed. People don't know how to hold him. Then a teenage boy with the tiny one. Detective recognizes now this must be Daniel, bent down to corral this little man, the forgotten redhead. He smudges Daniel's face, thumbing over the strong expression, sorry to look at it. He closes the album.

"Should we go for breakfast?" Nina asks, ready for a date. Detective sniffs her powdery entrance, wants her ruffled again. She is awkward with accoutrements, and sits so she won't bump into herself. "I thought, since you . . . ," she retreats.

"Yes. Very much. Just not yet." She can't get comfortable in the pale chair, ashamed of her color. The sunny red hair, green shoes, a parrot trapped in her plumage.

"You were looking at pictures."

"No," he lies. He wants to take her to breakfast, get on I-95 and hurry to Boston, or Binghamton. To be this make-believe man, hide in Nina's hair, dull on the map of her embarrassment. But he is here working. The doorbell will be his cue. Until then, they are alone.

"Nina," he starts, and the doorbell sounds. Nina ignores it, looking for space on the couch near Detective.

"Nina," from the kitchen. "My hands are wet." Nina angles to the door, finds Rookie on the other side. He is in uniform, collar too tight. The November cold shakes in.

"Ma'am." No response. Nina looks at him as though she hasn't opened the door. As if it's not too late to pretend no one's home. "I'm Sergeant Hrcek with the NYPD. May I come in?"

"Why?"

Rookie doesn't like her, wants to push her down or stick out his tongue. He feels eleven, locked out, wants to pound his fist. "This is the residence of Daniel . . ."

"What is it?" Mother barges in, her hands white with dishwashing suds. "You're letting all the cold air." Rookie leans his way in without an invitation, kicking the door closed with his boot.

"Ma'am, I'm Sergeant Hrcek of the . . ."

"We got all that," Nina cuts in.

"Fact is, we released a body of a Daniel . . ."

"Yes, yes."

"And it was picked up by the William H. Graham Funeral Home, with the billing address being the one here."

"My hands are filthy," Mom says.

Detective appears from the living room, puts his hand on Nina's shoulder. She relaxes. Rookie nods to Detective as he would to any stranger, but his nerves jump. He is caught in the spot. "That body was illegally released."

"What on earth?"

"The morgue released the body prematurely."

"We were contacted," Nina tells Detective, leaning back into him, almost feeling his holster.

"The deceased . . ."

"That's my son, young man."

"Apologies, ma'am. But your son's body is part of an ongoing homicide investigation."

"That's murder," Detective blurts, delivering his line badly.

"The body should have never been released. That's our fault."

"Why does this matter?" Bell presses, eager to draw the curtain.

"We have to exhume the deceased."

"No fucking way!" Nina stands clear. The mother backs into a chair.

"It's the law, ma'am."

"Fuck the law. You guys had him and you blew it, and now he's ours. That's my brother, you little Nazi. He's staying put."

Rookie backs toward the door, prepared to break Detective's cover. His eyes flash like police scanners. He looks to Detective for permission.

"You said homici— murder?" Detective reigns it in.

"We have reason to believe, yes, your son, brother, was murdered. We need the body."

"You contacted us," the mother explains. "When my husband gets . . ."

"The body had already been signed for. We will pay for any expenses." Rookie calms down, focuses on Nina, how good she smells.

"Who did this?" Nina imagines. "Who signed for Daniel?"

"Can't reveal that name, ma'am."

"I can," Nina turns to her mother. "Fucking Emma." Detective freezes, eyes fixed like a boy on stage. Rookie panics, his leader lost.

"Sign here, and here. It's over."

"No, it's not," Nina tells them. "Daniel is staying home today."

Rookie is not unhappy to be banished to the car. He is first-date nervous, and happy to be hemmed in. To hear police signals over the radio, a boy's secret code.

Inside, Detective's role is less clear. He imagined stroking a back, a quiet tone. Now, he has to wade through old anger. "I don't get it," Detective admits, both as policeman and car salesman. He is increasingly afraid.

"She," Nina starts while Mom washes up, returns. "Emma is this . . . this family curse."

"Why would they release Daniel to her?"

"Probably lied. Said she was his wife. And she is gorgeous. You've seen her. Seen them together. People give her everything."

"Daniel loved her." It is a guess, but his tone is reverential. He knows it is true.

"They were kids. He didn't know any better. He never spent time with another girl. Not even talking. She suffocated him."

"From the moment I laid eyes," Mom bites down, "I knew he was gone."

"You make her sound . . ."

"We can't possibly explain the . . . ," Nina gnashes, her pretty face crunching into a dark mask.

"She was never cruel to me," Bell defends.

"You're a man," Mom says, touching him. "That's why I kept your father away from her. He only would have encouraged." The room is heavy with familiar bitterness. Thoughts never spoken, but treasured, honed for years. Two sons dead and now someone to blame. "We should have never put him in that hospital."

"They released him, but he was in there till the end."

"They stole our son. She stole our Daniel." The regret and helpless accusations tumble out in block letters, filling the room. The women sit motionless, their mouths opening only wide enough to add to the construction. Soon it is a fort of responsibility and shame. They cannot move.

"Do you think she . . ." Detective won't finish. No answer. "I mean, I don't know, but it's a way to find out." He is gentle enough not to mention the probing of Daniel's shell, the breaking of bones.

"He should be left in peace.'

"What will they find? Murder." Nina mulls, hopes even. "She's so tiny."

"Poison," Detective suggests, sounding too expert. "Or something."

Mother won't consider it. She leaves them, shaking her head, scuffling out like a much older woman. "It's always up to me," Nina says, finding the couch, but not sitting. "Everyone leaves and there I am."

"I'm here," Detective comforts. He leads her onto the couch, their hands fitting together. He doesn't know who he is. Whether he's pretending or obeying. Each new word is a surprise.

"You know her." Nina squares, relying on him.

"Not really."

"You've talked to her. Know her. More than we have. Mom met her once. I'm the only one in the family who really spent a little time."

"But you hate her."

"You don't."

"No." Detective looks for things to smooth on Nina. Her skirt, hair, wrinkles. "I am afraid. A little afraid of her."

"Yes." This they understand. Rookie accidentally honks the horn.

"But I don't hate her. How can I hate her?"

"If you knew."

"But you don't," he counters.

"I know enough."

"Do you trust me?" Detective asks.

"Of course."

"I think you should let them . . . find out. Daniel isn't in there."

"I know. I know. I just . . . This family has seen enough death." Nina frowns to stop tears from escaping.

"You'll never know. They'll have this cleared up in no time."

"Will they arrest her?"

"I don't know." Detective can't decide. "Maybe it's the only way."

"I'm sorry. This is so much." Nina stands, backing away. "You probably just came up here to be polite."

He steps kiss close. "I'd love to have breakfast."

They exit, the Detective handling the Rookie for her, giving them a moment alone. "Academy Award," Detective starts, "is not in your future."

"Sorry about the horn."

"Calm down, kid. You had the easy part."

"Get her? She's a tamale. She's waiting for you?" Rookie strains his neck for one last look at Nina's weary beauty.

"Hey. We're going to breakfast. Don't look so friendly."

"What about me?" Rookie asks, pawing an empty donut bag.

"Start digging."

24. Emma set the building on fire. She was making scrambled eggs at 6 A.M. as an antidote to insomnia and it worked. She nodded off while on her feet, setting off a chain reaction that included her hair, the lace curtains, and soon the entire front wall, the window a mouth of flame. I woke to her screaming into the sheets. She had only minor burns across the cheekbones and forehead, but her eyebrows had curled in flight and her eyelashes had singed halfway down.

I calmed her down before I realized the front end of the apartment was white orange. The fire was so pretty it took time to accept the danger. "Am I all right?" Emma pleaded as I reached for the phone.

"Yes, Emma. You are golden. Go downstairs."

"Our stuff."

"You'll just break it later," I joked, and she ran into the hallway.

"Should I wake the neighbors? It's so early."

"It's never that early." 911. "Hello. I know you're busy, but we're on fire. First and First. The pig building. Yes. A pig roast." That was funny, I thought, throwing the phone into the fire. It made sense to appease the monster by feeding it books and flammables it was going to get eventually. I was handing over a dress of Emma's I'd always hated when the firemen chased me out.

On the street, joined by a mob of voyeurs, we watched the building light up from within, floor to floor, a six-story jack-o-lantern. We watched silent, occasionally gasping at a brutal crack or burst, in awe of the speed and hunger of the burn. The water of it, a fire flood.

They went through our ceiling with axes. Pipes dripped ugly sauce onto the frayed mess. There was no substance left to anything, only edges, all the centers burned through.

No one laid blame. Emma told the truth, but the firefighters showed only compassion. Neighbors came by with their cats to make sure we were okay. Emma received five bottles of skin lotion to look after her face.

We hadn't lost much aside from shelter. We weren't big on memorabilia and we'd overshopped the flea markets for years. The fire provided a much-needed spring cleaning, albeit an unorthodox one. The true pain was in seeing so many good people suddenly without homes. Nearly half of the thirty-six tenants, or burnouts as we dubbed ourselves, found friends to crash with, but the rest, Emma and me included, needed an outstretched hand.

We went to a city shelter. It was at Ludlow and Stanton, filled with single mothers and their buoyant children. There were chases and soda-spitting fights first thing in the morning when we got there. We were given the shelter rules and hours of operation, allowed to wash up, then pushed right back into the world. It was 9 A.M. on a Tuesday morning in May. We had no clothing, little money. We were homeless.

Having slept the night before, I didn't mind the fact that we couldn't get back into the shelter until 6 P.M. But Emma was nearly comatose, and the weight of her actions finally tore her down. "I burned everyone," she cried.

I rubbed cream on her cheekbones. Her singed eyelashes and shrunken eyebrows made her look like a salvaged doll. "Everyone's okay."

"All their stuff."

"People, Emma. All the people are safe."

"I've never hurt anyone," she said. "It's never been my fault." She had lived her survivor's life by never being to blame, by absorbing every blow but returning none. This time she'd done the damage, and nothing I could say would change that.

"It's not, Emma."

"There were babies in there."

"Everyone's alive."

She trembled on a bench on Houston. New York raced by, oblivious. "I am so sorry," she managed. "I don't know how to do this." She shook for an hour and a half. I was expected at Milano's at noon, but couldn't leave her alone. I wanted drugs for her, to still this, but she wouldn't have anywhere to sleep. There wasn't room at the bar. I called my mother.

"Hi, Mom."

"I don't believe it. I didn't think you got up before noon." She was vacuuming or doing some noisy chore and had to shout to hear herself. Emma held my hand and trembled against the phone booth. People gawked at us, charcoaled, quivering like junkies.

"Mom. We're in . . . Can you turn that thing off?"

"What?" she yelled.

"Could you stop?" Something clicked off, taking her attention with it.

"I'm way behind. We're having a party tonight."

I nearly hung up, the oncoming party enough to make any return home impossible. "I . . . we need help."

Long pause. "Oh, no." Mom instantly blamed Emma. The sound was unmistakable. "What did she do?"

"Nothing," I lied. "Our building burned down."

"I did it," Emma yelled toward the phone. I squeezed her hand hard enough to shut her up.

"Are you? Daniel, are you hurt?"

"Emma's a little, her face and her hair."

"Oh, my God." She turned the cleaner on again. Then off. On. Off. "Where are you? I don't need this. You're scaring me."

"We're okay. We're just homeless."

"Don't say that. You're not. No one in this family is homeless."

"We checked into a shelter."

"No."

"There's nowhere else."

"No. The shelter is, no. Knives. Drug addicts. No." Vacuum back on.

I asked the question, but wanted it back instantly. "Would it be possible to . . . ?"

"You could come here," Mom preempted, "but your father, there's a huge party here tonight. Clients. That girl, with a burned face."

"It's not that bad. We'll hide out in my room. I just need this one thing. We'll be invisible."

"People like to see the house. I vacuumed. You can't just shut your door. People get curious. Think something's odd." She was a thousand miles away, dusting, scouring, the vacuum sucking hidden dirt from the carpet in the hall. "And I . . . it's just too much. But you're okay?"

"Yeah, Mom. We're okay."

"I'll get your father to get you a hotel," she said like a travel agent. "For the night. Or two if she's hurt. Call him later. He'll tell you where to go." We hung up.

"I don't think we should . . . ," Emma stated, still shivering.

"We're not. We'll get a hotel."

"Money."

"My father. Right now, I just want to get you together."

"I am together," she protested.

"You know what I mean."

"I'm sorry, Daniel." Her shaking fingers tugged on my mouth. She wanted to get inside, be warm. Be innocent.

"You have nothing to be sorry about." We need friends, I thought, my mind oddly flashing back to Mahmed, wondering if he needed somebody to keep an eye on his food while he saved his final money. "Let's go to the movies."

In the womb-dark of the Angelika, Emma curled up and slept to the flicker of the film. Her heart beat in her temple. I could hear her shallow transparent beep, frail against the background of my own thudding heart. She slept straight through, so I carried her, like I would one day carry our Sophie, into the next cinema.

The second feature watched over both of us until an usher woke me gently. "If you're going to sneak in, at least watch," he said, smiling. "It's a good movie." Emma slept on, blaming herself, dreaming she'd wake up forgiven.

25. They eat breakfast like again they are strangers. Nina can't fix on such a changeling and she blames her intuition. It used to be so sharp, she scolds herself. You used to know men.

Detective feels transparent, on the verge of confessing. He's certain that every lift of the fork betrays his cop rigidity. His broken marriage. His runaway son, who is now handcuffed in a Canarsie precinct house. He is dizzy with guilt. He is so sorry.

"I am so sorry," the waiter says, switching coffees. "Nothing worse than mixing cafs and decafs."

"Forget it." Detective swallows.

"But you won't, if I do," waiter chuckles. He surveys the table like a finished blueprint. "We're all set."

"We used to come here on Saturday mornings for pancakes," as Nina smokes. Her cigarette is stale and takes coaxing. She stubs it out. "Until Warren was born, then it got a little complicated. If you knew how much I hate talking sometimes. Every time I open my mouth it winds up having all these goddamn double meanings."

"Everything has a double meaning," he tries.

"That means I'm either not that special, or doomed to repeat my stupid habits for life. A lot to look forward to."

"What happened?" He means between the car ride and the

omelets, but she hears so much more. Double meanings. She wants to scream.

"Everything okay here?" the waiter peeks in.

"Fuck off." Nina lights another cigarette, starting halfway up, burning the paper. "I'm a bit moody," Nina admits. "Not a real crowd favorite."

At the cemetery, they are yanking Daniel's casket like a root from the earth. It dangles over the hole, eager to dive back in. Rookie smacks at a November insect, or is it snow? The first flake disappears on the cool oak surface as they load the corpse for a free trip to the city.

Detective rubs his smooth, heavy chin. He doesn't want to sleep with her. He doesn't want to look at her at the moment. He stares at his home fries, sour in the belly. "I'd like to be friends," Nina says. "Just never quite got the hang of it. And with circumstances, it doesn't get any easier."

"I'll say yes. To friends." They are relieved though still confused.

"Daniel got lucky with you. He had Emma. That was all I knew of. My sisters, they chose marriage over family and I guess I just chose . . ."

"Yourself," with sympathy.

"Maybe. Yes. That sounds selfish." Waiter sends a busboy over with the check. "Boston isn't home, you know."

"You live there."

"That's all. I don't work. Still on the family payroll. I stay up there to pretend I got away." She fingers a lump of mascara, pulls it off. "I don't know why I still play dress-up."

"You're very pretty, Nina." He means it, isn't sorry he said it. He doesn't feel handsome enough to earn a return, so "And you're welcome to stay, if you don't want to go home."

"Stay?" As he realizes that there is nowhere for her to stay. No Binghamton ranch house with guest bedroom, fresh towels. Just a narrow apartment in a building with a pig on it that still has ashen halls. An apartment lined with canned goods, a cop's panic. There is no place he can take her, introduce, show her off. He doesn't exist. There is only this diner, the lies he tells to say good-bye, and nothing else. All that remains between them is a dead man neither of them knew.

"I mean," he searches, "I don't have to be back in Binghamton until . . ." The sentence ends with a kiss.

"Quality Inn," she says, and they leave without paying the bill.

Before they start their cars she calls him over. "I can't do this."

"Either can I," he exhales, apologizing to his wife for imagining this far.

"I can't afford to crash into you," and she says his fake name. "I really like you. I could come to Binghamton."

"Or to Boston. Me. I love Boston." He has never been. They kiss through the fog of themselves. It is gentle, very slow. They don't open their eyes for a long time. "Thank you," he says. It is the softest thing to happen to his face in years.

"You don't smile."

"I forgot how," and she kisses him again, touching his face with lonely hands. "Boston?"

"Boston," She agrees, rescuing him. She leaves him her number, address, and aroma. He wishes he could only inhale.

"Boston," he says out loud. The laughter is thick. It feels good. Laugh.

26. The hotel was downtown, the bottom of the city, at the Marriott Financial Center. Dad had booked us far from the action, at a place he probably never had clients stay. Because we saw each other so rarely and he had never laid eyes on Emma, he had to guess at how much of an embarrassment we actually were.

It was extraordinary, still. Far nicer than any accommodations we'd had in years. This was a hotel from childhood, where we had run the halls unfettered, made clandestine ventures to the ice and soda machines. Swam in indoor pools until breath was a brick in my chest. I felt twelve as I approached reception, too young to be checking in. I wanted to leave the grown-up stuff to Emma and go scampering, exploring. Emma, however, was unable to manage more than a "Wow."

"My father called," I explained shyly. We had no luggage, and the only assurance the staff had that we hadn't wandered off the street was that this far downtown no one walked the street.

"Last name?" which I gave them. "Very well. Room 2144," and the front-desk clerks sent us off, bobbing and waving behind their counter. Emma clung tight until we entered the elevator.

"Those people were awful."

"No."

"They weren't real."

"They're paid to be that way."

She grumbled. "I don't like it here."

"You don't have to. Just one night." The quiet bells, hushed hallways, carpeted walls, all suggested the hospital in its gentility, its absorption. Inside our room, the curtains were open, revealing a view of the Hudson and the Statue of Liberty. The building adjacent was covered with elaborate granite work, gargoyles, birds of prey with an eye on us. The bed was firm and enormous enough for me to make snow angels and not reach the edges.

Emma discovered the white-light bathroom, its wall mirror revealing every indentation in her burned face. I came in behind her and watched as she stroked the soft scabs that had formed, nature's Band-Aids, and realized she wasn't sad. "They're beautiful," she said. "Will they go away? I don't want them to go away." With the back of her thumb, she glided over the marks below her eyes. She was calm now, returning to herself. She filled the tub, and from the bed I could hear her rocking gently. She came out in a hotel bathrobe, quiet, healing, and curled near but not against me.

"This is how people live?"

"Some people," I told her.

"Not us."

"No."

"But you grew up with this." She found a charcoal mark on my shin and scratched at it.

"Sometimes. It's not bad," I finished, "but it's not enough."

She sat up, a little girl. "But it's not bad." Emma burrowed into me, folding us into one, like clothes in the dryer, spinning us down to the precipice of the bed. "Will they feed us?"

"If we're good. Remember, I'm paying Dad back."

She already had the hotel menu in her hungry hands. "He owes you."

"I'm paying him back." I got whacked with the menu for not playing along, and fell back onto the crooked pillows, giving up. Emma chatted with room service for way too long, until I started entertaining the thought that my father did owe me. The price of my disappearance, of not getting in his way. It was worth at least a dinner and a night in the Marriott. Yet I felt responsible. I should have stayed awake with Emma at the stove, should have had a bucket and extinguisher handy. I should have been prepared. By the time the food came, I was too guilty to eat.

"It's delicious," Emma teased, starting on my dinner. I gave in to the mini bottles of Smirnoff and the cans of Carlsberg. They went down easier past the lump in my throat. "I like not working. I never don't work. We should go away." The revelations came quick to Emma in that plush robe in front of her smorgasbord.

"We're not allowed."

"Why?"

"We're just not. Some people go away," I was certain. "And some don't."

"I'm going to Boston," she announced. "To see Nina. To hug Nina." It wasn't a bad idea. My sister hadn't completely forgotten us. There had been vague invitations lofted before, though it was family policy to politely disregard all acts of kindness as temporary lapses of reason. "Tonight."

"Tomorrow," I bargained. I could tell Emma had won. She had one foot on the train. "The money? Milano's?"

"They should bronze us there. I had a few hundred at home." Her face flushed, blending the burns into an auburn background. She looked like a sunburned wife on a Miami weekend. "How much is the bus?"

"Boston," I hummed, trying to remember it. "They have beer there, right?" A sock in the arm.

"They'll have me there, Danny boy, and that's all you need to know." She popped a kiss on me, then blew into my mouth, falling back, laughing in a new way.

"We should have more fires," I suggested, and stole back my meal.

27. Daniel's in the morgue, waiting his turn.

Detective finds his apartment poorly stacked, rearranges all the canned goods by food color, not alphabetically. He opts for visual patterns instead of words. He is beginning to distrust words. Next time he meets the woman and her child, he plans to keep his mouth closed, keep his questions behind his teeth.

In the mirror, Detective is younger somehow, the blue in his beard reflecting brightly up onto him. He decides to grow whiskers. They grow quickly, the Italian ancestors hidden in a nook of his family tree providing the almost instant lushness. Had a beard in the ninth grade, first boy in his class. Girls asked to touch it, tug it, standing lipstick close, then pushing off, giggling. He has shaved every morning since, sometimes twice before noon. He can hear them growing, pushing up out of the forest of his face. It is a race he has never let them win. Now, he is ready. His hair is boy-thick, his face, a man's, ready to be dressed up.

At the precinct they tell him he forgot to shave. "Amnesia," he answers, a rare joke, surprising his colleagues. Welcome to the jungle, they say by five o'clock. In ten days, his beard will be full enough to hide a pencil.

"I'm pleased about the body." The Captain squirms in front of

Detective. Captain is smaller today, a little nervous around Bell, short of breath. "ME says he can take a look in the morning." Detective acknowledges silently. "Growing a beard?" A nod yes. Captain wants something to yell about. His voice is fragile this quiet. He hates the sound of it, would rather write his questions down. "Rook working out?" Detective nods, not hiding in paperwork, staring at Captain, shrinking him. "Let me know anything moves the needle," he says, backing out. "And don't sweat the Murray Hill stiff. Wife's brother's on some goddamn board." By the time he leaves, Captain is dripping sweat. He clips to his desk, phones his wife just to catch his breath.

"Get laid?" Rookie asks Detective over coffee in Tompkins Square Park. No answer. "Broad is a looker."

"Broad?" Detective repeats. "Is that from the police handbook?"

"I'm just talking. Don't be a jerk." They drink sloppily, spilling on their thumbs and shoes as they walk. They stop outside the dog run, where puppies stand shy by their owners' sides. "Everyone's asking about you," Rookie admits. "What you're like in the field. Is it true about the old stiff. Curious." Detective likes the attention. He wants it to last so he says nothing. "I tell them, yeah, he's good in the field. Calm. And as for the old-timer . . ." Rookie trails off laughing, trying to share the joke. "Anyway," Rookie finishes. "You don't have to worry about me."

"I don't."

"You married? I saw pictures."

"Barely."

"Not easy marrying a cop, my girl says. . . ."

"Not easy marrying a person," Detective overlaps. Coffee's gone cold. "You have your money?" Detective asks, palming his wad of ones and fives.

"Yes, sir."

"See you in an hour at Teresa's. I'll be wanting eggs."

They split up and start their canvass. Detective stole two photographs of Daniel from his late teens, and they move among the junkies and homeless, flashing the pics like news from home.

Detective gets the occasional nod, and once the dollar bills come out, a circle of nodders. One, Detective figures, has met Daniel. But these are strangers. Detective feels bad showing Daniel off so conspicuously.

Circling, his identity now clear, Detective receives a wave from near the park's eastern exit. He traces it to the gate. It has moved on. The wave comes from the corner of Tenth and Avenue B, and is connected to a thin arm, an arm in a dress or an apron. A man's arm.

Down Tenth Street to a stoop two up from C. The arm belongs to a man with a matted beard and bald head. Scars across his forearms and scalp. He is clothed in dirt three coats thick, a perfect black, with flecks of flesh peeking out. His shoes are laced, no socks, jean cut-offs exposing wounds and furrows. His arms are sleeves of filth and he wears an apron that warns, DON'T FUCK WITH THE CHEF!

"Beautiful day, Officer," the man exclaims. "November can be good." The bitter bake of skin and squalor have Detective breathing through his mouth. He wants this over with quickly, knows it won't be. He offers Daniel's picture as his first comment. The Chef doesn't look.

"Is Daniel in trouble?" Chef's voice is strong from years of rest. It sounds prerecorded.

The photo pocketed, chin down, Detective's gestures answer the question. Grief clogs Chef's face, fattens his lips, but no tears. "When?"

"Few days ago."

"Why you?" Chef asks, wishing for a more familiar messenger.

"Murder. Maybe."

"No." Chef stands, his scent rising with him.

"Did he take care of you?"

Chef laughs, gesturing to his exterior. "Daniel did a better job than this."

"Do you know anyone?" Detective asks, standing, much taller than Chef. "Anyone he helped? Someone who might know."

"Officer, the ones he helped are gone. It is the ones who said no that remain." Chef checks his new golden laces, double knots, then steps down and away. The way his head bobs when he walks, Detective realizes he wasn't following a waving hand, but a bouncing head. Chef's skull is book narrow, squeezed by time's vice. He moves quickly, Detective scuffling to keep up.

"You could do some good."

"No one would hurt Daniel. Except Daniel." Chef stops, his ridged back to Detective.

"How?"

"Sometimes," Chef's laugh again, breaking the sentence, spilling out onto the street, "he forgot to eat." Chef moves on, his speed nearly too great for Detective. From behind it looks like a race or a lover's quarrel.

They are deep now. At the eastern tip, shanty town. Their feet mingle with refuse, animal and human. Aluminum tents, cardboard tenements, public housing without the funds. Some men notice Detective's arrival more than he does. They want his things. He clatters after Chef. "Why are we running?" Detective asks.

"You seemed to be in a hurry." Chef stops, and Bell sees he is in the center of a homeless fortress. It is dark under the highway, black coughs, night-ruined faces. He strokes his beard. "He has money," Chef announces to the hungry spectators. Detective's whiskers retreat. He takes a stance he wishes could launch him straight into the air. A whiskey bottle lands at his feet, spinning, seeing who gets to kiss him first. "But he has questions, and he is the law." Detective finds his gun, leaves it in peace. "He might also be a friend," Chef guesses, surprising Detective. They make eye contact for the first time, and Chef rattles off into the pitch. Detective forms a line, pulls out his money, and starts buying stories one at a time.

28. May 3, 1990, and a bus ride to Boston. No warning for Nina, just a plan to knock on her door. "I don't believe you don't have the address." Like everything else, it was being stepped on by city inspectors. "You have no idea?"

"Four one one."

"Four one one what?"

"We can call four one one."

"You're hopeless." That was why I never went anywhere. Too much pressure to find things, do things. At home, I knew where everything was. New York City was a backyard and I knew which trees to climb at the precise time of the year. I never chased anything. The city unfolded before me each day, friendly, loud, familiar. Boston was another planet.

"How come you never visited her?" Emma found a cozy nesting spot under my arm, and quickly softened her tone.

"Nina isn't," I realized as I spoke, "the kind of person you visit."

"Why not?"

"She thinks she's invisible." The steady heads of trees blinked by us. We were being yanked toward something, and I didn't trust the brakes.

"Is she? Invisible."

"We're about to find out."

The bus station was crowded with shouting parents, oblivious children, and whole groups of people who seemed to be stranded, left there years earlier, still unsure of what exit to use. I grabbed a phone, and pulled us safely into a booth. Emma read the graffiti while I located my sister. "They have it." I jumped, bumping my head.

"Sally is the one, when you need your zipper . . ."

"Hush," I cautioned, ending Emma's reading. "Four seven seven five. Got it." My fingers felt fat as I pushed the numbers. "Hello, is Nina there?"

"No, she isn't."

"Is she due back? This is her brother."

"Her brother!?" then a long pause as the roommate slowly remembered there were two brothers in Nina's life, one of them still alive.

"The other one," I tried to help. "It's a surprise." She gave us the address and directions and we fell back into the station. "Can we go home now?" I requested. Emma pulled me shirt first toward the taxi line.

The apartment was a good twenty-minute ride from the bus station. The Boston fare meter clicked by much faster than New York's, I complained covertly to Emma. She pinched me. "Don't ruin this," she laid down the law. "Don't even try." At the dropoff, Emma tipped too much and we hurried up the steps, knocking loudly.

Daisy opened the door. She was just twenty-one, a BU student who'd answered a boarder ad the year before. She had her hair pulled back, the way girls do when they're growing it out. Her T-shirt was long, past her knees, and she wore fuzzy white slippers and black leggings. A Boston girl. "I didn't even know," she said, leading us toward the kitchen. We followed, crowding in among open cupboards and the refrigerator door. "I was just going to make some tea," she pretended, filling the pot with too much water.

I wanted to go home. I wasn't sure what to say to Nina after such a distance, and I was only good with strangers when we were on opposite sides of a bar. Daisy kept bumping into us, like she didn't know the dimensions of her own apartment. We fumbled into the television room, waiting for the water to boil.

"Are you guys in school?" Daisy asked, her face stretched with enthusiasm.

"We're bartenders," I summed up.

"Cool. Good money."

"Good enough for a trip to Boston."

"You'll love Boston." She paused. "Nina's going to be so excited."

Six hours later, Emma was asleep on the couch. Daisy had given up all pretense of hospitality and was on the phone arguing with her boyfriend in Pennsylvania. I had the TV on mute and was flipping channels with my eyes closed, guessing what I was missing.

Nina pushed in just after seven from a bad day at a bad job. She was ready to disappear into a book, not crash into a relative.

"Your brother's here," Daisy yelled from her bedroom.

"What?" Nina's eyes got it before her ears, as I met her in the hall.

"Hey, Nina."

Emma woke up and asked me something inaudible. I looked at my sister for the first time in over six years. She had stumbled on a strange prettiness, her hair redder, mouth redder. She had been colored in. She hugged me more to not fall down than anything, then saw Emma over my shoulder. "Hi," Emma offered.

"It was her idea, Nina. To surprise you." Nina's face couldn't hide the flashflood fear she had of Emma. Years of misinformation from home had made Emma a criminal, a fact we always seemed to forget until it bit us in the neck again.

"I don't believe this," Nina sputtered.

"We've been waiting since one," as if to convince her of our commitment.

"No one called. Why didn't Daisy call?" she shouted toward her roommate's door.

"We didn't have your number. It was all last minute."

"I mean at the office. Daisy!" Nina strained. No answer.

"You look beautiful," Emma said, trying to hug my sister, who offered only half her body for the embrace.

"I don't know what to say." None of us did.

"This is a bad day," I attempted.

"No. No." Nina said this to herself. She wanted to feel good about it. She was trying.

"Why don't you take a bath?" Emma suggested. "I could make us dinner."

"She's an unbelievable cook." I smirked, seeing our building barbecued.

"I don't know," Nina started, looking between us, "what to do." There was the heavy quiet of strangers. I looked at Emma, angry that she banged us together, angry that I let it happen. Emma was not prepared for anything but goodwill. She backed away, touching her scab, feeling her burnt hair.

"What an asshole," Daisy blurted at us, her boyfriend the target. She stood outside our jagged triangle, T-shirt stretched, hair in her eyes, pretty in her ignorance. "Anyone hungry?"

Food was an ideal excuse not to talk. We ate pizza in a deep concentration, swapping oohs and aahs with abandon. I stood by New York pizza despite the excellent evidence in front of me, and Daisy blabbed about the frozen stuff she had to stomach once while

in Mechanicsburg visiting her beau. Nina and I were satisfied to let
the evening pass this way, visions of the bus station dancing in my
head. It didn't matter we had no home to return to. The spartan
comfort of the city shelter held a certain appeal. Emma had
different ideas.

"Our building burned down."

"No way," Daisy doubted between bites.

"Yesterday morning. That's what happened to my face, in case
anyone was wondering."

"I thought it was a birthmark," Daisy confessed, relieved.

"We lost everything."

"You're still here," Nina reminded sharply..

"This isn't why we came here, Nina, but would you mind if
we stayed a couple days?" Emma knew she wasn't welcome, and the
challenge made her dig in. I was willing to let Emma have her
Boston vacation and leave on the next Greyhound. Or take Daisy
out for many drinks to discuss bad haircuts and stretch pants. Nina
didn't bother answering. "Aren't you happy to see your brother?"
Emma growled. "I'm happy every time he comes in the room, and
you've been denied that pleasure for six years. At least."

"Who is she?" Nina asked me.

"Ask me," Emma interceded. "Because you're acting like you
know, and this isn't working." Daisy grabbed the last slice and hid
behind her bedroom door. There were breakables around. I took
position to protect them.

"Maybe you should go."

"No. Why?" Emma was coiled, Nina exhausted. My sister
was in trouble.

"Because you don't want to hear what I've got to say."

"We shouldn't have come. This is my fault," I said.

"If you even had the courage to say, 'I'd like to see my brother
without the bitch around,' I'd be happy to sit on the steps. Walk to

the bus station. I just want to see you acknowledge him. Look at him. This is your brother."

Emma did everything but bodily force Nina to look at me, but she simply stared at her plate and said, "See what I mean?"

"Where do they get this idea, Daniel? Where?" Emma scouted out vases, glassware. "They abandon you, then pretend you were stolen in the night. Guess what, Nina. Last chance. You don't get him back." Smash. A plate. Nina looked. An empty vase against the wall. Daisy peeked out to protect her stuff and closed the door just in time on a flying pitcher.

"Get her out!" Nina howled at me. Her face was puffy, neck rigid, the tendons like poles to her skull. I went into the other room and turned on the set. Emma wreaked maximum damage because Nina was afraid to touch her. The stereo, framed posters, pottery.

"Don't forget the TV," I added, sick of what was on. Emma jammed a coat tree through the screen, sending sparks out in flurries.

"I bet you burned down the building. Didn't you, you crazy . . ."

Emma pulled out the coat rack and pointed the smoking antlers at Nina's face. "And I'll do the same here." A confession. "You're going to count all the fragments when we leave. All this shit, and cry over how much you lost. You have no idea." Emma traded her weapon for her coat and tramped through the wreckage and out the door.

"Why?" I asked Nina, passing her. Neither of us knew. It wasn't Emma's shattering frustration. That was the sideshow. What made brother and sister into such strangers? I would have liked to have coffee, gone over old news, picked through the rubble with her, but Emma had closed that door. Nina had her villain. And in me her victim.

"I don't understand this hold she has over you." Nina's final volley.

"That's because you don't know who I am."

"Thanks for taking me to Boston," Emma said, noticing a series of small cuts from her rampage. "Exciting town."

"You don't always have to break stuff."

"Some things need breaking." She was right. We boarded the bus, a few familiar faces joining us. Maybe we had taken the Family Squabble Express. Same-day service, serving the entire Northeast Corridor. Surprise your loved ones. Upend their lives and be home before midnight.

"It's simpler for these people," I hoped. "Isn't it simpler?"

Emma looked out the window, her face steaming up the glass. "There's all this heat under my skin."

"Let it out, Emma." The window fogged, obscuring what we were leaving, pushing us home toward what we thought we understood.

29. Detective looks at his last one-dollar bill and lets it go in the wind. He bought them lunch. He handed out one hundred and fifty bucks to men who had never heard of or seen Daniel. They tried, they pretended for their lunch money, but he gave up, shortening their stories, allocating funds. A city charity event. Chef knew where he was taking Detective. He knew they'd meet again, but he also knew men were hungry. Lunch.

"Got a guy says he knew him," Rookie gushes at Teresa's while Detective salts his eggs. "Couple of guys."

"How much it cost you?" The eggs are scrambled just so.

"Whatever. They knew the guy, said he used to push dope out of his . . ."

"Eggs?" Detective asks. "Good eggs. Waitress!"

"I have these guys."

"Where?"

"In the car."

"Cuffed?" Waitress arrives. "Make Sergeant Hrcek a couple soft-scrambled, coffee, toast." Two sips and the waitress leaves. "Let them go."

"I've got positive IDs"

"Let them go, be back in time for your eggs. Or I'll eat them."

Rookie knows Bell's serious. "You are crazy," as he leaves. He returns red-faced. "They split anyway."

"You have them on the honor system, Sergeant?" Laugh. "Relax, have an egg. I got a head start." Rookie eats what's left of his meal as Detective loosens his belt, leans in. "Daniel didn't push dope or any other substance. He drank heavily and he did what we did today. Gave out free lunches. But without the questions. He ran a soup kitchen and a shelter out of his apartment. Finish your toast."

"Sounds like you like the stiff."

"It's allowed."

Detective finds the morgue cooler today, less menacing. Coroners sense he belongs, leave him alone. He spies the Doc who covered for him in Murray Hill. They wave. On a stainless-steel table in the second examining room from the back, Detective finds Daniel gutted. There are organs on a sliding tray. All gray. Daniel's compartments have been emptied, their contents displayed. Small flags assist the Coroner's search for particular signs, stresses.

This many days after death, the corpse seems more brittle, fragile. Detective wants to protect Daniel, put him under glass, underground. There are lines drawn on the taut skin. Places to cut, sections to dig. The body is both map and site, an experiment in cartography.

Detective's slide show runs across Daniel's expressionless face. Nina, mother and father, a tiny boy. Vacations, sleepovers, a thousand legs and arms in motion. For a flicker, Detective sees Daniel move, acknowledge. It is the ME, cutting into view. "What a face." This coroner is new to Detective, sudden, his movements all elbow and twitch. He chose his career watching B movies on Saturday afternoons. "Hardly a mark, even at thirty it's notable. You are the detective they warned me about?"

"Warned you?"

"Mentioned. Discussed. I have a terrible time with words. Can't get them to sit still for one minute." ME makes a confident cut down Daniel's calf. Varicose veins. "On his feet a lot."

"Bartender."

"Isn't this fun? I love guessing right." Corpse's feet are knobbed, blistered, the soles dull yellow with calluses. "Of course one look at the liver says he got his liquor free. That's a middle-aged liver, Detective."

"Did it kill him?"

"That's what we're trying to figure out."

"You enjoy your work," Detective surmises to the sound of another incision, the unzipping of a purse.

"Better do. At least none of my clients talk back." ME circles the body, making notes, poking, prodding.

"Poison?"

"Patience, Detective. Poison is very clever at hide-and-seek. Give me at least ten days." ME pokes Detective in the arm. "A live one. How odd."

"Am I in your way?"

"No, it's just that most of the boys in blue prefer to skip the unveiling. Too close to the bone, if you get my gist."

"I knew him," Detective lies. It is a comforting lie. He relaxes, trusts the ME.

"I'm sorry. Wouldn't have been so cavalier." Doctor checks to see if he made any unnecessary cuts.

"I don't mind. I know he's not here."

"Well, for my sake, he better be here. Why didn't your friend eat?"

Detective looks at the Doctor, sees the owlish head, low jowls. He notices his fingers, long as a pianist's, and the way his jacket is too short. Or his arms too long. Detective wants to ask Daniel the same question, to nudge him awake, all hollow, and hear his voice echo back. "He wasn't hungry."

"Sure as hell got thirsty. Feel that thing," handing over the liver. "It's okay, it won't bite. It might sip, though." It is rock heavy in Detective's hands, and slippery, though it's dry. There are some things a man should not hold. "It's a fossil. I didn't know better, I'd say that was transplanted in."

"Possible?"

"No scars, no medical history. Of course not. Just goes to show you how much damage we can do. Drink?" ME hands over a flask and they both partake. "To whatever his name is, toe tag number 11674. Rest in pieces. Just kidding."

"His name is Daniel."

"Was."

"Right. I need to know."

"Detective, thirty seconds before I do." They shake gloved hands and go to their corners. Detective removes his protection on his way out, and squeezes Daniel's hand.

30.

The fallout from Boston was a bill from my Dad. I figured he'd be covering all Nina's damage, so he cut loose the smaller tab. Emma opened it while I was at work, recognizing Dad's letterhead, and entered Milano's with a curled fist.

"Three hundred bucks, the bastard."

"Hi, Emma."

She scooted a misty-eyed regular onto another stool and shook the letter in my face. I read it while she railed. "And on top of everything, Nina gets all new things. Which she needed."

"You redecorated."

"And got charged." Her indignation lagged.

"We had a great time at the hotel. And we torched an entire building for free."

"You have got a point," she said, wagging her finger at me affectionately. "I knew you'd do it."

"What?" I refilled whiskeys down the row.

"Calm me down. That's why I came over. Besides, we don't have any stuff to break." I stretched my arms across the wall of liquor. "Just kidding."

"Stay." I took her hands, brushed at the dry healing flakes on her cheeks. She was regaining herself every day.

"Are you afraid of me?" she asked. I laughed, looked around at everyone ignoring us. "I'm serious."

"Emma."

"I get scared. Sometimes," she said.

"Of yourself? Don't. That's why I'm here." I pulled her up against her side of the bar, going on tiptoes to kiss her nose.

"I should call the Doctor."

"Nonsense, I'm the Doctor."

Emma waited the hour till I punched out and we walked home together. Our new place was on Tenth Street between First and Second. It was in a tenement building owned by our previous landlord. We'd been golden tenants for six years, so he let us move uptown ten blocks and move in without a security deposit. We were on the fifth floor of a six-floor walkup, with little more than half the size of our pig-building place. The kitchen was really just a sink in the living room. The bedroom had enough area for a bed and a lamp, or more fitting, a flashlight. The fact that we could be at opposite ends of the apartment and still touch only added to the romance.

There were still a handful of our former neighbors who had been unable to secure housing. They were living in the shelter, or in some cases in Tompkins Square Park, since it was spring. First out of boredom and then for fun, I started going down to the shelter nights, to swap stories or help out in the kitchen. Emma was working, and for some reason, I didn't tell her I was spending so much time down there. It was the first secret I'd kept from her, and I couldn't figure out why I remained silent.

I started meeting other families, many Puerto Rican and Polish, who were stuck sleeping on cots, with no jobs or small-time day gigs that kept them in the hole. They taught me to cook elaborate soups, beer bread, roast chicken, meals in every language. I'd stay up late playing backgammon with the fathers or listening to broken English stories about the glories of Old Krakow or San Juan. The freedom. The blue. They greeted me with hugs, expectation, shouting my name, waiting for me. I was becoming a regular, developing a life separate from Emma, cheating on her. I still loved Emma, cherished what little time we could meet awake, but I was most alive at the shelter, or in Tompkins Square. I had found something I barely remembered. Family.

On Thursday nights, I would bring a book to read to the little ones. A story to take the steam out of their legs and let the adults catch a smoke, a coffee, a minute to breathe. "Tell the one about *el gato*," a boy said. He was ripe brown, his face flecked with dirt from wrestling with his older brother.

"*El gato en el hato?*" I said, pulling out a fringed copy of *The Cat in the Hat* I'd found at the flea market.

"*Sí, el gato en el hato!*" came the cheer. Seven, eight, nine, ten children circled me.

One mother started sitting in. She was in her early twenties, Puerto Rican–Filipino mix, with a little boy she called Trevor. He was three, a fierce, brown-skinned boy, who liked to run naked through the shelter, grabbing whatever he could on his journey. I called him Velcro. Velcro had attached himself to my leg for the story, and his mother, Maria, was too close behind. I had noticed her presence since they came to the shelter. She was quiet, but often stayed late in the kitchen, helping clean up, or lingered after story time, always on the verge of conversation.

"Hello, Maria," I said as the kids ricocheted toward their beds.

"You know my name." She had a laugh that came before her sentences. A clenched, involuntary giggle that started her motor. Her hair was impractically long, past her spine and china black, with uneven bangs dangling over her face, branches blocking a view.

"I didn't know you were American."

"The Bronx. We're just passing through."

"Where's the Dad?" was a question I'd stopped asking.

Mothers and children were the couples down there. I imagined Sophie mixing it up with these wild ones. I wanted Emma near. "You make this place okay."

They're my friends, I realized.

"You don't have to come."

"Yes, I do."

"Trevor and I got an apartment," she mentioned, sitting closer. She had just put on perfume. She smelled like other women, something I'd never sensed before. "In Queens."

"Congratulations."

"It's a start." She held her hands out in front of her, palms up. "Now if I can just start learning to hang on." She closed her fists.

"Hang on," I said as Trevor tackled me and stuck.

"We'd like you to visit us." Her voice cracked and leveled. "Isn't that right, Velcro?" Maria kissed me on the cheek. "I'll call here when we get a number. Don't forget us, Daniel." I stood amid the screech of cots and prolonged goodnights. Someone led me to the door, letting me out into the unfamiliar. It was eleven. Emma was working and I needed a drink.

31. Detective goes to his mother's grave. It's a thirty-minute drive from the precinct and he leaves the windows down. She was buried in Trinity along the Hudson, amid the dead flowers and thorn bushes twenty years before. Detective was twenty-four and he didn't cry like his sister. He signed the papers, paid with what his mother had allocated, and crossed himself before he left.

He and his sister didn't tell their father. They couldn't find him, even if he would have cared. Wyoming. Idaho. He'd vanished somewhere cold where people forgot who they were as a matter of habit.

His mother died quickly of some rampaging disease that left her enough time to regret and none to fix. They buried her here because it was close. There was no reason to visit, no family history. Her third husband, Bell, took all proof of her life years earlier. Photos, calendars, even canceled checks. He went into estate sales at flea markets in Florida, using Detective's mother's pearls and cameos as capital.

Today Detective wraps up against the sudden river chill and steps over dead flowers and long-forgotten names. He is pulled through the maze of gray and spent green to his mother's plot. Emeline Bell, 1927–1976: "A widow in life, a bride in death." A quote that honored her will, meaning nothing to her son.

Detective delivers the yellow roses, yellow like the flash of Sophie's hair, and props them against the stone, knowing the wind and threatened snow will claim them once he's gone. He looks out over the blur of granite, wondering why people bury what they don't understand. He wants to exhume his mother, set her bones in a row till they make a sentence that explains. He wants to soak the ashes and paint symbols on the ground. To switch skulls and femurs till someone fits. All these clues, he thinks, all the answers, and the earth, the great conspirator, swallowing evidence till nothing remains but the name. Bell, he fingers his mother's grave. Bell. Detective crosses himself and stays.

This time he cries.

32. The invitation came. Maria left her new number at the shelter and I was handed it without fanfare. I waited three days to call, finally using a pay phone on the corner of Broadway and Broome.

"Why aren't you calling from home, Cowboy?" Maria laughed. Before I had an answer, I had an address. "Take the E train from West Fourth."

"When?"

"Now, if you want, Sugar. But I'm around." I heard Trevor making helicopter sounds in the background. "Hey, Daniel," she said and left it at that.

I hung up, my heart banging. What was I doing? I was making a date. This wasn't charity, or to check on a little boy's progress. There was a pretty woman a train ride away, and we wanted to meet.

I felt I'd been cheating on Emma just by going to the shelter, but now the castle door had opened. I would never do anything to hurt Emma; that concept was secure. But with Maria's voice over the phone line, something shifted, my sightlines obscured. Everything fell into a matrix of "What if . . ." and "Maybe, but . . ." I needed someone to ask, but there was nobody. My family would have driven me to Maria's and baby-sat. Everyone at Milano's knew

Emma, and everyone at the shelter knew Maria. I decided I would ask Emma herself. Right after I took a ride to Queens.

Maria was busy in the kitchen and yelled for me to come in. It was late October, too deep into fall to let the air in. Trevor was of course naked. He smashed into my knee as hello, and continued his private journey through the kingdom. Maria came out, wiping her hands. Her body was looser, more comfortable in her own space. "Nice to see you, Daniel. Nice to see you."

I felt watched, and Velcro's dive off a couch arm confirmed my suspicion. "It's almost nap time. I didn't think you'd come right away."

"Something in your voice," I said, not meaning to.

"I like that." She grabbed her son by the ankle and took him out of the room upside down. "A man should come when he's called."

While Maria bedded her frantic child, I eyed the boxes and remnants of a displaced life. One label had four addresses crossed out before it got it right. There were a few toys scattered, but Trevor's landscape would have to be his imagination. The neighborhood had too much iron and broken glass for such an active boy. His mother would have to keep him behind doors for years.

Instinctively, I finished the dishes, even put away some things, in the wrong cupboards. Maria caught me going for a mop. "Stop that," she scolded. "Make a woman feel like a mess."

"Bad habit. I have trouble waiting."

"Me, too." Maria took my face with both hands, pulling me in to deliver a delicate kiss. She held me there, our lips just open, air escaping in slivers. "I couldn't not kiss that mouth anymore." She released me. I stood still and she hopped up on the counter. I had no idea what to do. I sensed my face turning colors, a kaleidoscope of bewilderment and bliss. I wanted another. "You look happy." I wanted the room dark, so we couldn't see how things looked, only how they felt. "You want some more?" I nodded and she came back to me, her hips pinning me against the refrigerator, her hands locked with mine, stretched straight down. I tried to kiss back, but felt so unprepared. We stopped again. "Daniel," she whispered. "You don't know how good this feels." But I did. She pushed her forehead against my lips, and walked me five steps, then turned. "You have a girlfriend," she reminded me. "They told me. At the shelter." I still didn't have words, my mouth malformed by such kisses. "And I have a son." We stood there in our division, eager to get close enough where space could be erased. "I wanted to know I was pretty again."

"How could you not?"

She smiled and took my face, pressing the bruises of sleeplessness out with her thumbs. "You're so nervous," she whispered, my ribs quaking from the inside out.

"I've never done this."

"I know." We walked to the couch and sat, limbs crossing, hands admiring. "I wasn't fair. I do like you. But you are so in love."

"It's all I . . . she is my . . ."

"Don't tell me her name." Maria requested. "I don't want it."

"All right." I appreciated the privacy.

"I know I can't have you, but will you still visit? For Trevor?"

"Can we kiss some more?" I bargained. Laughter threw her into me, her hair in my eyes, the aroma of waiting. So we kissed. For the hour Trevor napped, Maria and I found a thousand ways to undo facts and bend our lives till they curved and bloomed on our lips. The boy's crying was a sound track to our final touch. She gathered Trevor and brought him to the door to say good-bye.

"What's wrong with your face?" he interrogated.

"Ask your mother," I said, backing out of the apartment. She waved from her side of the door, and I fell into the afternoon burr. I had the train ride home to figure out what to say to Emma as soon as she noticed my face.

"I want to make love," Emma said, already knowing.

"No."

"Are you leaving me?"

"No."

"Take a shower."

"I didn't."

"I can smell her perfume from here." Emma had her back to me. She refused to turn around.

"That's all. It's nothing." Her shoulders rose and stuck. "Her name is Maria."

"Stop."

"She has a little boy," as if that explained everything.

"Is that why?" Emma half turned.

"She's from the shelter. We became friends. Her boy likes me."

"She likes you."

"Yes, but she doesn't get me."

"Why not?" Part of her face became visible, the cut of her chin.

"Emma, you know."

"Tell me."

"Because I have you."

"You have me?"

"I love you. I need you. I am . . ." I wanted to be back where there were no words. Maria's lips, Emma's belly, somewhere that talking didn't count.

"You said she was from . . ."

"The shelter. I go there." My secret life unspooled, this the bigger betrayal.

"Why? When?"

"To volunteer. A few nights. Most nights. It's like a family. The kids. I read stories. I hear stories from the *abuelos.*" I spoke fast to quicken the blow.

"Take me," she said, offering her face. It was crooked from crying and waiting and guessing. I didn't recognize her. I'd seen her angry, weeping, burning down the house, but not this way. "Will you take me?" Of course, I meant to say, the words getting jammed. "How long?"

"Six months. Since the fire. Five months." The weight of not being told fell on her face again, pressing everything down. Her eyes closed, jaw hung. I couldn't hold her. I didn't have the right.

"You are leaving me. You already left."

"No." I stepped toward her, but she folded in half on the couch, pulling the afghan down for cover.

"Sophie will be so disappointed."

"There is no Sophie!" I shouted.

"Go away, Daniel," Emma managed from her bunker. "Go away."

33. The death is in Queens. Detective drives over the Triborough, past all the Indian and Arab cab drivers racing home. Rookie sits beside him, anxious and quiet.

The scene is busy with NYPD from the borough. They look through personal items, keep the family at bay. There is loud talking, louder music. A paramedic's rap competing with the household's Persian cacophony.

Detective muscles in, Rookie behind like a proud son. There are arguments about jurisdiction, then they clear the room. Corpse is bubbled up, gorge to belt. His face is all surprise, no preparation. Skin is bundt brown, lighter where the stretch marks line his circumference. Hair is short, black. In every drawer, cash. Hundreds of thousands of American dollars. Not neat. Crumpled, handed over. The money isn't stacked, but stashed, under carpets, in the ceiling, sock drawer, in the pipes of the unused sink.

Rookie can't decide whether to slow down enough to take notes. He is Christmas-morning excited, looking under every item, shaking boxes, pulling curtains.

"Name," Detective finally asks.

"Mahmed Abdullah."

"Occupation."

"New York City cab driver."

"Time of death."

"Cousin found him like this three hours ago."

"Sure as hell wasn't robbery," Rookie grins, displaying another drawer full of bills.

"Where's the ME?"

Pictures are snapped, the flashbulb polka-dotting the barren walls. "Just like on CNN, Detective," Rookie bubbles. "Don't call the cops, call Unicef."

"Not funny," Detective cautions.

"Sorry."

The kitchen is bare. Cupboards empty, nothing in stock. "Where's the food?" Detective asks the cousin, a small man with bad teeth and worse English.

"No food."

"Why?"

"Never home." The cousin lives next door, swears he never sees the corpse. Swears he came over to "borrow" money. Swears he never does this. Sometimes. Once a week.

"When was the last time you saw Mahmed alive?"

"Never home," cousin answers, a cigarette cradled in his gums.

Taxi dispatch says he worked last night. There are $402 in the back pocket of his trousers. He is a rich dead man. "How much," Rookie wonders, "if you actually counted it?"

"Put it back."

Rookie does.

"He didn't see it coming," Coroner says, popping corpse's eyes open, playing piano across the face. "Whatever it was, it surprised him."

"But the belly?"

"Classic malnutrition. These hacks don't exactly eat right. Though this is extreme. You want to run this as murder?" Doctor quizzes. "Or natural causes? I could go either way."

"Murder," Detective gets. "I need the body."

They throw a sheet over Mahmed and gurney him into the street. Neighbors gawk and point. "She was pregnant," some say.

"He," Rookie corrects.

In the car, Rookie is calmer, almost sad. He gets nothing from Detective, a wall today. "Like the other?" Rookie tries. "Like Daniel."

"No food in the house. Neither had food in the house. Like they just forgot."

"I think the cousin did it, be honest." Rookie enjoys hypothesizing. He scoots around in his seat, talks into Detective's ear. "All that cash. No prospects. We should have checked his fridge."

"Mahmed dead, well runs dry. No one shuts down their own bank."

"Then what?"

"We need to talk to Emma."

His name was Mahmed, the note begins. It is pinned to Detective's blotter on his desk. The handwriting is familiar, like a signature he's seen. He was a friend of Daniel's, is the second line. Detective yells, asking, Who dropped this off! Who opened his door? He reads the note out loud: "His name is Mahmed. He was a friend of Daniel's. Keep looking." Emma and Sophie.

34. I spent my twenty-fifth birthday alone. Left Emma asleep on the couch, and went to work. Quit. Went down to the Spring Lounge, daytime empty, chafed tables and schoolroom chairs all to myself. I played the entire Van Morrison's Greatest Hits in the juke, and started getting drunk. "I'm here for one reason," I warned the satchel-faced bartender.

"Obvious." He poured the first shot of Jack and backed away. "Wave when you need me. And don't forget to tip." I saluted his integrity, and dug in.

Five shots of Jack soaked into the loaf of Wonder Bread I'd had for breakfast. The sugars swam in a stream of delight to my brain, breaking off into tributaries, drowning motor skills in the flood. The Budweisers slowed me down, twelve ounces an ocean compared to the puddles of whiskey I'd been splashing in. "Today's my birthday," I slurred, getting a free shot in return.

"Sorry to hear that." The bartender was taking on a certain bulldog beauty, a kindness, a loyalty. I knew I could trust him.

"Today's my birthday. Hey, Dennis!" It wasn't his name, but I'd decided it was easier to pick one and stick with it. "What the hell's wrong with the jukebox?"

"Out of quarters." He was gentle with my impatience.

"Well, then feed it," I belted, shoving dollar bills his direction.

"On me." He scraped a fistful of change out of the register and dialed up Ray Charles, The Pogues, and a bunch of groups I couldn't name under such duress.

"I'm taking a break," I said, tripping to a table, laying down my soggy head. I napped till the wind blew in the mailman. "Dennis," I shouted. "You guys get mail?" Snoozed for another few minutes, then sat up, a group of children playing ring around the rosy in my head. "Ashes, ashes," they sang jubilantly. "All fall down."

"That calls for a drink."

"I think I'll join you." It was 1:30 P.M. and all that pouring had built up Dennis's thirst. His face was a gallery of bumps and pockets. More than time had gone to work on him; things that punched out from within, leaving scoops of skin and rusty stains.

"How do you get a face like that?" I said out loud, not meaning to.

"You've got a head start, pal." He smiled, filling my glass with amber poison.

"Why does the head feel it first and the liver last?"

"The liver is a beautiful instrument," he confided as one who knew the intricate behavior of his organs. "It's like a woman who never complains, no matter what you put her through. And then, one day, she just quits." His jowls quickened. "No worry, no wondering. Solid as a rock till the day she says good-bye."

"Then what?" I asked, pulling his sleeve.

"Then you die." He opened us each a Bud, toasted, and drifted into a phone call.

The friendly smoke of other customers chased me away just after two. I left Dennis way too much money and walked west on Spring with one eye closed for balance. Needing food, I wobbled into a Cuban dive, where they plied me with black beans, white rice, and Tabasco sauce. I chomped my buttered bread, drank Pepsi in gulps, and tried to sober up enough so I could start getting drunk again.

In my tumult, between inebriation and overeating, the other diners appeared to be rushing at me from the sides, questions on the ends of their forks. Their eyes spinning into cherries and sevens and stars. But when I'd turn to confront them, they'd sneak back to their casual postures, their sustenance. Coffee, pork sandwiches, fried plantains.

"Leave me alone!" I yelled.

"Hey, baby, you're okay," the waitress soothed, a blacksmith forged cook appearing behind her.

"I'm okay." I agreed. "Today's my birthday."

"Happy birthday," as she cleared my unfinished plates. "You don't look crazy. Why you want to go acting crazy?" Her smile was hospital white, and I tried to believe her.

"Sorry," I said, dropping a twenty for a four-dollar check.

The weather had turned against me, an uninvited November bite in the air. In a nameless bar I threw back pints of Bass ale and an array of liquors to chase the cold back into the atmosphere. The tender had long red hair and a defeated Irish face. She was bad at feigning interest and I saw her mostly from the other end of the bar. She visited when I waved, but took her tips joylessly. Maybe it was her birthday, too.

I swapped forgettable stories with a series of locals, always steering them away with some rendition of "Happy Birthday to Me."

"You're drunk," the bartender labeled me.

"Since noon," lifting a glass toasting my accomplishment.

"Think maybe you've had enough."

"I was seeing who'd give out first."

"I quit," she said, her only smile breaking open that face. "Make it home okay?"

"I can make it home," I told her.

Like a man on a train, I exited, hands out in front for

protection. I'd entered a tunnel of my own making, lights and cars tearing by, blackness in a cylinder all about me. A Japanese grocery owner caught me from collapsing on his oranges. They looked so warm. "Home," I said to him, his face folding into a confused origami. "Home."

I kept the mantra up, hoping an interior compass would obey and overcome the illegible street signs and traffic lights. It was dark inside and out. Maybe a cab.

I don't recall saying the words, but the cabby dropped me off at Grand Central Station. The mania of commuters had passed and there was an odd calm, as if they had expected me. I bought a ticket by rote, and a team of candy bars to settle my stomach. The train came and rocked me to sleep, a metal mother, nudging me awake at the proper stop.

Swaying onto Peck Avenue, I stutter-stepped the last few blocks to my parents' house. It was late in the evening, but not the end. The crisp grass of the neighbor's lawn broke beneath my feet as I stared at the people trapped inside 16 Thistle Lane.

Dad sat in his chair in the den, illuminated by the dull spotlight of the TV. He had the remote in one hand and a drink in the other. He lugged the glass to his mouth for the occasional pull, the strength to manage all he could muster.

Mom buzzed room to room, a dragonfly, drawn by the light, the chore, the undone. I could see her dusting, tying, fixing, a hurricane of actions. She never broke the seal of the den. The netting was up. No insects allowed. Finally, she sat down at the dining-room table and looked out the window. Not at me, but past me, her eyes fixed on some impossible point, locked onto that promise, that soldier coming home.

"Today's my birthday," I reminded the house, and then jimmied the garage door open and pulled down blankets and towels kept there for camping trips we'd long forgotten. They had the sting of kerosene and fish, and weren't allowed in the house either.

In the back seat of my father's car, I made a fort, alcohol still thick on my tongue. Inside, lights went out, covers pulled like bandages. A brutal silence descended. "Happy birthday, Daniel!" my sisters and parents and Warren shouted. I shivered into sleep.

I woke up just in time to scamper out of the garage and hide in the neighbor's bushes, leaving the blankets in a lump. My father grumbled something about them toward my mother, who was still in bed, then pulled out. He looked my way, even slowing down, but puttered off unknowing.

I was stuck in Rye on a dreary, drowsy, nausea morning. I wasn't sure I'd make it through the back door as I snuck into the house. I took a box of cereal down, but replaced it as my stomach canceled breakfast. I could hear Mom padding around upstairs, and didn't want to frighten her. My only desire was a few more hours' sleep, but the threat of having to explain my presence was more daunting than my blues. I snuck back out and walked to the train.

I caught the commuter, which kept me on my feet, surrounded by suits and oversplashed cologne. I could smell the hurry they had left in. They stood, many with their collars askew, ignoring each other, pretending they weren't all marching off to their doom. So solemn they were in their gray and black and brown, so earnest in their invisibility. I would have had fun with them, sung out loud, compared briefcases, if I hadn't been so dazzlingly nauseated. Heat pricked up in columns along my forearms and neck. I strained for anything cool to lean against. The silver doors, the trash receptacle, even the cool of a gentleman's Rolex, until he noticed. The last thing these men needed was vomit on their shoes, and I did everything to avoid disaster. Another minute, I kept telling myself, one more minute, too guilty to strike a deal with anyone. I deserved punishment. I would serve the full sentence.

The train crept along, sneaking up on the city. "They don't

know we're coming," I said, getting no response. "Pretend they don't know we're coming," my comments hastening the exit of my end of the car.

Back on familiar turf, I got dragged, bumped, and yanked on my way to the bathroom. Homeless bathed in preparation for their commute, up Lexington, then over to Central Park. They had a rugged dignity I couldn't match as I dispersed my goods in the nearest toilet. "He's all right," came the word from over my shoulder. They let me clean up in peace.

I bought coffee and a bagel to arouse and soak. The 6 train to Astor Place and the quick walk home. It was 9:15 A.M. Grand Central time. Emma would be asleep.

"You quit," she said, the door shutting behind me. She was in the bedroom, actually in the bed. She had the covers pulled up to her chin. These were the first words she'd spoken since Maria. I readjusted to the quiet splendor of her voice. "Dennis called from the Shark Bar." His name was Dennis! "He recognized you from Milano's and phoned worried. I got the message from Paul." Her body wasn't moving, just this talking head and all the blankets.

"Are you cold?"

"Where were you? You look awful. Get in here." She lifted the blankets and scooted over. I toppled in, barely getting off my shoes, so grateful was I to be near her. Under the covers, she let her body linger close enough to warm me. "They're not letting you quit. They already rehired you."

"Do I have to go in today?" I moved a fraction closer. She didn't mind.

"I'll cover. I didn't work last night, I was out looking for you."

"Emma."

"Of course. It was making me crazy. Happy birthday by the way."

"You, too."

"Tomorrow."

"In case you're not talking to me."

"Hush." She rolled me over with surprising strength and started warming my other side. "Where did you go?"

"I got drunk."

"You smell like you drowned." She pulled off my shirt, pants, socks, made me gargle, even combed my hair. "You'll shower later. Just rest."

"Get back in bed," I hoped, needing her near. She crawled in from the bottom, stopping to kiss my knee. "I've missed you. I thought you were gone."

"I was," she said, still not holding me.

"Are you back?"

"Are you?" she emphasized. My stomach had settled and I was beneath familiar cotton with Emma to my right.

"Yes. I'm home."

35. "Nina, it's me," Detective says from his apartment phone. It is night, the bark of sirens busy out his window. He stands with a cup of coffee too hot in his free hand. He is wearing old jeans and a T-shirt. Things he hasn't worn in years. They arrived today by UPS from Carroll Gardens. He is so young he wants to run, to call up girls, to find someone.

She is happy to hear from him, but afraid of surprises.

"Is this a bad time?" he apologizes

"No, not at all. You called. This is great." He doesn't believe her. Wonders if she found out his identity. His youth begins to fade. "I'm being a jerk," Nina says. "How are you? I've had a weird day."

Detective relaxes, sips his coffee, finds a chair. His finger tickles the edges of albums his wife sent. Groups and songs whose sound is long vanished from his memory. These must be the boy's, he thinks mistakenly. "What can I do?"

"You already have. Calling. Thanks. How's Binghamton?" Her voice finding its range.

"How's Boston?" he answers, nearly telling her about the dead Muslim with her brother's gut.

"When are you coming?"

"Soon, I hope. Maybe next weekend."

"Oh."

"Or not."

"Just warn me," Nina shuffles, looking in the mirror at her new haircut. "I'm lousy at surprises."

"Can I ask you a question?" Detective scoots forward on his chair. He pictures Nina, looks into her eyes, holds her. "It's stupid, I know, but it's been bugging me. Like when you hear a song and..." He overexplains, spills the box of records, sending them spinning across the floor. "You know what I mean?"

She's more patient than he thinks, doesn't notice his panic. "Good, I like helping with these."

"Emma," he starts.

"Yeah."

"What is her last name?" There is a long silence, too long for a phone call. Detective feels caught.

"That is a weird question."

"It's just been bugging me."

"I don't know," Nina cools. She knows why he called or at least why he didn't call. She glares at her reflection. She's ready to hang up, but instead, "Maybe Mom knows. I never bothered."

"Yeah," he says, his jeans now too tight. "Stupid question."

"I have to go."

"Nina, don't be mad."

"I'm not," she lies.

"That's not why I called. I'm bad over the phone. I do want to come up." He hurries this, sounding foolish and sincere.

"Give me two weeks," Nina allows. "I look like shit."

Detective listens to the dial tone until it becomes staccato beeps, then a woman's voice describing how to make a call. He keeps waiting for Emma's last name to signal through, or for this last conversation to be erased. In two weeks he'll have a beard, he consoles himself. They'll both look different.

He waits a long time before he gets Rookie to call Daniel's mother. It is a simple procedure, one he could have arranged at the start. But that was when names didn't matter. Only colors and shapes, the sound with the volume down.

"Clough," Rookie tells Detective. "Like dough, with a C-L."

"I don't like it."

"So what?" Pause. "Sir?"

"Get me an address and call me in the car. I'll meet you there."

"I'm in the middle of a sandwich, Detective."

"Then you'll have to wait to see how it ends."

The address is on Tenth Street between First and Second. Fifth floor. Detective and Rookie take the steps gingerly, guns drawn. They draw breaths outside her door.

"I got the papers moving for a warrant," Bell whispers. "But tonight we'll need an invitation."

"Emma Clough," Rookie growls, knocking. "This is the NYPD. Please open up." Behind the door, a scuffle. The officers feel the weight of their weapons. Fear. "Emma Clough!" Rookie yells as the door opens on a beautiful woman with a child at her side.

"You woke my kid," the woman says. "And you can put away the toys."

Her name is Maria Iglesia. She is lovely. The officers struggle to be sorry enough. At her side, his eyes wide as buttons, is her son, Trevor. He wears no shirt and his belly arcs out the way eight-year-old bellies do. She makes them tea they don't want but can't refuse. They need to watch her in motion. The boy stares at Detective, speechless.

"Do you know an Emma Clough?"

"No," Maria says, her sheepishness arousing Detective. He wants to send Rookie home, move in, care for the boy and his mother. Detective bites the inside of his cheek.

"I'm in love with you" becomes "Not familiar at all?" just in time.

"Her name is on the lease," Rookie stabs. "We're not selling Girl Scout cookies."

"I'm sure you'd do very well." Maria scowls. The boy stares on.

"What's wrong with your son?"

"He's not used to seeing men, I think."

"Yo lo conozco," Trevor says.

"What's that?" Rookie tenses, distrusts the curve of the child. Looks for arrows.

"He says he knows you," Maria tells Detective. Mother and son swap Spanish code, excluding Rookie, soothing Detective. "He says he knows you."

"That's all?" Detective asks, not recognizing the son of the beauty. He needs his whiskers rough across her face, to hear her say his name. His name.

"La fragrancia."

"Like a dog," Rookie half laughs. He can tell he'll be asked to leave. Tries to hang on. "Back to our mystery guest. Emma. Clough. Like Dough, with . . ."

"I do not know *la mujer.*"

"How did you get the apartment?" Detective inquires. She trusts him. He loves her. The boy inches closer to Bell.

"A friend. The same as always."

"Who pays the rent?"

"I do. Not the state. I work."

"The boy," from Rookie.

"Day care."

"Ought to have a shirt on," Hrcek parents.

"He just started wearing pants last year. I take what I can get." Maria's mouth quivers with the invasion of her home. She wants these men far away. Her son dives onto Detective.

"Velcro!" Trevor yells, frightening them all. Detective peels Trevor, and leaves him on the ground. The boy crosses his legs and sits beside Detective.

"Who got you the apartment, ma'am?" Rookie closes. "Let's start somewhere."

"Daniel," Maria nods.

Detective moves close, ready to catch her. "He's dead."

A secret grief overtakes her. It is battering, causing small explosions on her face. Maroons and purples splash beneath her eyes, at the corners of her mouth. She bends without breath or sound. Trevor blocks her face from the men, forcing them to look away. He leads his mother into the bedroom and shuts the door, returning to sit on Detective's lap.

"Daniel is our friend," Trevor tells them. Rookie's belly cramps, shuts him up. Detective puts his hand on the hot of Trevor's back. They even each other's fevers, and wait for the grief to subside.

Detective decides to meet Maria the next day while Trevor is in day care. Detective walks Maria down Second Avenue and up over to Round the Clock for breakfast. Her eyes are scorched behind sunglasses, cheeks still swollen, lips bitten and sore.

"When I cry, my whole face goes," she tells him, though he still finds her beauty unbearable.

"Can you eat?" Detective is tender, his whiskers softer. They sit and look into their coffee cups for answers.

"He was the most beautiful boy," she begins.

"You were lovers."

"I loved him," she answers. They wait for a storm to pass. "Did you know him?"

"I found him. I'm getting to know him."

"I can't believe." She removes her glasses to press the ham of her hands into her stubborn eyes. Tears run out over the sides, forming a line down her pinky.

"When was the last time?"

"I didn't see him much. Three, maybe, no. Six months ago. He just took care. I knew he was around."

"And Trevor?"

"Like a dad. An uncle. Stories, they'd wrestle. Goddamnit!" Maria pounds the table, bending a fork.

"Somebody killed him," Detective says for the first time. He wants justice for this woman and her boy. For himself. He needs a crime.

"You were there to arrest."

"Emma."

"That was his girlfriend," she guesses. "Wasn't it? I never met her."

"You knew of her."

"Only that she had enough to keep Daniel. More than me." They wave off the waiter again, their coffee now cold. She adds cream to clear her thoughts. "She didn't . . ."

"We need to talk to her. I think she knows."

"Who?"

"Or what. Yes, who. It might be her. We need to talk to her, and she's very slippery."

"I used to think she was imaginary," Maria recalls. "That he made her up because he was afraid."

"Of what?"

"Whatever. Us, I guess. Him and me. And Trevor. Having a child. A little boy." She waves her hand like cleaning a chalkboard. "It's because I never saw her."

"I've seen her," Detective says. "And I've thought the same thing."

They order and eat in silence. Maria is relieved to hide behind her glasses, let food fill up all the space for words. Detective can't quite picture Emma. Just geometry without boundaries. He hears her voice as though it were his own, but he cannot see her face.

"Was there a funeral?"

"There'll be another one," Bell predicts. "Too many people didn't get invited."

"You would've liked him."

"We never would've met. Can you tell me where to look?" he asks, foolish near her beauty.

"The shelter on Ludlow. They got the best of him."

"I can't believe how beautiful you are," he breaks down. His throat tightens despite the release. "I'm sorry. I find it impossible to . . ."

She holds his hand, takes off her glasses, her eyes black and gold with grief. "My son does know you," she realizes. "I am Maria, Detective. What is your name?"

36.

Emma and I fell back into our routine, except that she knew about my visits to the shelter. I only had to reassure her once that the woman I'd kissed was no longer there. She asked no other questions.

We were making enough money to allow Emma to quit her day job, so we actually saw each other in the morning before I went to Milano's. She was groggy, but made an effort to have breakfast with me, or at least we clung to each other for a half hour or so.

New Year's Eve, 1991–1992, I took Maggie's shift so we could bring in the new year together. Just after midnight, after the streamers and photographs, after the drying of the Guinness tap, a familiar face walked in. He swerved through the obstacles and found a stool around the back curve of the bar. Emma was filling tequila shots for five Danish tourists who wouldn't stop singing "My Way," so I snuck back to reintroduce.

"I know you," he preempted. Then a hand extended. "Mahmed. Mahmed Abdullah."

We shook vigorously. I grabbed his shoulder. "You look great."

"I feel very good."

"Happy New Year!"

"Not my holiday," he corrected. "But happy to you. New

Year." He turned down my free drink offers, his face dark as the back room. It absorbed all the light coming from the front, flash-bulbs, smiles. His was an absolute seriousness.

"It's been a year, right? This is a new year."

"Yes."

"So you've quit," I assumed.

"No." He pulled his flimsy winter jacket close around the collar. The door kept opening, hitting us with a boomerang wind.

"I thought you said . . ."

"One more year," he corrected. "I will work only one more year."

"What about the . . ." It felt ridiculous saying it.

"Only one more year. It will be good. It will be okay."

I had no reason to convince him otherwise. I thought the whole idea was loony, anyway. But his expression showed a be-trayal. He had let himself down. "You can stop any time," I consoled.

"Any time," he repeated. Emma waved from her end, still caught in a tangle of foreign arms and orders. The whole bar was now singing "My Way," but in Danish.

"Why did you come in here, Mahmed?" He didn't know, his shrug to ward off the chill his answer. "How about a Coke? Water? I'm glad you stopped by."

He hurriedly gave me a piece of paper, closing my hand over it, then stood and pressed against the bar. His eyes were faraway birds that suddenly raced and perched before me. There was a slow panic in his breathing. "What is your name?"

"Daniel."

"Daniel," his head turning to ensure privacy. "This is my address. Come and see me in one year."

"Did you follow me?" I began to figure. "How did you know . . ."

"One year. Promise me."

"Why?"

"To stop me. To make sure I stop." He was halfway to the door, my hands fumbling with only an address.

"Mahmed," I yelled, my throat full of questions. "Happy New Year." He pushed out into the snow, his black hair turning flakes to ash.

"Who was that?" Emma asked, washing shot glasses five at a time.

"A friend," I guessed. "You know him, too."

"Oh," and she shot back to her heavy tippers. "*Godt Nytar*, honey," her voice sneaking through the mayhem.

I waited only a month to go to Mahmed. February 2, 1992, an ugly day, concrete sky, mean earth, a bruising day. His apartment was on top of a storefront on Astoria Boulevard, not three blocks from Maria and Trevor. I decided to make a double visit.

Mahmed's door was open, I discovered after rattling my knuckles on it for five minutes. I called his name and got only my footsteps in return. It was a large place, but devoid of furniture except for the television, which was on. There were no other signs of life, the kitchen empty, no dishes in the dish rack. The refrigerator, which I couldn't help but open, also bare. Through the floor I could hear the merchant sounds below, change, music, the register bell.

One lamp stood guard in the front room, and I snuck past it to the bedrooms. To my right was an empty room, big enough for a king-size bed. Fresh paint was drying, the drips and scuffs of a sloppy job evident. The ceiling had been left bone, while the walls were electric white. It was like standing in an elevator.

The other bedroom door was closed three-quarters, gray light striping the hallway carpet. "Mahmed," I whispered, pushing it open. If he wasn't asleep, I knew I'd be waiting as long as twenty hours. "Mahmed."

A miniature man. Earphones. Cash. These things registered separately, they were so incongruous. The man had his back to me, his short spine curled forward. The back of his neck and his bald spot were of such different pigments it didn't seem to be the same person. His head was so pink his scalp appeared to be blowing a bubble. His Walkman was turned up loud enough to cover my entry. He just kept counting. He separated the money by denominations, making sure to siphon off every third or fourth bill into his pockets. They were overstuffed with cash, sprouting green front and back.

He was too casual to be a thief, but there was clearly the sense that I had caught him at something. And if he had turned, I would have been caught, hard pressed to explain my sudden arrival around so much money. It was absurd, more bills than I'd ever seen. The cash drawer at around 4 A.M. had always made me nervous, seeing shadows as shotguns the few times I'd closed. But this was a vault. It lined the walls, filled shoeboxes, smothered the bed the multi-colored man counted on. There were even twenties and fives at my feet, Mahmed's life work, spread like trash around his desolate apartment.

"Hello," I said, surprising myself. Then louder, "Hello!" The sound out of his mouth was prehistoric. It had the high screeching of a trapped T-Rex, his arms flapping the cry out and around. He stood, but was so short it made no difference. He tried stuffing money under things, or back where it came from. He emptied his pockets, a look of shock at the money's presence on his face. He spoke gibberish. Not a foreign language, but a new one comprised of rapid head movements and long repetitive sentences, in which the words smashed together till they were dizzy.

Twice he started to run at me, then retreated. His pink, hornless head unprepared for battle. Finally, I stepped aside and let him bow and scrape by, his nonsense apologies trailing behind like the cash tumbling from his pockets. With two waves and a final bow, he was gone.

In the bedroom was the shed Walkman, one bed, a few clothes in the closet, still in their original bags, and the hurricane of cash. "I hope this is the right address."

Two hours and ten minutes after I'd planned my departure, Mahmed walked in. Through half-mast eyes he greeted me as if he came home to strangers every day. His knuckles were monkey bent from holding the steering wheel, and he walked with the nursing-home shuffle.

"You met my cousin," he filled me in. "He left a message at dispatch."

"Not much of a talker."

"He steals from me." Mahmed looked into the empty fridge for a full minute, willing food to appear. "Want to have some lunch?"

"He didn't look like your accountant."

"I leave the door open. He doesn't work. He is afraid of people. It's okay. Not too much. And he keeps the house clean."

"Great painting job."

"He tells me he is too short for the ceiling." An exhausted laugh. "Let me buy you lunch. Where is your wife?"

"Girlfriend."

"I thought you were married."

Mahmed led me to McDonald's. He ate fries in fistfuls, taking charge of a vanilla shake and a Coke simultaneously. "I haven't eaten," he defended, "since two days."

"You don't even stop to eat?" The grease shone on his fingers.

"It's not so easy. That's why I found you. But you're early."

"No, you're late," I told him. "You were supposed to stop already. Granted, I don't know what I'm talking about. I'm not sure why I came."

Mahmed finished his meal, ordered two more cheeseburgers, and finished my fries. He moved like a lion at the kill. "When I was nineteen, my father said there will be seven years fat and seven years lean. Prepare for the lean."

"What does that mean?"

"Famine." He inhaled the last burger, his mouth slamming down over it.

"Like in Ethiopia?"

"But in New York. He said only those with enough will survive, and their families."

"So you work," I said, seeing all his money, the fear that stacked it there.

"I believed him. Five, six years, I work till my eyes burn in my head. Driving blind. Saying thank you. Telling stories to tourists from Philadelphia and Los Angeles and Missoula." Fatigue pulled on his edges. He needed to sleep for a year. "And all that money. That is why I leave the door open. I wish to be robbed. I dream of it."

"You don't believe your father."

"No. I do not know. No." Shame bowed his head. "He is dead. I should believe."

"Just because he's dead doesn't mean he's right. Look around. See anyone starving?" The shelter rose before me. The uneven cots, the distorted faces. "Although I do know what you can do with some of your money."

"I am afraid, Daniel. Afraid he was right. Afraid I will not stop working. Die behind the wheel."

"I can't help you," I said.

"I know. I need to tell someone. If it is true."

"Famine isn't like an earthquake, Mahmed. We'll see it coming. You'll have enough time." Customers lined up, traded cash for a promise to satisfy their hunger, and we sat there. Stupid and full.

3 7. Chef is waiting. Cleaner somehow, rested. The blackness on his skin nearly sheer, revealing life, pink underneath. He waves to Detective with that bobbing head crossing the street. They are outside the Ludlow shelter, both glad to meet.

"I knew you'd wind up here."

"Thanks for taking my money."

"The city owes it to those people," Chef says like a lawyer, betraying his past.

"Your apron is clean."

"They hosed me down." He pointed inside. "Not many who know your friend in there. Administrators. Don't hassle the others."

"I'm practiced at this," Detective prepares him. "Good to see you."

"It will happen," Chef says, bobbing down the street.

"We heard," a gray-haired Hispanic woman says into Detective's badge inside the shelter. The main area is piled high with stacked cots. The room is bruise brown, and the woman does what she can to block Detective's view.

"He'll be missed?"

"Already. See those dishes? Daniel. And tonight is Wednesday. Would be chicken with Daniel. Pork and beans." She had the faintest trace of heritage in her accent, like she was doing a bad imitation. "Don't bother nobody. They don't know."

"Who does?" he asks, returning to her desk of flowers and flux. Through her door they can see a sliver of the disappointment that dominates the place.

"They come and go. We don't keep records. That's the proof," straightening her posture. "That they're not here."

"Some stayed. He took some into his home."

"Maybe." She shuffles papers, looking for nothing. *"Yo no se."*

"Come on, don't play over the border with me. I'm a friend."

"Look like a cop."

"Pretend I'm a friend."

"My imagination ain't that good."

"He's dead. There's nothing I can do to him," Detective reminds.

"Then leave him be. He was a good man. He is gone. *Finito.*" She stands, having nowhere to go. Her bun reaches Detective's third button, but she's as wide as he is and not moving.

"This the guy about Daniel?" a black kid under twenty-one crashes in. His head shaved, mustache wispy.

"Yes," Detective opens.

"I'll take a walk with you." The woman scowls at the young man as Detective follows him through the morning maze of toppled juice cups and dirty paper plates. "Dude was weird," he lets on. "My name's Broderick, yo."

"Detective Bell."

"Cool first name, Detective. Have to remember that." Broderick walks one step sideways for every two forward. Detective has to follow him to avoid getting run into the cots. "About a year ago I came on, you know what I'm saying, do my community service, service to the community, how it is, and everybody's talking Saint Daniel. Gave me the nerves." There is a wrinkle on the back of Broderick's scalp active enough to be a mouth. Detective listens to it as he trails. "He came in and did good shit, but . . ."

"You didn't like him."

"He was cool. Quiet. Stuck to the clients," he says referring to the homeless. "Didn't say much to me. Feels weird, 'cause he's everybody's golden child." Broderick takes Detective into the kitchen. They stack dinner plates and put away silverware as if routine. Bell likes the feeling of lifting and stacking. He wants to stop talking and work. Do dishes, mop the floor. He sees things that need a shine. "I think in the end he came in here to recruit."

"Recruit," Detective repeats, absentmindedly.

"Spy the less fortunates. Special cases. Little kids. Especially kids. If a mother or father had a kid, you know what I'm saying. Bam. Daniel was on it."

"And then what?" Bell's focus returning.

"He took them home." An argument breaks out between two male clients. They are large and close enough to punch. Detective leaves his gun holstered. "They'll chill," Broderick predicts. "Just playing alive."

The squabblers don't shake hands, but part without blows, curses lingering in their wake. The Hispanic woman comes to the kitchen door to punish Broderick for work not done. The kitchen is clean. She withdraws, beaten. Detective is curious. "I don't understand."

"Home, man. As in took them from the shelter to his own shed."

"And the shelter?"

"They didn't mind. Opened up beds. I just thought it was wack. Taking strangers into your home. Sometimes eight, ten at a go." Broderick hopes Detective will be as surprised. He searches for any connection. "I heard he gave them money. Clothes. Man, people started lining up when they heard green."

"Free lunch," Detective recalls.

"Exactly. Ain't no such thing. Must've been getting something." Broderick plays detective, batting theories in his head.

"Don't try too hard, Broderick," Detective says gently. "There's not always a reason." Detective is afraid this is a lie. He wants to leave.

"Yes, yes. Mama said there's a reason for everything, even when it don't make sense."

"Broderick," the Hispanic woman calls from a distance.

"She doesn't want me. Just me away from you."

"Thanks for your help. It is strange," Detective gives Broderick.

"Damn straight," he smiles, thrilled. "About time that shit got sussed." Broderick bounces to his duty, jubilant from his testimony.

Detective wanders among the faces he has always ignored. A woman with scabs on her knuckles and knees, a blue flower in her hair. Two black boys wrestling over a Charlotte Hornets jersey, fists like gavels. A frail man, thinner than Chef, his arms flesh accordions. The ugly, maimed, hanging on by nubs and their daily bread. There is room in his car, he counts, for at least five. More with children on laps. He pictures Trevor here, cutting his bare feet on a nail. Maria, curling her beauty down into a knot in her belly so no one will notice.

There are a few strong, angry, look like they've been given bad directions. They too have perfected the art of looking away, fading into furniture. They spot Detective out of liver-yellow eyes, turn their backs on his clean clothes, new shoes. "What time's dinner?" one shouts at him, facing the wall.

"I don't know," Bell answers immediately. "I'll go ask."

"Fuck it," the hungry man changes, stopping Detective in his tracks. "It's just a joke." Detective walks on, knowing he's the punchline.

The knob turns, Detective bends beneath the crisscross of police ribbons. Daniel's apartment is deserted, a wallet-thin gap in the bedroom window inviting in a sharp draft. Detective leaves it open. The bed is gone, no blanket for him to curl up with. Where do they take everything? he wonders, mystified that he has never found out during twenty-odd years on the force. He feels like dancing.

The phone lines are cut, sockets pulled. The only thing getting in or out is the persistent chill. A gust rattles the pane, snow spraying up and by. Detective searches for signs of those who have lived here before. He scrapes at the paint with his hunting knife. Pries up floorboards in the back bedroom, looks up the chimney, pulling on the flue like it was God's tail, getting a faceful of soot in response.

He unscrews the bathroom-sink pipes with his bare hands. Old water sneaks down over his shoes, spreading clear brown across the tile. The closets contain no secret compartments, nowhere to play hide-and-seek. He slices the cable line and rips the phone jacks completely out of the wall. He is looting an empty house, his pockets full of nothing. There must be something to discover, as he jabs the knife into the front door.

He sits down to listen. In the middle of the apartment, twenty-foot ceilings giving him breathing room. Crosses his legs like a boy who obeys. Nina first, her sour seduction, the cruel friendliness of her voice on the telephone. Daniel's mother, flat, overprepared. Maria, he hears the sound of her face, of blouse against skin, Trevor leaping, shouting, *yo lo conozco!* Rookie, frustrated, trying to be funny, always a sentence behind. Then an infant's breath. Also Emma, below mute, but clear, calling him back here. A trail of whispers and denials, each tremble of her throat an answer to a question not yet asked. The voices come one at a time, refusing to mingle, each surprising the last one away. Except for Sophie and Emma. Detective listens; swallows his breath and vision to pay attention. One voice is missing. A sound he has only heard spoken of. A tremor so familiar he fears he won't recognize it when he comes. So he sits still, and listens.

38.

"I'm here," I said to the charging Velcro. He tripped feet away, and somersaulted right into my arms.

"Is this your house-call day?" Maria asked, dressed to go out.

"Are you on your way?"

"No. It's freezing in here. I can see your breath."

"Don't get personal." I untangled Trevor from my legs and kissed Maria once on the lips. "And don't get me started."

"Feel my hands." She put them against my neck.

"They're like icebergs."

"The heater broke and the landlord's in Acapulco."

"You need to move anyway. This neighborhood. I'll keep an eye out."

Despite the temperature, Trevor ran in mad circles, wearing only a T-shirt and Bugs Bunny underwear. He was heated from within. Maria moved tired. Her eyes flashed, but the body didn't follow. It was more than the cold. "I got demoted." She paused, waiting for Trevor to pass. "Actually. Fired."

"What?"

"My boss put his hand on my back and said he could guess my bra size. I poured coffee on his shoes."

"He guessed wrong?" I teased. "Coffee on my shoes sounds nice right about now. Let me take you out of this polar expedition."

"Trevor."

"Isn't there a neighbor or something?"

"All the baby-sitters try to put clothes on him and he hides under the bed."

I rubbed my hands together, hoping for sparks. "You've got to get out of this place."

"Can I move in with you guys?" She slid her hand between my knees. "I can be your cook. I'll be really good. I'll only kiss you when she's at work."

I grabbed Trevor, his skin boiling, and took him to his room. "Help me get him dressed. We're taking a walk. It's warmer outside." The boy flipped like a fish on a deck, but the two of us managed to get him suitably bundled. He didn't complain. He knew it was a game he could get away with. He wiggled until he got bored. Maria already had all her warm clothes on, so we forged outdoors. It wasn't warmer, but I had them captive, so I decided to make a day of it. "Mind going into Manhattan?"

"Not with you."

"It's a field trip."

We took the E and got off at Fifty-third and Fifth, then cabbed up to the Met. I hadn't been to an art museum since I was a schoolboy, but I knew we could sit in the lobby for free and it would be warm. "I came here with my class once," Maria said as Trevor raced up the steps on hands and feet.

"Me, too."

"We laughed the whole time."

Inside, Trevor hid behind a woman's fur coat, then bolted out, laughing hysterically, the woman oblivious. "Think they'll arrest us?"

"If we're lucky they'll arrest him." The ceilings seemed a hundred feet high, and large paintings hung on several of the lobby walls. Each had darkened with age, the subjects peering out at all of us, weary with suffering and stillness. Groups of students swirled, checking each other out. Guards stared blankly, seeing nothing.

Brochures were distributed and dropped. Everyone was mesmerized. Except of course Trevor, who had snuck into a plant bed and was digging for something. He came up with a quarter.

Aside from the kids, the congregation was primarily elderly and unemployed. Most had come for the reason we had. Different climate, different scenery. The art was mostly an excuse to get out of the apartment. It would be framed by coffees and trips to the bar, the real reasons for going out. The museum was a way of helping us believe we cared about something outside our own appetites. People sat down aching, their legs and backs rebelling, and spoke lustily of where to go next.

Trevor petered out just as we tired of looking at everyone. He put his head on Maria's lap, his feet on mine, and promptly fell asleep. "Why did you come today?" Maria asked. "You don't, you know. As much as I thought you would."

"I think about you. It's better that I don't visit."

"You're a bastard." She smiled. "Because you're right."

"I was in Queens to see a friend. He thinks the world is ending."

"Soon?"

"Five, six years. That there won't be enough food."

"Overpopulation."

"Something like that." I pulled up Trevor's socks. "I wonder if there's enough now." The boy's belly rose like a jack-in-the-box that couldn't open, his breathing deep and loud.

"I think I would like to be rescued," Maria announced. She looked around to make sure strangers heard her. "Are you people listening? I am now available for rescue." I wanted to quiet her, embarrassed that people might think I'd abandoned her. And the child. I didn't like being noticed.

"Stop it, Maria."

"I look at this little man, and I have no job, no heat." She pressed hard on her nose. Eavesdroppers stopped paying attention. "Then you say the end of the world and I want Superman. I want to be held while I sleep. I want to be fed and bathed. And I think if I move fast enough, maybe I'll catch up with my past. Be a little girl again."

Our position was too awkward for a hug, so I squeezed her arm. "Then there's you," she jabbed. "And I can't have you. And that pisses me off." I started to explain, but she stopped me. "Don't. I'm just whining today. I was going to call my mom. You get it instead." We gawked at the floor. "I want to check out the paintings."

"Can we leave him at coat check?"

She handed Trevor over to me and grabbed her purse. "I'll be fast. I just need to see." Maria shed her boy and her life long enough to go look at colors, forms, and fragments that fit inside a frame, hung on a wall, drew people in, and left me with a lapful of disarray. Trevor slept dizzily, too young to dream of anything but running in circles.

Maria was gone more than two hours. Long enough for Trevor to pull me like a wagon up and down the steps, over to the pretzel vendor, to the edge of the fountain. He was four, and I hung on unless he let go to chase a pigeon or tackle a larger child. I kept apologizing, scurrying after him, making sure he didn't find the street.

His mother met us at the foot of the stairs. She looked full, and too tired to talk about what she'd taken in. Trevor and I were flushed with February's fever, breathless, happy even. "I like this place," he let Maria know, pointing with the whole top half of his body to clarify his emotions.

"Me, too, little man."

We crossed the street, passing an elegant building of rusted brick and limestone. "I always loved that top apartment. I imagined wonderful things must go inside."

"Would you like to come up for tea?" Maria pretended. "I'll have Joseph prepare the guest room."

"Very good," impressed with the royal accent.

"I watch public TV." I took her arm and we walked like lovers down Madison, child at our side. She glowed when she described the paintings she'd seen, the artists' names familiar on her tongue. I was proud of her beauty, her joy, her son.

"My parents would like you."

"Yeah," she said, allowing a glimmer of hope. We were quiet all the way down to Sixty-eighth and Lex. "I can get the Six here," she repeated my thoughts.

"We could grab something. Something warm."

"It is cold back there," she recalled, marching in place to stay warm. "But there's nowhere for us to go." We kissed quickly to push off the hard truth. I spent extra time saying good-bye to Trevor, just to be close to her, listening to the shiver I could not still. Ten steps gone, Trevor broke away and latched onto my legs, trying to climb the rest of the way up. I lifted him to eye level. He was trying not to cry. Little bubbles burst in the corners of his mouth and at the nostril edge. He started several words, but they all came out as "H . . ."

"Hey, buddy. I'll see you soon. I'm Velcro, too. You can't get rid of me." Maria stood where he'd left her, commuters bumping past.

"Daniel," Trevor spat. A wet victory. "Daddy."

I put him down, dumb with sorrow. His familiar size, his dependence. I was skating toward something immense and immovable. I had to release him before I crashed. I pushed him into the crowd of knees and bags, nearly toppling him. He found his balance halfway to Maria. "I love Daniel," Trevor said, spun around, a bit confused. A passerby rubbed Trevor's head, straightening him.

"I love you so much more." But they were gone, and I was lost amid the whirl of strangers, with nowhere for my tears to go but in.

❢   ❢   ❢

I borrowed a razor and lather at the shelter, shaving and showering in time to grab a gyro on my way west. The snow had frozen, turning the sidewalks into narrow rinks. Head low, I sliced to the corner of Houston and Mulberry and waited by the light for Emma to come to work. I spotted her on the north side of Houston, just before Elizabeth Street. She wore a long white dress, snow white, with a navy peacoat up top. Her hair was long again, flying in chestnut curls behind her. She walked with the fear of falling clenching her jaw, her hands stiff navigators on the treacherous terrain. I yelled her name when she was inches from the door, running the gap between, then falling, riding my ass the last ten feet to her porch. "Get up," she said. "How was your day off?" She put her hand on the door to open it, but I pinned it shut. My face yanked in different directions; eyebrows up, mouth crooked, eyes straight ahead. "I'm ready." She waited.

"Emma." I stood taller than my frame had seen. The wind stopped, ice melted from all my steam. "Will you marry me?"

For the first time in recorded history, they shut Milano's down. Only for an hour, but it remained a landmark event. Maggie, John, and Paul, who was in to clear the safe, were so overjoyed I'd finally asked they locked the doors, poured the booze, and pommeled us with kisses, hugs, squeezes, and tugs. "Did you say yes?" John asked Emma.

"A long time ago."

"You poor lass." Paul played us "Tom Traubert's Blues," and we danced to the saddest love song ever written. Emma had the look of a weary traveler who'd finally arrived at the station. I was electrified, small pops and big bombs going off at steady intervals. I kept checking the mirror to see if I was the same boy.

"February 2nd," Paul lilted, his hair blocking all vision. "What an off day to get engaged."

"This was the only day," I answered. "Ever." Regulars

pounded on the door, threatening through the glass that they'd find a new bar to abandon their paychecks.

"You'll wait and you'll like it," John barked.

"Dance again," Maggie prodded. "I'll turn off the neon." Maggie pulled the plug on the beer signs and punched in Sinatra's "The Best Is Yet to Come."

"Everything's on the offbeat," I told Emma.

"Just like us." So close she was less a stranger and more a second heart, one I needed beating to keep my spirit alive. Her unknowable face, the subtle mouth that housed all the secrets, hers and mine. The pulse of her belly, pounding out the rhythm of a child, sewing sinew to bone, threading our future. She stood on my toes to whisper in my ear. "Thank you for staying." The song ended and we danced on, our colleagues quiet, only the knocking at the door as syncopation. She would be my sustenance, the weight on my skeleton, my hunger and my food. There would be no boundaries. I would yield to the flood. I needed her to know.

"I know," she promised, and we made a pact that neither of us could survive outside the skin. It was my last chance to block the doubts. There was only room for Emma inside me. And Sophie, and if I promised this symbiosis, I could forget Maria and her son, if only as a means of survival. Emma passed though my skin and vanished within. She was the antidote. I never stopped to think she might also be the poison.

39.

Chinese kid on a skateboard nearly takes off his door. Detective doesn't remember this, not in Carroll Gardens. "Should be in school," Bell grumbles.

"Sorry, sir. On my way," boy says, incredibly polite. Detective wonders why he didn't have a Chinese son. He checks the address again and walks up the steps. The brownstones hide family activity. Exiting kids and parents ambush Detective on the sidewalk, make him edgy. He doesn't know this street, though it's near a house he once owned. A high schooler with scars on his face stares him down. Not his son. Detective is alien here, like he never lived in New York, never ate a Sabrett's in the Yankee right-field porch, never tore an axle on a Hudson Street pothole. He resents the disrespect. Gets his gun and badge ready.

"I don't believe it," Bell's wife says from the top of a set of cement stairs. She is wrapped in a thin housecoat, slippers, bare blue legs. Only curlers are missing. Detective checks to make certain he's the target. She doesn't appreciate the joke. "I don't look that bad. Get in here."

She takes his arm, pulls him into the house. Television hollers an ad at them as she searches for the remote. He turns it off on the set. "Don't do that." She nods. "That'll screw me up later. Tray on my lap. Where is that thing?" She finds it, fixes his error, lures him into the kitchen. "I was in the middle of Cheerios. I never get up this early. Looked out the window, saw you." The words come out like scarves in a bad magic act. "Get the boxes? I see the shirt. Always liked you in that. You never wore it." She is whipping him with these words, hoping to subdue any animosity he drove over with, instead sowing new seeds.

"Shut up," he says. "Eat your Cheerios." She finishes her bowl, goes to pour more, but stops. He waits till she finishes chewing. "I was thinking," he starts, standing. "About when we met."

"I like the beard."

"About the records we owned. That I can't remember the tunes."

"You used to sing to me. Or was it me to you?" She scratches where a curler should be.

"And I was thinking how I can't remember anything. Until last week."

She leaves the room and returns with photo albums, opens one. "I should have sent pictures. Pictures always help."

Detective slams it shut, bending a Polaroid of them at Coney Island, sunburned and squinting. Wife sits straight, more scared than angry. Sorry she got up so early. Remembering she wanted to watch something today. "Not amnesia," he barks. "I didn't come here for a slide show."

"Please don't yell."

"Maddy," he simmers. "I'm sorry. I was fine. Nobody recognized me. Leave the Gardens for a year and everybody forgets. . . ." He stops, reels himself in. "I just wondered if you remembered."

"Honey, what?"

"Who I was."

This worries her, reminds her of things she can't quite name. "Who you were?"

This she knows. "I was Madeleine Aldredge of the Yonkers Aldredges, and we met because your sister . . ."

"My sister."

"Because Ruth was two cubicles away from me at Kraft, and she had a picture of her gorgeous brother, and how would I like to meet you." Detective paces the kitchen, realizing he's never been here before. That he's talking to his wife in a strange home. He checks the other rooms for eavesdroppers. They are alone. He soaks through his shirt, can't sit down. "You're making me nervous. Honey."

Detective stops, looks right at her. "It's not the details," he emphasizes. "It's the fact. The fact I have no idea. That I feel only days old."

"Since you left me," Maddy mopes.

"No. Before that. It's why I left. Why I'm here. Maddy. You loved me?"

"Still."

"But you let me leave."

"There was no way to stop you." Sadness bubbles up around her simple explanation. She cracks a knuckle that's never been cracked.

"People do things." He gives up. "Our son?"

"He's at school." Pause. "There are bills." He hands her an envelope full of cash. "Will this be your regular cash drop? I'll remember to wear this outfit." He pounds the table at her sarcasm. She loses a slipper getting up. "What are you doing?"

"I met a woman," an arrow she can't dodge. "Two women. With children." Detective pulls at his hair, needs to kick out. "They say they know me, and I thought . . ." He unclenches, looks at his wife, sees a coarse beauty, something familiar. "I thought, then you must know me, Maddy. So I came." He pushes the money toward her and tries to leave, finds it difficult. He waits for her voice, wants to hear it.

"You are my husband," she quavers. She will finish this. Fingernails dig in. "The father of our son. A detective with the New York City Police Department, Ninth Precinct, Homicide Division."

He doesn't recognize.

"And your name is Daniel Rowan Bell." Detective weeps at the sound of his name. Finds a chair and weeps. Maddy stands behind, scratching his back, tending to him. She eyes the cash and knows that's all he'll leave her with today. "It's okay, Daniel," she coaxes, his sobs banging harder, the cries of a little boy.

40. That weekend we went shopping. I called Mahmed and talked him into taking a day off. Practice, I told him, for the coming years. He agreed to not start work until 6 P.M. Then I asked to borrow his cab. "I'm making her my wife," I explained, as if she were a kit needing assembly.

Emma and I drove in the potpourri-scented taxi all over Manhattan in search of antique- and thrift-shop bargains. When I was a kid my sisters used to go to great lengths to secure seemingly decrepit furniture, rough-shined vases, forgotten trinkets, anything for sale. Then the women of our house would make a circle and gape and chat. Dad would tell them to shut up. I never understood until Emma and I started junking up our place on First and First. It was fun to buy leftovers. Everything had an impossible color to it, sanded and coated countless times, worn down to essential elements. We spent years cluttering our space with stuff we just liked to look at.

But since the fire, we'd made only two purchases. A bed, and an old couch we actually found on the street, paying homeless men five bucks to guard it while we ran home to measure whether it would fit through our door. It didn't, but it was worth sawing two feet off one end and gluing it back together once inside. Of course neither of us ever sat at that edge of the sofa. We could hear the glue creaking, expanding, and shrinking with the weather, the far end preparing to secede and start its own love seat in the corner.

Thus with empty apartment, empty cab, and an engagement to celebrate, we went in search of stuff. There were stores all over the city, but after reluctantly accepting our budgetary limitations, we wound up right back in our neighborhood, the taxi unnecessary. The East Village was flush with homey shops. Owners cajoled from doorways, showing off chairs, lamps, stand-up fans, leaning a little, crumbling a bit, but still worth a look, a touch. Many times I followed Emma's frantic waving into a cobweb corner to see a wagon or a music box. "They hide all the good ones in the back," she said. She was the expert in these dark halls, her eye cutting through the maze of furniture firewood to find the singular item or items that would move in with us. "No," dust a signal of her sudden rejection. "Too ugly." "Too brown." "Too expensive." "Too, just too."

"Can you believe that last bench?" She laughed, as we stepped into February's stiff arms. "The only good thing about sitting on it was that you covered it up." Of course it was the last store that captivated us, filled the cab with things we could have carried home. A yellow bucket. A water-blue chair, broken. An ottoman covered in rose-colored stars and hunter-green moons. And a vintage trunk too fragile to take on a trip, but perfect for filling with stuff we didn't want to see anymore. Emma kept clapping her hands gently as I loaded it all into Mahmed's temple, careful not to tear the upholstery. "I should run the meter on you, lady," I quipped. "Man could break his back."

"Get used to it," Emma fired back. "Husbands carry."

We left the cab and huddled into a little restaurant the proprietor had recommended, Friend of the Farmer in Gramercy. It was a quaint spot, stolen right out of the countryside. Macramé and needlepoint dotted the walls. Butter churns, farm implements, and handcrafts cluttered the sunny room. And they served jam with everything. It was homemade jam and they were committed to moving the product. "Would you like some jam with that?" they asked.

"No. Just the coffee."

Emma settled in among the bric-a-brac and highbacked chairs. Her quiet spirit rose to the surface, and she blended in so well it became difficult to see her. I just looked toward the direction of her voice, but that wasn't much help either. "Where are you looking?" she asked.

"At you. Aren't I?"

"Everywhere except," she stated. "I like this restaurant. The way it feels. I could live in the country." She said it simply, devoid of urgency or some unquenched desire, but it sounded loud in my ears. Emma and I had always lived in the city. I assumed we always would. The noise, the confusion, they were essential to my balance. When I got too far into the green, even a few hours in Central Park, I got jumpy. I needed cement beneath my feet. We hadn't discussed it, but I thought Emma was as addicted as I. Yet there, among the cotton and pastels, the quiet hum of neighbors spreading jam, Emma was being absorbed without difficulty.

"My parents," I made my case, "live in the suburbs."

"That's not the suburbs' fault." She was right. "And I don't mean the suburbs, tract housing, one-car garage. Look around, Daniel. I mean breathing. Being outside. Horses."

"Horses?"

"You know what I mean."

"No, I don't. Horses?"

Suddenly I saw the finest sliver of Emma's past. She had so many padlocks on what came before us that I'd given up, but there in the blinding similarity something slipped out. "Never mind," she said, yanked back into focus.

"You had horses."

"I said never mind," trying to stay casual, darkness rising.

"It's okay. Horses are okay," not wanting to scare her off. "I just never knew." Emma searched for a joke to make, but she wasn't practiced at being offhand, so she sat with her mouth shut, mind wide open.

"What kind? Of horses."

She stabbed the jam for a minute to punish herself for being vulnerable. She had broken her own rule. There was no one to blame, so the jam paid the price. "Just horses." Emma was rich, or at least born rich. We'd never seen any of it, her working two jobs. There were no horses in our East Village stable. "Can we talk about something else?"

"Did you compete?" No answer. "My oldest sister won a blue ribbon when she was . . . I forget. It hung, still hangs, in the bathroom. Right over the magazine . . ."

"No," scooting her chair forward, engaging me. "It was two horses, and they were gifts. Friends. I never rode them. A few times. They were my friends." I saw Emma standing on a hay bale, whispering secrets into a private ear. Real secrets. "Can we go?" She stood. "Let's go."

I paid the bill and chased after Emma, who was tapping on the roof. Beside her, the passenger-side back window had been shattered. "Maybe the country's not such a bad idea," I quipped.

"Let's go." Nothing had been stolen, the window just got in the path of some kid's boredom. Emma sat in the car, neck stiff against the new wind, and I gathered as many remnants as possible. Mahmed would need a new cab for the night.

She pressed against me on the short ride home. It was more than the cold, it was a message. Her pool-ball shoulders sank into my ribs, letting me know I'd crossed the line. "We got good stuff, Emma," I said to her scalp. She bruised me further. "I'd say it was a success." The window gaped, swallowing the brutal wind, freezing my surface. Emma dug in. "We're almost home."

41. Maria isn't home. Nina doesn't pick up the phone. Emma floats in his periphery. Detective tries to gather his women but no one comes. Afraid to be alone, he goes to the precinct, though he's all caught up. Calls Rookie. At home. Wakes him up. Apologizes, tucks him back in.

There is a basketball court where young men play till winter calls game. It is on Sixth Avenue and Fourth, by the subway, a court Detective has never played. He puts on sweats, high tops, makes an appearance. The day is a surprise, only small puddles at the free-throw line a sign of weather. Brothers dry it with old T-shirts and newspaper. There is a long line, game in progress as Detective approaches. He is glad to be around people, hear the rhythm of their profanity. He smiles at strangers who grimace back. He is ignored.

Out comes the badge. The middle of a game he steps out, asking for a go. Laughter at his audacity. He shows them his shield. Number 1019. Several on parole bow out. He checks the ball in.

At first, no one fouls Detective, his occupation a seal around his drives and jumpers. He doesn't miss, feels a bit savage with his onrushing beard, the way he demands the ball, most shots falling. The other team is roused. They snipe at each other. Cover the mother, can't arrest you for playing defense. Three, four opponents

take on Detective's elbows and thrust. He is impossible, everything
in the net. He has merged with the playground, entered the mythic.
He will be discussed for years. Fucking cop, they'll remember him
as, and wait, though he will never return. Now, he is laughing,
mouth slack as he makes his move. Giggles sneaking out after each
basket. High-fives. Strangers thrilled to be near him. His sweat is
sweet, age forgotten. Everything is in his hands. The world is
round, the universe striped and fenced in. He bounds over stars,
eludes quasars, rises to where breathing turns to crystal, the
planets to glass. Held, cradled here, gravity's brother, he rises,
rises, leaving everything behind.

Emma is waiting at his apartment. "I used to live here," he hears
her say. He follows her upstairs, inside. "Building burned," she
mentions.

"They told me. The apartment had been empty for years."

"I did it." She shows him the patched line in the ceiling,
where the firemen came in. The char painted over, the water
damage. Tells him where all their antiques were, some stacked
because it was so narrow, like his food.

"I went shopping." He blinks. She is still there.

"Have you met Sophie?" He is afraid to touch her, his hands
too heavy to lift. "You have been playing."

"Something" is all he can say. There are a million things. He
forgets them all. To ask her, tell her, arrest her. "I'm Daniel," he says.

"I'm Emma." There is nothing he can do. Food, no cookware.
Records, no stereo. Yearning, no words.

"Thank you for your note."

"Mahmed never stopped," she says. Sophie yawns, her mouth
a perfect circle.

"I've been looking for you."

"Don't." It doesn't sound like a threat, more a promise that
she'll appear.

"Was Daniel murdered?" Detective asks, amazed the words came out in order.

"Murdered?" Emma shifts Sophie.

"Killed."

"Yes." They stand in the lonely apartment, cans rising like sculpture from every corner. Detective is losing her, her edges blurring, features migrating. He doesn't have the strength to continue the interrogation.

"Emma," Detective trembles. "Have you been waiting for me?"

"Of course." Sophie now asleep.

"For how long?" She helps him toward the door. He seems the stranger; it is his time to go. In the hallway, he turns to her and Sophie, still in the doorway.

"Beware," Emma says. She will shut the door on him, lock him out.

"Who?" he finally asks. "What?"

"Beware." The door closes. Detective fumbles for his keys, checks the apartment number, knowing he will get an answer this time. Courage bumps up toward his heart. She is trapped. He will threaten arrest, wake the child with his tone. He is strong again, certain. The key fits and she is caught. Call Rookie, he reminds himself, turning the lock. Inside, the window isn't open; the hole in the ceiling still sealed, no tunnels, no trapdoors. Detective turns in circles till he's dizzy enough to know. He is alone. Beware.

42. The wedding took shape. It was planned for June in a vacant lot on Houston and Elizabeth. Emma and I bought an old-fashioned push mower, and with help over the fence, cut the grass on an April Saturday, frightening rats and mauling trash. Emma planted begonias and rhododendrons around the outside, the absentee landlord ignorant of the garden we were building for him.

One Sunday, Mahmed, his window repaired, helped in picking up the endless parade of old bottles and cans. Practice, he said, for the collecting he would soon begin. Very soon. I flashed on inviting Maria secretly, to tell her of a playground where Trevor could motor free, but buried the notion before it bloomed.

It was decided that eight people would attend the ceremony. Decided, of course, by Emma. Paul, Maggie, and John were Milano's people, so they had to come. Minus the Justice of the Peace, that left room for four. Never did such a small wedding party have difficulty filling slots. There was no inviting my family, as much as I wanted them there. To prove something. My health, my peace, but they weren't interested in who I was, only who I wasn't.

Mahmed was invited, but he was working. Our garden was being ignored. "Do you want me to invite," Emma asked, handing me hedge clippers, "anyone from the shelter?"

"No," I knew to say, passing the test.

"You can."

"No one," I repeated, slicing the head off a dandelion.

"I'd like her to come," Emma stood before me. "And her son."

"Why?" To show off was the answer, but she wouldn't tell the truth this time.

"We need bodies."

"What's wrong with four? People we know and love."

"Invite four people from the shelter," she ordered. "I don't care who. Something this important needs to be witnessed."

There was a man who played sentry over the shelter doors from midnight till dawn. He was vein thin and his head wobbled when he walked. Always in an apron (but never holding food), I dubbed him Chef. He had appeared one morning with an elaborate set of rules written on long scrolls of two-ply toilet paper, a contract. The script was illegible, but ordered. Chef had relayed the details while unspooling his commandments in dirty powder-blue piles at my feet. He asked if he could keep an eye out for those inside, linger on the steps, signal for help if necessary. I bought him a flashlight and made sure that coffee and an egg sandwich were waiting for him at the end of his shift. We never had a break-in with Chef on watch. He spent a week in the hospital one winter, and twice thieves stole from the poor. He was our moat and alligators, our arrows in the air. I couldn't imagine a better man to guard the first step of a marriage.

I had made countless connections among the shelter guests, but the city kept them in motion, and once they made a break, they rarely returned. Occasionally, a familiar face would order a pint at Milano's and they'd light up with tales of jobs and housing. Whether they were lying was easy to figure, but I never stole a man's happiness while it was still in his mouth.

Thus, we had five bartenders, including the bride and groom, and one Chef. We needed three who just wanted to partake. I told

Chef to grab three people, the first three to agree, and get a cab on me up to the wedding. It was a Friday morning, cinnamon sticky, in early June. June 5, 1992. I bartered bread from the bakery across the street from our chapel, gaining several bakers in the process. Our little gathering had momentum. "Is it okay if we have more than eight?" I asked Emma, a country bride in her bare feet and pale yellow dress. "By accident?"

"I like accidents," she said, beaming.

Running extension cords to the bar next door to the bakery, in order to energize our speakers, I attained a few more revelers in the mood for a wedding feast. John and Maggie filled two tables with fruits and homemade goodies. Paul, of course, brought the Bushmill's and stout, and the wire cutters that gave us a doorway to the celebration.

The Justice arrived late, ten past eleven, his black suit tar amidst the flowers. His hands were ten years older than his face, and his bureaucratic doom quickly caved into a spontaneous friendliness. "No reason I can't take the afternoon off," he said, foaming at the mouth from a gulp of Guinness.

Chef appeared even later, towing three stunned newcomers with him. One couple were in their forties, from Guadeloupe, Mexico, and had arrived in America two days before. The other was a shelter regular, Harkey, who had clearly just showered and shaved, shaving cream still behind his ear. "Cleaning up," Harkey explained their tardiness. "Haven't seen a wedding since my own. Wanted to smell okay."

"You smell fantastic." I hugged him. "Everybody here?" The small gathering nodded in unison and the Justice began. I stood by his side, blind in the sun, about to do something so familiar that I thought I might forget my lines. Then Emma.

John, a nickel-haired box of a man, led her up the path we'd planted ourselves. He blushed with the beauty on his arm, his eyes thorns in the rose of his face. A child's suppressed grin tricked the corners of his mouth, his chin quivered. There were lilacs in a row, and John stepped on one till Emma returned his balance. Later, he would apologize for his imperfections, but it was gorgeous.

I know why I was born, I thought, as I caught the shine of Emma. Her movements were strong and serene. She came toward me without motion, appearing to my left as a message, a whisper, a hint. "I do," I said to her as John departed. "I don't care what he says. I do."

The Justice laughed and took us through the language to certify what we'd never needed words to say. There were yeses and nods. Some phrases repeated, two thrift-store rings. It wasn't until we kissed and heard the row that we realized what had formed in our garden. From buildings and bars, antique shops and markets, people had appeared. They clung to the fence, snuck in like cats, honked from parked cars. A police car rolled by, sirens and lights saying congratulations.

Swarmed by our friends, new and old, we turned up John Coltrane playing something unspeakable until the lot jammed with neighbors now invited to the feast. Parisi donated bread, Paul kept the liquid flowing, and we danced with strangers under the surprised June sun. "It's almost eight guests," I tumbled into Emma. "If you use the new math."

"That's why I only wanted a few," she explained, her breath like flowers. "I knew this was going to happen."

The couple from Guadeloupe taught everyone the Mexican Hat Dance, John and Maggie illustrated the waltz, and the Justice volunteered to teach us how to clog until we shut him up with whiskey and goodwill.

By five o'clock, it was a block party. Emma and I had been kissed by everybody except the mayor, a new reception line forming everywhere we stood. We decided to separate to survive the onslaught, and I saw only my wife's fringes until the sun went down.

The cool air began easing people home, revealing that our paradise would need another week of cleaning come morning. Strangers swapped numbers, new lovers snuck away, someone gave the Mexicans an apartment, and Harkey couldn't stop crying for joy.

I found Emma tearing a fresh piece of bread in a far corner of the grounds. She was a shy firefly in the hovering darkness. I followed her flashes, directions home. "Hi."

"Hey there." I took her in. I couldn't believe she'd be going with me. "Want to go home?"

"We just met," she teased.

"But I've known since the second I set eyes on you there was nothing else."

"You say this to all the girls," she prodded.

"There is only one."

We kissed to the sound of people searching for us, others departing, the end. "I'm happy," Emma said, letting go. "You saved me."

I rested my head low on her shoulder, looked up at the pure splendor of her face. "What do I do now?"

43. "Nina," Detective says into the answering machine. "Nina, pick up. It's me." He waits. Phone is answered as he repeats his name over and over, like a child's game.

"What time is it?" she asks, groggy, her vision not working yet.

"It's time."

Nina obeys. She cancels her one appointment, takes the train to New York. He will meet her at Penn Station. They are going on a tour.

Detective paces like an expectant father. He wears jeans, sweater, fits in with the travelers. The station is clean, free of vagabonds. It doesn't feel like New York. He buys a paper, tucks it under his arm. Two packs of gum, some Certs, minting his breath. There is a hurry to Detective today. Weight shifts one foot to another. He doesn't want to be late.

Nina is. Her train caught in snow rain just outside the city. Thirty-minute delay. Detective goes into Dunkin' Donuts, likes being anonymous. Guilt free. He eats crullers and watches people. Realizes he never looks at anyone. At a crime scene, yes: the body, families, suspects. He'll stare into a killer's eyes until he absorbs his last cell. But in the world, he is blind. Vision shaved to pinholes. The earth spins on beneath his feet.

Today is different. A couple kiss and spill coffee good-bye near
Gate 14. An old man drags a suitcase on three bad wheels. Two
boys in college sweats trade acid for cash. "Don't," Detective tells
them, flashing his badge.

Nina rises from the station guts, red and awake. Detective
doesn't notice her newly short hair, hunter's eyes. He is by
Houlihan's, eyeing the hostess, who finally smiles back as Nina
bumps him alert. "Forget me already?"

Bell snaps to attention, still not registering this woman. He's
been interrupted, his new focus blurred. Sour juices clot in his
throat. Her hair is smooth to the head, shorter than his. Her face
looks more bruised this way. Exposed. The nose is a little left and
the color of the eyes, less brown, more rust. She is worn down,
partially erased. Her hair had been a flame, setting off the rest.
Now, Nina is difficult to see, except for the damage. But she is no
less pretty. Detective is glad to have this woman so near, he just
doesn't recognize her.

"Yoo-hoo," she chirps. "It's still me."

"Yes," Detective answers, still not caught up. "Hello."

"You are such a weirdo." Now, the voice registers. Detective
touches her for proof. "You hate it. I knew you'd hate it."

"Wow." He hasn't said this word for thirty years.

"Thanks," she kisses him on the rough cheek, still letting
him touch her hair, then face. The Houlihan's hostess looks on,
trapped behind her podium, armful of menus, missing everything.
"I love the whiskers." They paw each other tenderly. "I thought
I'd lost you." He takes her bag and they walk toward the wrong
exit.

"I was watching."

"Not that," she fixes, squeezing his shattered hand. "I mean
for good. The last phone call."

"I always was going to call. Just waited for the right time."

On the corner of Thirty-first and Eighth, he remembers his

policeman's parking space in front of Madison Square Garden. He'll have to leave the car.

"Where are you parked?"

He answers by opening a taxi door.

She sits close in the backseat, jacket off, the pull of her sweater making perfect curves. Her thigh is a matchstick next to his. He wants to touch her hair, her everything. He sits on his hands. "You don't live in Binghamton," she says.

"What do you mean?" A twitch.

"You're always in the city."

He can maneuver out of this. He squares to her, releasing a hand, thumb on her chin. "It's really hard not to touch you."

A kiss, cold and sweet. Mint. "Don't strain yourself."

More kisses, closer examination as they follow potholes up Eighth. "I'm at the point," Bell says into Nina's mouth, "where I can get away. Leave things to my lieutenants." He has to grin at his pun. "And I wanted to show you something."

"What?"

"Who I am."

The cab releases them at Ninety-seventh and Madison. A husky lunging, snapping at Nina. "Me and dogs," she recoils. It is the first sign of an unfriendly neighborhood. It is early afternoon and the wet snow bangs down. She shivers into him. "Where are we?"

"Home."

They walk east on Ninety-seventh away from Central Park. The husky snarls behind them, its owner pulling meagerly on the chain. The street is hot with decay, melting the snow in doorways and on stoops. Faces without eyes stare from open windows. Crack keeps the bodega hopping. Locals notice the strangers' arrival.

Signs made of bedsheets and spray paint hang from windows, cursing absentee landlords in Spanish and English. Rats, shin high on their back legs, do their search and sniff. More faces in the windows. Nina draws close, wanting to be inside Bell's jacket, missing Boston, a town she hates.

One fifty-six East Ninety-seventh. The door is chained, building empty, guarded by derelicts and squatters. The stink of humans sneaks into their open mouths.

"Are you afraid?"

"I don't know what you're doing." Nina hears the husky, turns around to nothing.

"This is where I grew up. It was a little different. I'm not trying to scare you."

"Is it safe?" He doesn't answer, touches his gun, reassuring only himself. A sudden boot to the lock and they are in. Now Nina knows they're not covering for him upstate. Selling Chevys to pay his bills. There are no men in bad suits and old ties telling automotive lies on his behalf. She is halfway up a rotted staircase in a forgotten building with a total stranger. "What's your name?" she has to ask.

"Daniel."

"Don't."

"Daniel Bell."

Up two flights, occasional groans and conspiracies reaching their ears. "My sister and I," Detective starts, "used to chase each other up and down, up and down." He toes the step that tripped him at age six, first broke his hand. And his ankle and collarbone. Hears his sister crying, mother running, father snoring.

Apartment 3R. Another kick to enter. Nina's questions are stacking. She doesn't want to know until she has somewhere to run. There are three rooms, identical size, and a small kitchen. Rodents ignore their entry, wrestling over the tiniest of crumbs. "My father left us here," Detective says, pulling up a floorboard, then two more. "I used to hide under here when he came home, pretend I was out playing."

"He hit you?"

"I just wanted to see if he noticed I was gone." Bell stares into the hole, amazed he once fit. "There was a letter." Detective wanders, picking off scabs of old paint. "Two weeks after the phone calls and the police visits. From Montana. Idaho? 'Sorry.' That was it. And he signed it." Detective laughs, Nina's hand on his chest. "His autograph."

In the kitchen, Detective kicks a rat like an empty can, sending it spinning, stunning it against the far wall. The rat shakes it off, and seeks more docile surroundings. Nina hears the grunt, the swoop of the kick, and her ribcage locks, imagines the blow. "We waited here three years. Until we were evicted. Or mother found a new husband. I don't remember the order of things."

"It wasn't like this."

"No," he promises. "The rats were smaller." Bell takes her to the window. It is broken, shards like teeth in the gaping mouth. Snow sneaks in, white-capping baby rats. "Fire escape. They'll be waiting for us out front."

"What do you do?"

"You're safe, Nina." She believes him, and they slip down the steps and ladders, landing in the alley behind. "Next stop," he offers. "Are you with me?" She wants to punch, hugs instead. Bell smiles, leaving the building behind again.

Waverly Diner. Downtown now. Spaghetti, bread, warm booth. Even full, Nina can't manage the questions. "I'm sorry I lied to you," Bell says. "It wasn't a plan."

Waiters, the owner, know Detective. Smile, wave, won't let him pay the bill. "You're somebody," Nina tells him. Laughter coughs out of him.

Outside against a painted brick wall, detective pins Nina. He backs away and she stands still. The brave push past under the umbrella of snow. He waits till they are alone. "I was fourteen, same age as my son."

"Your son," she repeats. Her jacket and boots are not enough. The chill comes from within.

"There was snow, like this. I was inside, paying the bill. I had his wallet. He let me pay. I liked to pay." Nina tries to step away from the wall, but cannot. "This was Mom's second husband, but a real father. They shot him in the heart." Still Nina can't move. "I don't know who. Why? No clues. No proof." Nina looks at her feet, sees an outline in the snow. "I had his money. They just left him there." Detective shows Nina a small chip in a brick that stands the height of a fourteen-year-old boy. His second broken hand. He pulls Nina free.

Nina understands that she is walking across Sixth Avenue, rubbing shoulders with a cop. "Do you think she did it? Emma?"

"Yes. There's one more place."

They walk. Past the stubborn pushers playing Caribbean music in Washington Square. Past the NYU students and the stores and hot-dog vendors, cops and robbers. It is not yet three, but the sky is black with snow. Below Houston then east. Broderick meets them at the door.

"Detective!"

"Hey, Broderick."

"And who is this lovely home wrecker?" They swap intros, brush off invisible flakes, pound boots. They can't stop moving. "Any dirt?" Broderick investigates. "I've been keeping an eye."

"We're closing in," Detective assures him. Broderick returns to setting up cots, pulling down pots and pans for the volunteer cooks.

"Pork and beans," the Hispanic woman tells Detective. He pulls Nina away. They stroll the thin expanse of beds and blankets.

"Where are we?"

"Six weeks. Every day I took that walk over to the Waverly, certain someone would be there. Celebrating. Showing off. Every day that we lived here. Were stuck here." Detective takes Nina behind a curtain where they stack chairs, tables. In the corner, they kneel. "Daniel knows who did it," Bell reads aloud. The sentence is etched into the wood, deep enough to draw blood. "Took me ten days to sneak the whole thing on there. I thought maybe if I wrote it, it would happen." They stand, hidden by the curtain, confessing. "Thirty years since I'd been here. Forgotten. Erased. You know it still smells the same. And I still feel embarrassed."

"That woman," Nina needs to know. "Broderick. They know Daniel. You."

"I want you to know how sorry I am. Your brother was . . . he is missed."

"I didn't know him." It is an angry admittance, shamed. It tears out of her like shrapnel.

"You would have liked him."

They take a cab back to his car. It's all snow when they arrive, his sleeve clearing the windshield, her hands the headlights and back glass. "I can't go home," she says, having no idea what she's referring to.

"Either can I." They drive to a hotel where Detective has never seen a homicide. He is tired of ghosts and wants to lie down, spend money, know nothing. The valet takes his keys. No luggage. Inside, Nina marvels at the lobby furniture, the brass railing up the staircase. It reminds her of childhood trips. Chasing down hallways, reaching skinny arms up soda machines to steal Pepsis. Tearing One-Hundred-Thousand-Dollar candy bars into thirds to share with her sisters. Teasing Daniel till he committed a family crime like tickling, then making sure he got punished.

Detective checks them in, calls to her from the elevators.

"I didn't know this place existed."

"It's a secret," Detective warns, certain his wife is hiding in a maid's cart.

"I'm good at those." Nina steals soap. "We used to stay at Marriott's," she recalls as they enter their room. Gargoyles stare at them from the adjacent building. Across the river, the Statue of Liberty lurks. They are downtown, the sole of New York. The room smells familiar. Nina finds a robe.

"I am tired," Bell admits, a sigh climbing out of him, Nina's shape evident behind the V of the robe. He is too tired to look. Her body is alert, ready to be seen. She opens the knot as he closes his eyes. Stretched beside him, she takes his broken hand and rests it on her belly. Her skin is smooth, untouched. There is a tiny tremble in his fingers, the quiver of crooked bones. She lets this be his affection. She will discover him this way. This time she will pay attention. "Nina," he says evenly.

"Yes."

"Daniel knows who did it."

44. "There is something different about a wife," Paul said to me. My shift was over, Emma due to replace me. Paul had arrived instead.

"I don't know what that means."

"It's true," and he started collecting empty pints. "Go home and find out."

We'd been married a year. Our twenty-sixth birthdays had come and gone, and I was pretending everything was the same. It was the end of June, and Emma was painting. Again. She had started four weeks before, a surprise gift for our anniversary. She painted the bedroom the same tangerine color I'd used on First and First to prepare for Sophie's arrival, but somehow, my face had not registered the ideal emotion. She hadn't stopped redoing it since. She'd wait a day or two for the enamel to dry, then back at it, covering midnight blue with buttercup yellow. Sloshing oxblood red on top of mint green. The result was inches of paint shrinking our bedroom, and a color so close to mud it felt like living in a foxhole.

On this day I found her speckled with white paint, an attempt to get a clean start going badly. Her hair in fact was the only proof of all the colors she'd tested. A catalog of panic on her curls. "Hey, you," she said while dipping. Half of one wall had been attacked, and the former brown refused to give in.

"I expected you at work."

"Not today," she said, undaunted.

"No?"

"Today is painting day. Can't have this awful brown. Today we start over."

"We could use the money."

"No. I'm sick of all the fumes." She still wouldn't look at me. "The customers open their mouths and all that propane comes out. And we're filling them with it. When they burst into flames, who's going to be responsible?"

I dropped my beer in the sink. When I got as close as ten feet, she wheeled and pointed the bristles at me. Her knees bent, stance hardened. "Emma."

"Quit interrupting me, Daniel. I'll never finish."

"I'm sorry, about the tangerine. I was just caught off guard."

"No problem there. All covered up." Her eyes fished for focus. "I'll find one you like. It's out there somewhere."

I was on her faster than expected. The brush fell from her hand easily, her blood-thin arms at her side. Her eyes found mine and stilled. She'd been waiting a month for me to do this, pin her down, stop the butterfly wings. "We'll move," I said, hoping there were walls out there without any paint. Only raw material. Space to begin again.

"I can't."

"Emma." She began to shake from the inside out, her limbs experiencing it last. It was an audible rattle, the click-clack of bones coming loose. "I'm right here."

"I can't wait any longer."

"We'll call the doctor."

"But Sophie."

"I need you first."

"I was okay," she said, too sad to cry. "For a while I was okay."

"You still are."

"You can't leave me, you know. We're married."

"There is nowhere else to go," I explained. We stood inches apart, my grip soft against her wrists until the rattling stopped and I could hear her breathing again. "Can you tell me?"

"No." I released her, watching her fade into the background she had painted. "I should finish." Emma took the fresh can of white and doused the walls. It ran in fat lines down to the baseboard, staining the floor. She opened the two remaining cans and did the same. The vapors rose like a witch's brew, stinging my lungs. I let her complete the work, watched her body surrender, taking her directly into the shower for the collapse.

I peeled her clothes, laid her transparent body down, and bathed her. "I needed to finish," she told me. "Thank you." Her body slackened, though her eyes fought hard to see through the mist. Her teeth clicked once in a while to prove she was strong enough to make a sound.

In the tub, shower water raining down on us, the architecture of her organs came clear. Her heart was tiny, the size of an infant's fist, and too much blood burst through the chambers. Her lungs were golden, not pink, because she was made of air. Veins carried the flood through every secret channel, greedy for oxygen. There was a violence to her survival. Relentless.

The paint came off easily as I washed the residue from her surface. I touched my wife's familiar body with the soft wonder of a nurse. Noting every mark and curve, the bent geometry, and what remained. A cramp made a crescent of her foot until I made it straight.

The skin below her neck had rarely seen the sun, allowing an impossible color: secret white, like frosting, snow. I had to make sure she didn't melt. I washed and smoothed every tendon and cusp till her expression requested an embrace. Wrapped in towels, I led her to the couch, the bed still dripping paint. "I'm ready," she murmured.

I kissed her like a starving man, my lips feeding on her exhaustion, drawing it in. "Tomorrow," I promised her, insatiable.

There's something different about my wife, I thought, on the subway to Seventy-seventh and Second. Emma was too weak to travel, and having received permission from her doctor to pick up the prescription myself, I stuck Paul with another shift and went in search of a cure.

Dr. Brunn's office reeked of Brut. He was a tall man with long hair for a professional, which he worked his fingers through at regular intervals. He was giving his receptionist a neck rub when I entered. He said a vague hello, still massaging. "I'm Daniel," I announced. "Emma's husband." Dr. Brunn laughed, as if I'd told a joke, then snuck back to his office.

"Can I help you?" the receptionist asked. She was an unspectacular girl with thick glasses and dry lips. I wanted to help her.

"Emma. Emma Clough. She was, is a patient of Dr. Kleiner from River Glen, and Dr. Brunn has been contacted."

"We're your pharmacy," she said bluntly. Neither Emma nor I had ever consulted Dr. Brunn, but our suburban physician had referred us here for local medication. Good friend, Kleiner had told me. Racquetball. As if that were the qualification I was looking for.

"Did Dr. Kleiner call?" She handed me a written and signed prescription for five refills of Sinequan. The paper seemed heavy and sharp. I handed it back to her.

"No, no. This is yours." She scolded me like I was an idiot.

"It's just a joke," I said. Behind his office door, Dr. Brunn laughed. The phone rang, giving me cover. I grabbed a stack of *Sports Illustrateds* and snuck into the back hallway. The other doctor in the office was golfing or such and his office door was open. I entered, tried the couch, sitting, lying. He had a human skull and a gorilla skull on his desk. A hunter. There were maps and diplomas nailed too high up to read. Books lined the shelves. I pulled down a leatherbound copy of *Great Expectations.* It was a cigar box. Taking one, biting off the tip, I heard Dr. Brunn laughing behind me.

"He won't notice," he said. "Doesn't smoke." The long-haired psychiatrist put his arm around my shoulder and pulled me into his own office. It was full of light, mostly black-and-white photographs on the wall. People blurred, in distress. He had no books and an empty frame where a diploma belonged.

"Still studying?" I asked.

"Keeps them guessing." He was handsome in a brutal sort of way, mixing compassion and menace in each sentence. I didn't trust him. I didn't leave. "We've never talked. Never met," he said.

"No."

"Why for?" He was playing at something and it irritated me.

"I'm done with doctors."

"Someone's still looking," he said, eyeing the prescription in my fist.

"There's something wrong with my wife," I blurted. I expected another nasty laugh.

"She could come in." Tenderly. "If she doesn't want to make the long trip I could have Don send me the file." He leaned forward, elbows flat on his desk, nearly resting his chin on his fist.

"You scare me."

"I'm sorry."

"Your face keeps changing." Brunn stopped his fingers midway through their hair run. "Emma's in trouble."

"How long has she been clean?"

"Years."

"But she's falling back."

"I knew how to deal with this when I was . . . but now it scares me. I feel stupid. I've always known before." I balled the prescription up, jammed it in a pocket to keep from throwing it away.

"It's okay, Daniel. That you're not sick."

"She's not sick," I hurried. "She's going to be okay." Dr. Brunn's appointment arrived. He had her wait by the magazines. "There are things I need to know," I explained. "Then I could fix it."

"You're the doctor," he accused.

I am, I thought. I couldn't say it. "There are things I need to know."

"She won't tell." He knew. He pulled out his address book. "Give me your number, take my card. In case you can't fix it." The edge was gone from his voice. He knew I would fail, but he was willing to let me do it alone.

"We met at the hospital, Dr. Brunn. I need to know before."

"That's with Kleiner. And it's confidential."

"I'm her husband." His silence told me I had no rights. I knew Dr. Kleiner would have the same monotone expression. "All these doors," I fought him. "No key." He shook my hand without getting my number, but stuck his card in my shirt pocket. "Fill the prescription. Give her some balance. Then ask her." He didn't understand. He'd never seen the fortress, not been shredded by the barbs. His hand in the small of my back, he guided me to reception. It was ten degrees cooler, and his laugh followed his good-bye.

"He scares me," I warned the next patient.

I returned to Emma with $125 worth of pills that promised to sandpaper the edges. She refused. "I'm better," she swore, watching television. I turned it off. I'd never seen her look at the screen before.

"You asked for these." I hated them, too. They made us tired and submerged.

"Now I'm just saying no." The circles under her eyes were

coffee black, and stretched corner to corner. "I have to get ready for work."

"Should I take them back?" holding the bottle like a grenade.

"Do what you want," pushing past me. "I'm fucking starved."

I bought us some vegetable tempura and rice, and by the time I got home she was painting again. This time with makeup. Thick coverup makeup made her circles the color of sand. She had rouge on, and lipstick, red as a pack of Pall Malls. Her eyes were lined with thick black streaks, and green eye shadow lay like moss over her lids. I was afraid to say what I thought for fear of setting off another month of repainting.

"I didn't know you had all this stuff."

"A girl likes to dress up." She was wearing cut-off jeans and a tank top.

"Emma, let's stay home tonight."

"Gotta work. You said it yourself. We need the money." She was speaking loudly, the veins in her neck making a tic-tac-toe pattern below her jaw. "Especially if you're spending a hundred twenty-five bucks on dope. Unless of course you sell it. Then we're set for life."

"Stop it."

"I can't."

I went to grab her again, shake her, but it wouldn't work. The rail had slipped. She was being harsh to keep from feeling the loss. I was the only one with a chance. "Will you try one?" the bottle still sealed in my hand.

"I look pretty."

"Always."

"I'm on the bend," she knew. "And I never got to show you a thing."

The tears fell because her eyes couldn't shut. The greens and blacks and reds made tributaries that ran toward her open mouth. I took off my shirt and smeared the disguise, holding on for my own sake. We walked around the box apartment, touching walls instead of speaking, calming her, isolating us both.

"Can you hang on?" I begged, slipping a pill under her tongue. She swallowed before the water came.

"Sometimes it's just not possible, dear Daniel," her arms straight up in the air. Hang on.

45. "You're married," she says as he exits the bathroom unshaven. His body is hardening from disobeying his hunger. He has the straight lines of a younger man.

"Yes." Nina is still in the robe, sitting facing him, the robe undone enough to invite inspiration. He looks out the window to dull his desire. "She is a good woman who let me stay in the house long after I didn't belong."

"But you like me."

"Very much."

Nina dresses near Detective. Slowly. Nothing is waiting for her, nothing needs her attention. She takes time to feel the silk panties slip on, jeans up against a clean shave. The way her bra makes it easy, how good her body feels. She hands him her sweater, the last temptation. He pulls it softly over her head, hands lingering at the waist just long enough to be a compliment. Younger now, she pulls him close, kisses his ear. He feels it in his hip.

"Good-bye."

"I'll drive you," he insists, not wanting to separate.

"Now you see me." She laughs. "I'm going to my mother's, my parents' house. You know where it is. Thanks for the tour."

"Nina. My name is Daniel Bell. I'm a Homicide Detective. I'm looking for your brother's killer."

"I know."

"I had to say it."

"I know." There is a second when they are so lonely it is one sword piercing them both through; the only way to connect, a pull across the blade.

"I can call you when I find her," he commits.

"Who?"

"I don't know."

Poison. Detective hears this as good news. He was right. He has his killer. "Can't identify the crafty sonofabitch," twitching Coroner explains. "Worked like, a little like strychnine, a little like hemlock, for crying out loud. Sure I'm not working on Socrates?" Bell doesn't get the joke, circles ME in his office, wants something physical to look at. "You've got that show-me look on your face. Can't you just trust me? Leave the boy alone?"

Back in the lab, ME shows off Daniel's damage. Curdled tissue. Involuntary canals. Clotting. Implosions. Cracks in the casing. A murder. "If I had the body right away, maybe there'd be prints, but this poor soul was stuck in thrust for at least three days."

"There was no scent," Bell recalls.

"Can I put this boy away?"

"After three days there'd be a stench."

"Bet your bottom drawer," ME says, sneaking off his gloves. Detective halts him.

"It was clean. Nothing." Detective reinvestigates the evidence, looking for initials left on a bone, a confession carved in the marrow. "There was no scent."

"Maybe he was just sleeping," ME deadpans. "Hell, he's still asleep. Sorry, kid," as he looks at Daniel torn open like a Christmas present.

"Is there something that will do both? Kill and preserve?"

"Not in my textbook, Doctor." ME looks at the body as

though he's never seen it before. It is a strange creature, peeled, bent before him. He doesn't trust it. Its secrecy, its refusal to admit death. Even now, uncovered, looted, it seems alive, dormant maybe, but ready to spring. The agony of the back, face without wrinkles. Striated muscles, bloated belly. It is a lie, this body, refusing to submit to the knife. Buried and brought back from the tomb. There is no grave this shape, ME thinks, backing away from his work. "I don't believe you," he says.

"There was no odor."

"Everything decays. That's why there's enough room on the planet."

"Maybe some things are just harder to kill."

Detective waits for Maria to get home. She mounts the last flight wearily, her footsteps too far apart to belong to one person. Bell meets her halfway, taking the four grocery bags. "You should have been in the circus," he compliments.

"I thought I was." Inside, without Velcro, everything seems possible. They are a couple returning from the store. They are strangers on a first date. She has caught him breaking into her home.

"He was poisoned," he says, smiling. "I'm sorry. I had to tell someone." Maria stops putting away groceries.

"I won't like you," she says. "All the bad news."

"It's proof. We can find someone. Punish someone."

"Trevor will be home soon. Don't make me cry." She digs a heel into her foot, staring at him.

Detective finishes filling her cupboards while she sits, rubs her foot. He is losing track of which kitchen he is in, afraid to call out the wrong name. A philanderer who never makes it into bed. "Did he take drugs?"

"No." The answer is sudden.

"Prescription. Medication. My partner went over his checkbook."

"You take everything." She sharpens. "I'll bet you even have his body. Thieves."

"A couple years ago," he presses on, "there were a lot of checks to a local pharmacy. Maybe he was pushing."

"Detective, you are so far off base you're in the bleachers." Maria stands, bitter and sore-footed, anger soaking up the tears.

"You weren't with him. I'm just trying an angle," he back-pedals. "Maybe the girlfriend. We have another death. If it pans out the same . . ."

"Like Daniel?"

"Identical. Malnutrition. No injuries. In Queens."

"Danny had a friend out there." Maria closes in, mind clicking. "Used to visit him when he first came to see me. I don't know. Not even where. Close by, I guess. I'm not helping." She paces, too tired to sit without dozing.

"It takes time. This woman keeps slipping through my hands."

"Emma?"

"I see her. Every few days, but she . . . I can't act."

"That's how Danny was. I think she has this power." Maria is standing by him, behind his guard. He steps back to avoid kissing her. "Can I make you dinner? Trevor's gone till eight." She doesn't have to approach to see his nervousness. "I won't poison you." She smiles. "Promise."

Detective lifts the phone, holds it between them. "All right," he says, so hungry he could pass out. "Nothing big." He pulls the phone cord into the bathroom, sits on the edge of the tub. Pots and pans clang into place, the sound of Maria's movement enough for him. "Hrcek?"

"Detective! You are a hard man to find."

"Fieldwork, Rook. You won't believe."

"Hurry up, because I got a doozy for you."

"Poison," Detective announces too loudly, shuts the door.

"And I've got a witness says Daniel had a friend near her in Queens. Could be our cabbie."

"Sure," Rookie says. "Only a million friends to interview in Queens."

"Spit out your news, then I got a favor I need."

Rookie clears his throat, an oral drum roll. "Married," he rumbles. "The sonofabitch was married."

"Emma."

"Can't take her in for falsifying, Detective. She is the Mrs. June 5, 1992. Pictures to go with the certificate. They got married in a fucking vacant lot." While Rookie gloats, Detective remembers a wedding, flashing his lights, blaring his siren on a drive-by one summer. The bride a shimmer, groom dumb-happy by her side. "Not bad for a Rook, huh, Detective? Now, what's the favor?"

"I need some assistance. Backup," Bell admits. Maria yells his name from the kitchen.

"I could send a unit? What for?"

"Detective?" she calls out, striding toward his hideout.

Then into the phone, Bell's reply. "Dinner."

46. A leave of absence. That's what I told John and Maggie. That Emma needed a little vacation. They didn't mind, considering that recently she'd been given to the occasional whiskey dumped in the middle of a Guinness. Or staring at a customer until he fled. The veterans had gotten nervous around her, knew she needed time. I decided to take her night shift and they would hire someone new for the daily drunks. I suggested Maria. As long as she's off by seven, I negotiated. They called her in for an interview.

Emma took her medicine. In fact she took it too well, finishing the first bottle in half the allotted time. The refill I brought her was kept hidden in a shoe box under the bed. Doctor Daniel would control her intake.

After such a long time off the loop, the drugs took an inevitable toll. Emma slept. And slept. When she was awake, she managed the narcotic shuffle into the front room, held a book in front of her, as if reading. It also worked as a shield from my concern. I had her under constant surveillance without even trying. Neither of us could escape the routine. Work became my relief, but Emma didn't seem to miss the bar, didn't mention it. Once she asked if they found anybody, the answer being no. Maria had turned down the job.

When I would return after a night of nearly slugging intoxicated young men, I'd find Emma too asleep, mouth loose and wet, eyes sunken, looking like another version of herself. Last year's model. I'd fold her into comfort and drift off, holding her together. All those years, watching the vault dissolve from the sheer spark of her hope, her determination, seeing ever more of her true face, polished like a white stone. And then the darkening. More than the girl I first met. Guards in the towers, alarms, impenetrable. The dope soothed the jangle, but also threw a further curtain across my Emma. The closer I held her, the harder she was to see. I had had the patience to wait for innumerable secrets, and the faith to believe they would do us no harm, but they had refused to come out to play. They hid inside her crooked frame, doing the damage from within, where I could not make them yield. I was feeding her pills that refused to cure. Stealing her identity, trading an explosion for a coma. But there was no one else for Emma. She was mine to raise.

River Glen psychiatric hospital was a thirty-minute train ride from Rye. It had been over six years since my last visit to Dr. Kleiner. Like a man returning to elementary school, everything seemed smaller. The trees, bushes. The fence, easy to hurdle. The pond, a puddle, and the main building made of children's blocks and pick-up sticks. I was not afraid.

The lawn, peppered with pine cones and lazy August leaves, looked like a salad. A few hospital guests, heads hung, baby-stepped to the main entrance. The term "guests" had always amused me. As if we'd come for vacation, making sure not to miss the Thorazine daiquiris and electro-massage therapy.

Inside the smell was everything. It was the aroma of ice. Something perfectly sealed. So cold it burns, with invisible bands closing everything tight. Teeth hurt, a sudden headache, then the sound. Rubber soles on pristine tile. Squeaks and squeals, the song of caged birds. I checked the front door to see if it locked behind me.

No eye contact. We were all shadows, no one was ever home.

It was a place you came to find yourself, but while in its confines you were never actually there. Far down the hall, doors opened and closed by themselves.

Before meeting Kleiner, I took a walk onto our old ward. No one lifted their eyes from their shining white earth shoes to notice me, so I could move around as if I belonged. I didn't need signs to guide me beyond the Doctor's offices to Ward J.

Ward J was a special section for those with a chance to move on. The only thing heavier than the medication was the philosophizing. There were endless guests who'd snapped in the middle of a college religion class, or whom wealthy parents had talked in off ledges so the driveway wouldn't get messy. We were a crazy mix of the neglected and spoiled, with enough funding for an unlimited stay. We were on insurance-company scholarships. The privileged.

They taught us crafts that involved blunt tools. There were sports for those willing to forgo competition and reach a purer goal. Sweat. There were even classes offered, as if River Glen were a university that had simply gotten a bad reputation by letting in a few disreputables.

At twenty-six, no chemicals putting corduroy on my brain, I decided to peek in on a hospital class in session. The "teacher" didn't notice my entry, and I found a chair in back. She seemed to be a patient, the constant repetition, slow speech pattern, but her clothes and jewelry said otherwise. A stick pin, high heels. A well-cut suit. Sharp objects that belonged to the outside world. "So in this story we have the rising action. Rising action." She spoke as if coaxing a child out of a dangerous situation. "The rising action comes just before the . . ." and she hung the sentence out, refusing to finish, to admit no one was listening. Private dialogues sprang up around the edges of the classroom. She had abandoned them to their thoughts. Failed them. She was here to stuff them full of distraction, till they were bloated with others' ideas, enough to squeeze their own poisonous ones out of their pores. I went to finish the sentence, but in the stale, familiar air, my tongue wouldn't work either.

"Twist," a cow-faced teenager said from the corner, like he was ordering a drink. I wriggled out of the tiny desk and out into the hall. "They don't know us," I told a passing nurse as she bowed her head. "They have no idea."

One more place to visit before Kleiner: the supply room. Our first bed. I knocked in case two new kids had found sanctuary, then jiggled the locked doorknob. Blood shot from my heart to my extremities, and I surged with the sense something had been stolen from us. The empty hall swallowed the sound of my sneakers cracking the lock, splintering the door. I shouldered the rest of the way in.

Inside I felt a criminal pleasure looking at ten pushcarts, eight feet high, festooned with sedatives of every flavor. It was a Baskin-Robbins of medicines, from liquid to powder, pills to inhalants. And in the fluorescent flutter, it was clear that these substances were the biggest lie of all. They were supposed to speed recovery, but only delayed everything they touched. I knew Emma was home, robed in Sinequan, stupid with it, more dull than dangerous, but still not my girl. I wanted her back. I wanted a cure that didn't sneak in by capsule, or spike the human cocktail by syringe. I wanted something I could do. Steps to follow. Bread crumbs back to the house.

The first cart I just toppled. It fell, drunk with its own bounty, making a loud complaint on contact. The others I used for sport. Getting running starts, hopping on, skitching till the crash. The glass split with triumphant clamor, floating in the spill, beaching onto piles of powder, pills like rafts on the surface of the river. I kept waiting for the insistent hurry of an orderly's Adidas, but the only noise was of my own making. Smashing, stamping, smashing again, giddy and grateful.

My head out the door, I laughed at how professional they were at ignoring. I squished down the hallway, crunching pills on my way. Again the smell. Clear, vicious, reminding us all that no one was home.

Kleiner's office was at the far north end of the hospital, away from the other doctors. He only dealt with J ward patients, and fancied himself a healer, not a shrink. I entered expected, and his wide face expanded with a smile. "Daniel. You are a man." His hands were padded and hairy, like shaking a paw. He guided me into a showroom leather chair. "We have ducks again," he gestured out his window. "Geese, I mean." We'd lost fowl privileges in our day. A lifer had strangled and undressed an unlucky duck, then presented it to the cook at dinner.

"Hello," I finally said, unable to swap stories, tell jokes, lie.

"Must be strange." He stood at the window, spying on the geese.

"Nothing's changed."

"Except you." I nodded, kicking the desk. Six years had tricked part of Dr. Kleiner's face. His chin had gone weak and puffy and his lips had all but disappeared. His hair was too short, exposing his folded ears. Yet his eyes still glimmered, carried a gladness. His office stole fragrance from his bowl of fruit. He bit into the apple I turned down.

"You have to tell me everything," I explained. "She's on her way out."

"She should see me." His face a mask of concern.

"I'm the only one."

"Hold on, Daniel. I understand your passion, but you have to try and understand."

I stood. I was bigger than him now, too. I remembered the symphony of breaking glass, was ready to break something new. "It's so simple," I said. "What happened before. No one ever told me, and once I know, she'll be all right. Please."

"You must discuss this with Emma."

"I'm the husband."

"I can't do it. Bring her in. We'll all talk."

I pounded his desk. "It's not words, Dr. K. I've always known how to do this. Go in a circle faster and faster, but I have to know what she will do." Dr. Kleiner reached into his files and removed two patient histories. Mine came first.

"How long has it been?" he asked, trying to calm me.

"No fucking drugs!" His hand reached for the phone, then withdrew. "I'm sorry, but I know exactly. Emma is losing something. You can help me get it back. Tell me, Doc." I sat down again, woozy. "Tell me who she is."

He shifted Emma's file to the top and surveyed it. Uninterested, his finger lifted tabs, poked at reports. Faded writing called for his glasses. He started to hum. "She needs to see me," he stonewalled. "It won't kill her to visit the old homestead." He had no idea.

I was over the desk like a panther, my fists so ferocious that three blows did the trick. I propped him groggy by the window, blood frowning down his face. I grabbed both dossiers and in capital letters wrote my name on his desk for proof: Daniel Rowan.

I ran until I burned, igniting what was behind me. My right hand pulsed with the dull promise of a break. I held on to Emma's secrets and sprinted toward a separate coast where I could make her whole.

47. "She a good cook?" Rookie asks as they drive through Queens on an empty November day. The streets are clear, few cars taking spaces. The pavement is sick gray, as they step into their jobs. Detective doesn't answer, tastes still mingling on his tongue. "What are you afraid of?"

"He got her an apartment, tried to get her a job." Bell fires. "Was good to the kid. But she never won."

"So she did him? Slipped a mickey into his daily dose of nothing." Rookie likes being on the gentle attack. He bumps shoulders with Detective. "You're starting to see things, Detective. Truth is you were over there for a little more than Sara Lee." Detective has to smile, caught.

"But I was good. I'm a married man."

"She is fine. She like the beard?" Rookie strokes his baby skin. "Thinking about growing one myself."

"You couldn't get an ingrown hair. I'll lend you my trimmings." They bump again, accidentally, and tell each other to cut the nonsense. Police work ahead.

Mahmed's cousin is either performing a religious ritual or watching a soap opera, Detective guesses, finding him yoga style by the TV, candles burning, tears fat down his cheeks. "Karim," Bell reads from his notes. "Can we have a word?"

"Ashley is in the hospital," he points at the tube. Rookie helps him up, his legs straightening. Rookie shakes him till they drop to the floor.

"Not finish," Karim complains, pointing again. "Ashley."

"Did your cousin know a man named Daniel?"

"Daniel?" Karim says, adding syllables.

"Yes. Daniel."

"Yes. Daniel." Karim repeats.

Rookie perks. "Yes? He knew him."

"Yes," again. "He knew him."

"Were they friends? Did he come by the house?" Rookie bends in low, seeking focus. Karim drifts toward Ashley in ICU. "No, no, little buddy. Daniel. We're talking about Daniel."

"Who is Daniel?" Karim asks, Rookie releasing him back to his initial position.

"Take the place," Detective orders. And they do. Every crevice and divot, pulling out the last remnants of a forgotten life. Under the mattress, inside the toilet, their fingers eyes behind the furnace and refrigerator. And while Karim weeps, Hrcek looks in the mirror. Slipped into the space between wood and glass he discovers a taxi receipt. Hands it to Bell, who reads what is written on the back: MILANO'S 51 E. HOUSTON.

"Hey, Detective. How about a drink?"

Paul is bopping to "One Mint Julep," in unison with Ray Charles's chant every time. It is just past noon, and the first customers are cops. "My Irish bobby," Paul salutes Detective, reaching for the Bushmill's. "Good to see the force getting an early start." Bell's raised hand says no.

"Daniel," Detective begins.

"Where's that bloody eejit been? Just because he quit doesn't mean he can forget us. I was the best man at his wedding, you know." Paul beams. "There's a story."

"His wife, Emma."

"You know her? She stopped coming round, too. Are they in a scrap? Seems they were always in a scrap."

"Daniel's passed," Rookie tells Paul, saving Detective the strain.

"No," from Paul, like it's a joke. "Fuck off."

"They drink here?"

"They bloody well ran the place. Days for Daniel. Nights with Emma. I don't believe you."

"Last week. He worked in this bar?" Detective takes that whiskey, Paul's shaky hand delivering.

"Years. Oh, my Christ." They hand him this sudden sorrow and Detective's card.

"When you're ready," Detective says. "But soon. Two dead and the trail led here."

"And tell the others," Rookie demands. Outside they bundle up to no avail. Snow. "How'd you like to die," Hrcek asks into a gale, "and nobody cares?"

"Nobody knows, you mean," Bell fixes.

"Same thing." They walk the wrong direction, forgetting the car. Headed east on Houston toward Detective's apartment. Detective realizes this, but hides the mistake, wants the company, plans on lunch. "Hell of a bar," Rookie attempts. "Tender knew you."

"No," Detective lies.

"It's okay."

"No. Bartenders pretend," Bell explains. "It's their job."

"Like cops."

The snow is relentless by the time they reach Second Avenue. Rookie gets his bearings, pushes off, promising to meet later, lunch with his girlfriend. She is getting serious. He might need backup, he teases. Detective gives him the car keys, heads home. There is a chance someone is waiting.

At the street entrance, fresh footprints escape down toward

A. There is wet snow up and down the steps as he rises to his place, listening for neighbors. Silence. He struggles with the keys, hand brittle from the chill, drawing his gaze down. Only a foot in the door does he see the note. Same block letters. Same signature: ONE BODY REMAINS—THEN EVERYTHING—EMMA AND SOPHIE.

48. Three, maybe four miles. I ran long past pain and cramps. Past cotton at the hinges, heart out of blood. Past houses and lawns, shut doors, open garages. Leapt over Big Wheels and dolls, toys the color of rain. Between swing sets, through sandboxes, over hoses and FOR SALE signs. Ran till my legs were wires, sending short-circuited messages.

My hand was swollen and curled, a boxing glove. The files were scrunched but whole, and I surrendered my pace. I walked as I tried to read till a curb invited a visit. I threw my legs in front of me into the street, willing to have them run over. Behind me was a yellow house, blinds drawn, windows shut. I read mine first.

The first several pages listed medicine, hospital voodoo, a record of my sleep patterns. There were monthly reports with elaborate details, such as "Improving." "Quiet." "Truant." They made playing hooky sound like an attribute. I had to dig into the back sheath to find who I really was. The sheets had crispened with age, nearly nine years locked in Kleiner's cabinet. The ink had sunk so deeply into the paper they seemed to have been created as one. This was my résumé. It read as follows:

Rowan, Daniel Patrick, age 17, 5'10", 120 lbs. Blue eyes. Brown hair.

Prescribe Elavil. 300 mg. Inj. Isn't speaking. Ribs exposed. IV fluids. Possible spoonfeed. Extreme exhaustion, dehydration. Check address—from Rye??!? Confirm insurance. Sister, Nina Rowan, drop off. Voluntary. Parents due. No previous psychiatric. Detached. J Ward, resident wing. Won't swallow. Confirm address: 16 Thistle Lane, Rye, New York. Contact parents. Where has he been?

The door opens behind me. "Get out of here," a woman says. I limp fifty yards, take refuge behind a bush, remove my shoes. Bright silver blisters draw water from the air, filling into tiny blimps. Where have I been?

The only other notable paper was my release. It was unremarkable, except, like my admittance, my father had signed it. Law required he visit the site of his embarrassment at least twice. His signature had none of the studied curve he brought to checks or business documents. It was a few long lines, interrupted by bumps of consonants. A man in a hurry. A man not paying attention.

Emma's didn't open so easily. My right hand was useless. I shook it open with my left, scattering a few papers on the smooth suburban macadam. I gathered the missing and struggled to take a deep enough breath.

More drugs. Emma, who had been admitted one year before I was, had been administered a relentless diet of hard-core antidepressants from the day she arrived. Several months in a row the dosages rose, a snake on her chart, tailed by a doctor's annotation of "Addiction?"

There were long, rambling discourses from Dr. Kleiner, full of vague doubts and hopes. More than once he mentioned how attractive she was and how she was not using the benefits. Not "allowing her face," he called it. I was glad I hit him. Emma displays this. Emma displays that. The notes flowed in great looping letters full of ignorant surprise. Considering the dope they were loading her veins with, she was lucky to hold a conversation, much less have a breakthrough. But for all his rambling, his winking while treating, there were almost no specifics. The notes illustrated a commonplace depressive with some hope to turn the corner. As before, the treasure was on the admittance form. They didn't know what to do with us inside the walls, but when we arrived, they knew what they saw.

Clough, Emma Lauren, age 16, 5'3", 89 lbs. Eyes? Hair brown.

Arrived by ambulance from United Hospital. Soft restraints. Attempted suicide by hanging (fractured larynx) in hospital bathroom after admitted for Darvon O.D. Vitals returning, emergency watch. No parental admittance. Check insurance. Gave birth to stillborn two weeks prior to first suicide attempt. Profoundly dehydrated, malnourished. Anemia. Anorexia nervosa. Small heart (x rays), jaundice? hepatitis? pancreatitis? Yellow. Confirm address: 5 Larkspur Drive, Rye, New York.

The street where I grew up was made of children's noise and touch football in the street. There wasn't a window that hadn't received the insult of a line drive or an electric plane. Families knew each other mainly owing to accidents, parents trading barbecue invitations while sweeping up glass. The mayhem of youth brought the sedentary adults together. We were the web they all got caught in.

There was a house up the hill, dull yellow, with four pillars and trees guarding the porch. There were two older boys that lived there who played dirty with anyone who wandered onto their yard. G.I. Joes were snapped in half, tricycles never returned. It was the house of tears, sending lost little ones scampering home to the echo of cruel teenage laughter.

One day a girl appeared on the uneven porch. She was waving good-bye to her brothers, who were taking their nastiness on the road. She stood alone, waving long after her brothers had vanished. I was ten, but I remember thinking it was more than a wave. It was a signal. The house was hers.

I remembered so clearly because she had never appeared before. She arose from the exhaust of her siblings' departure, full and perfect. A bright flag. An announcement. I waved back the split second she turned to go inside. I never saw her face again.

Rarely, I'd catch the back of her head in her parents' Volvo on her way to Resurrection Academy. Or see her pulling the blinds after I'd made a spectacular catch on the fringe of her lawn. Her parents didn't socialize, weren't part of the neighborhood association, took vacations whenever we had our block parties. They often came home to eggshells and toilet paper, further isolating them. After some years, it was as if the house didn't exist.

Then Warren fell. The ICU, the cemetery, all the crackers and cheese slipped into a blender of memory. No color. No sound. One thing remained. As we left the church, there was a girl in a yellow dress. Her back was turned, and she wore a black hat over unruly curls. Just past arm's length, my mother yanked me back to the family grief. I was swallowed by a torrent of arms, rough skin, and ugly sweaters. The spent yellow flashed up out of the sway, a weary sun, then dipped out of view. As I fell into the car with one last glance, I'm certain she returned my wave.

Emma Lauren Clough, my wife, grew up three houses away. She owned a yellow dress and knew how to wave. On August 14, 1993, after having been in love with Emma for almost a decade, I finally knocked on her parents' door.

The porch had been repainted recently, but it still had a tilt like standing on a boat deck. The knocker was a lion's head, with a blunt bronze shine. The blinds were drawn as always, but there was a car in the driveway and her parents' ancient Volvo out front with expired plates. Another knock and then an ugly face. It didn't seem possible that the man at the door learned to swim in the same gene pool as Emma. He was in his midthirties, hair gray and wax thin. His brow hung over his face like an awning and his nose was too big to take cover. "You're Emma's brother," I told him.

"Who the hell are you?"

"She's my wife."

He grabbed my collar, pulling me inside instead of punching. "Sorry," he said. "We don't like leaving the door open." The house was empty. No carpet, no pictures, a single bulb gave light from the staircase. The hallway was long, leading to the kitchen, and the light from the back windows made it look like we were holding flashlights.

"What's your name?"

"I'm the older brother," he admitted.

"My name's Daniel. Emma is . . ."

"Mother!" He yelled this, the echo banging upstairs, hardening any softness the word ever had. "Somebody."

And the mother responded. She moved on piano legs down the steps till she was upon me, smelling like all the neighborhood mothers. A combination of Giorgio, nerve, and salt. "What? The house already sold." She had a hint of Latin in her walk and talk. "How did you get in?"

I looked at older brother, who got a smack on the arm. He wasn't happy when he looked back at me. "I'm family," I said stupidly. She stared.

"Says he's . . . uhm, the husband of . . ."

"I was napping," she belted, belying the speed of her entrance.

"Emma, Mrs. Clough." Not a blink. "Your daughter."

She pinched me behind the elbow, ushered me to the door. My firm stance surprised us both. "No daughter. Get out."

I yanked my arm free. "Emma Lauren Clough." I dug in. "Beautiful and smart. The little girl in the yellow dress. My wife."

"No daughter," she said to her son's Adam's apple.

"No sister?" I asked him.

"Go home, kid. These are old bones you're digging." His brow softened. He looked sorry for everything.

"I'm your brother-in-law," I claimed, as if we should swap gifts.

"My daughter died a long, long time ago."

"No, no, she didn't. She got better," I bragged, an auctioneer, the words rolling faster and faster. "Ten years since, and she's strong. Has a job. Got married. She's okay. She's good."

The woman looked at me like I'd broken into her house to tell her a ghost story. She nodded to her son and he sheepishly guided me to the exit. "The yellow dress! Let me see the yellow dress!" I was on the porch in seconds, my buckled hand no help.

"Forget it, kid," my brother-in-law said, and slammed the door.

"No!" I kicked in a window, my sneaker a trapped bird in the blinds. I needed that dress to remind Emma. To show her we were together before everything. Before the deaths and the lies and the drugs and the distance. That we were connected from before time, placed houses apart to keep watch. That our love was born before we were. That we were enough.

Big brother stepped outside. "Don't do it."

"Beat me up!" I yelled. "Fuck you. You've got a baby sister."

"You have no idea," he spat, his face hardening into an anvil.

"No one deserves to be forgotten." I charged him, but he shut the door on me again. I pounded with both hands, rearranging bones. In the driveway, I kicked and elbowed all the car windows to dust. All but the back glass of the Volvo, where I'd seen Emma's ten-year-old head bob off to school. "Give me the goddamn dress!" I was exploding like Emma had over my family.

The helplessness made razor marks under my skin, leaving me in ribbons.

From the highest window, older brother shouted down. "Go to the hospital. I don't mean for your hand."

"She's beautiful," I cried up at him. "You'll have to see her." He closed his eyes, then the window, leaving me with everything broken.

United Hospital was more waiting. I spent two hours switching floors, waiting for supervisors, all the time keeping my hand in my pocket to avoid guaranteed but unwanted attention.

"You look pale," a maternity nurse said. "When is she due?"

"Can you help me?"

"I'll try." She wore her nurse's cap like a party hat.

"My wife had a baby in this hospital."

"Congratulations!"

"Stillborn." Her tricked face didn't know whether to rise or fall; she covered it up, smothering her apology. "I know. It's terrible, but no one will help me."

She reached out her hand and instinctively I gave her my right. It had hardened into a purple ball. "What on earth?"

"Plus I'm walking around here with a broken hand." Her compassion broke warm across me. I had my saint. She walked me personally over to records, overriding obstacles with a gesture to my hand. At the final desk they needed ID. "Her name is Emma Clough. I'm her husband, Daniel Rowan. You can call the city."

"But the birth took place before you were one in the eyes of the state. Was this your child?" The administrator wasn't buying the broken-bone story. She had a pile to sit on and she was going to stay king of the hill.

"Emma's in a crisis. We need this information."

"Bring her into the hospital."

"It's not that simple."

"Look, honey," she related, "I know how it is with men,

always wanting to know who else came to the bake sale. But this is ten years ago. Time to move on."

I pounded her desk with my bad hand, sending a howl out of my throat that scared us all. I wavered on the edge of shock. My saint nurse held me steady. "He goes into shock, I got you to mention," she told the administrator, who trundled off to finger-walk. When she came back I was on a gurney, ready for my free ride to ER. She showed me the birth and death certificate, allowing me the certainty. "Sorry, sugar." The child's name was Sophie Claire. And the space where the father's name belonged was blank.

49. "We've got a body," Detective barks into his phone, tracking down Rookie. "She's three for three." Detective doesn't want to believe that the woman who shimmers and shines has been eliminating friends and foes, but the writing is on his wall. She is leading him home one death at a time, the child at her breast an unlikely beacon.

"Serial," Rookie says as they skid up First Avenue.

"I don't know."

"Just because it's a woman," Rookie challenges. "Your problem is you like everybody too goddamn much."

"No." Before last week, Detective didn't like anybody. Now he is collecting friends, memorizing addresses, phone numbers, spending time. Something is at risk.

"Think it's too late?" Rookie pries. "Belly's already swelled."

"Either that, or we're walking into the knife."

There is no answer at Maria's apartment door. It is a logical first step, and Detective expects the slow wail of a motherless child to rise from under the door. He kicks it in. Ten steps each way and the place is clean. No Maria. No Trevor. Detective feels a tremor of relief. "I was sure this was it."

"You look sick."

"Call the lab."

The twitching Coroner is calmer on the phone, his gesticulations not giving him away. "It's easier knowing what to look for," he says, Mahmed undone in front of him. "But I need a minute or two. Similar effect. Neither boy ate their dinner. Both got sent straight to bed."

"There's another one coming," Detective says.

"I don't like this case," ME confesses. "It reminds me of something."

"Only one more. She promised."

"Hope it's not you," Coroner hangs up. Detective checks for swelling below the sternum, above the belt. Hasn't eaten since Maria's dinner and then not really. He is hungry and nauseated.

"Where else?" Rookie asks, fiddling with the destroyed lock.

"Call the locksmith and get a uniform up here. My pocket." They wait for security. Detective opens the window, giving the snow passage. "Too much for November," he says, meaning the snow, but also the hunger and the dying and the ache that he can't escape. The fact that he cares what happens and is already sorry. Desperately sorry, as if he could have stopped all this. Saved these strangers from their poison and longing. And he knows nothing. His ignorance is painful, and he knows he'll need more than clues to soothe. More than the work, climbing the ladder, sleepwalking through each day. For the first time he must know. Or he will starve. Swell to the size of his own death. Burst open on the Coroner's metal bed. "It's funny," he says out the window, Rookie still on the telephone. "It happens inside," explaining malnutrition, starvation, tightening his belt a notch, "before it shows up on the surface." There is a hollowing around his eyes, something recedes. He is weak at the neck, his hair too heavy for his head. Shoulders loosen in the socket, ligaments pull and cross. His left knee cracks loud enough to hear, and he pockets his hand to stop the throbbing. "And then," he turns to Hrcek, flush with duty, "it's too late."

Though he is weakening, Detective's still in charge. He

demands immediate contact when Maria returns, and drives down to the shelter. Chef is waiting. "Keep an eye out," Bell enlists Chef. "And don't forget to eat."

"Thanks for remembering us," Chef responds, an empty plate in his hand. "But there's no food today." Inside, Broderick is calming nerves, making promises without legs. "City forgot us today," he tells Detective. "And Mrs. Hubbard stocked our cupboard."

"How many?" Bell asks.

Rookie is eager to move on. "What about the sister?" Detective pictures Nina, a globe of skin where her perfect belly was. Around him, forks become hammers; the homeless clatter for food.

"In a minute," Detective scolds Rookie, too many mouths to feed, then to Broderick, "How many?"

"Sixty-five today."

"Twenty minutes."

They go to The Hat. On the corner of Ludlow and Stanton, Rookie, Broderick, and Detective rouse the cook and waitress from their afternoon lag and order sixty-five chimichanga specials. Rookie hustles across to the bodega for Cokes and lemonade. It actually takes half an hour with the bagging, paying, and carrying, but the shelter residents could have waited much longer for a meal like this. One client shouts, "Yes!" after an especially delicious bite of beans and melted cheese and chicken. Rookie is no longer in a hurry and Detective elbows him, saying, "See?" Broderick smiles, is sorry there aren't leftovers. Aluminum foil is the only proof of food as the men, women, and children close their mouths on their finest meal in weeks.

Bell takes Rookie behind the curtain, shows him the etching he'd made as a boy. "I used to live here," he says, not ashamed.

"Who did what?" Rookie asks, eager as a little brother.

"We're about to find out."

†   †   †

There is a call at the station from Maria, grateful for the new lock, the best in the building. Detective shuts his door and calls the Rowan house. Mother answers. "Hello," she says, forgetting his name. "How's the car business?"

"Nina didn't tell you?"

"What?"

"Have a new job."

"My husband was saying the car business is a tough one."

"It just wasn't me." He laughs to himself. Nina picks up the phone. "I was telling your mother."

"Don't tell her anything," Nina sounds so familiar. "She'll just forget anyway."

"How's your mouth?" he flirts, unable to resist.

"Lonely. When can I come to 'Binghamton'?"

"It's not safe," turning serious. "Emma made an appearance. Promised another . . . I wanted to make sure you were okay."

"God."

"I don't know if it's already done, or if it's around the corner. I can't tell who she's after, but it's probably not a stranger. Nina?"

"I need to see you."

"I prefer you stay put. Or even better back to Boston."

"I need to see you," she repeats, the voice heavier, less friendly.

"She's carrying a little girl, not a gun. I shouldn't have called."

"Thank you," she rushes, more Nina. "Don't be sorry. I don't hear these things very well. I'll stay here. Call me here."

"I'm going to find her, Nina. She's not getting away any-more."

She starts to say "I love you," but bites it off halfway. "Bye, Daniel," she savors. "I like saying your name."

From the background, "Daniel?" the mother eavesdropping. "Daniel?"

"I won't let you down." Hang up. He's made this idle promise a thousand times: to weeping widows, little children, even fellow cops. Never meant it. This time it hurts. Not just because he means it, but because he's saying it again, to all of them, a twenty-year payback.

A knock, Paul and John enter. They are small out from behind the bar. John, his boxer face leading the way, waiting for a punch, is hunched. His spine asking a question. Paul's hair stays in his face, veiling all emotion. They sit, shrinking further. They have come seeking comfort. "Maggie's on day," John gruffs, assuring all that Milano's is still open for business.

"I don't know Maggie."

"Hell of a dancer." John's hair is slicked and parted. He looks dressed for church. "Never seen you."

"I said you'd been 'round," Paul explains.

"To drink," and eat paper, Detective thinks. "I didn't know about Daniel." They squirm in their seats, three men with nothing in common but a death. They're at a funeral with no corpse. "When was the last time?"

"Had to be three months."

"Four," John jabs the air, his fingers blue with arthritis. "I remember because it was the third of July and Danny said happy Fourth and I said you're early and he said just in case." Paul looks at John. It is the longest sentence John's ever spoken. "Paul was off. It was Maggie and me. Ask her. She'll be by." The regular rhythm returns.

"Somebody killed him," Paul says.

"Thieves. Boy didn't have money. Shot him in the street." John speaks as if he's the cop, picking the crime that fits his fears.

"Poison," Bell corrects. "We have a suspect."

Paul. "I don't want to know."

"Because you do?"

"I don't want to know." Paul sits straight.

"You have an idea, Paul," Detective tells him. "And it's probably right."

John looks back and forth, wanting in. "I don't want to know," Paul repeats, the sentence taking on a certain music.

"I do," John's fists in front. He goes to smooth his hair, realizing too late it's oiled. He retracts his hand as if stung.

"Emma," Detective states. Paul is mute.

"Emma what?"

"Emma, John," Bell is now standing, hovering. "Emma."

John stands too, shuffling back a step, ready to land a jab. "What is he saying, Paul?" John seeks permission to hit, to shut Detective up. "She's a lovely girl. I walked her down the aisle. The path. Whatever you call it. I have pictures."

"So do I," Detective says. "And I also have a confession." Bell is bluffing. He has notes, theories, signatures. No confession.

"I don't." John stops. "Believe."

"Where is she?" Paul unlocks.

"You're not surprised."

"I tried to tell him."

"She worked hard," John challenges. "More than lovely. There is nothing in such a girl. Nothing like that. Poison? You're making it up. You cops know how. Emma," he nearly shouts. "No."

Paul pulls his hair back with both hands, revealing a face younger than Detective expected, but old enough to know. There is a wedding band tight around the proper knuckle. He looks at John, who doesn't recognize this angle. "John."

"No."

"Tell him," Bell prods.

"There's something different about a wife."

50. Surgery lasted two and a half hours. I'd broken four bones in my right hand and my middle finger. They put me in a cast and promised me early rheumatoid arthritis. They asked me what I had done. I told them I didn't know yet. For some reason, I wasn't worried about Emma. Sleeping, I thought. Oblivious of her husband's running, punching, breaking. Deaf to his futile shouting. Blind to the shape of his desire.

I called when I was still groggy, expecting her to wake me up. It was 8 P.M. No answer. I asked a nurse to dial, not trusting my aim, and got the same result. Asleep. I counted her remaining pills in my head. They didn't seem enough.

Why no father? What had stopped Sophie's heart? I took a walk to ICU. The wing had been dressed up since my last visit. Pumpkin-colored walls and new freckled tiles. They stopped me halfway down the hall. "Family members only."

"My little brother," I lied. The nurse put a finger to her lips to quiet herself, apologize. She turned around and left me alone. From behind beige doors, solemn machines beeped out heart and brain waves. Families gathered outside rooms, handing out tissues, starting small arguments. I peeked inside a few times, finding an old woman, hair and veins both blue, receding. Then a teenage boy with half his face bandaged, hiding an ugly surprise. There were fat businessmen who would outlive their stitches, enjoy another scotch. And see-through women, praying for death.

Visiting hours were ending, and my nurse signaled softly for my exit. I was granted one final minute. On a bed barely dented was a boy down to one leg. He was awake, but a morphine drip was pulling him under. His fourteen-year-old face didn't have a mark, save a fish-hook scar on his chin. His unbearable injury seemed a mistake. "I'm here."

He turned his drowsy head, grateful for company. "Hey," he said. He had decided to recognize me. "Where have you been?" I raised my cast as an excuse for my tardiness. He nodded. "Know how you feel."

"You're going to be okay," I told him, a crutch.

"You're a little late."

"I should have been there. I didn't know."

"Either did I," his mouth dry and sorry. "Will you help me?" He asked me to hike his hospital pajamas up over the stump. They had taken it just above the knee. "I want you to see something." I did as he asked. "Isn't it beautiful?" There were tears from one of us, looking at his shortened leg, somehow lovely. A reminder that so much more remained. "My name's Eric," he said, admitting we were strangers. "Thanks a lot." I left him there, grateful for his shape, and ran home to the rest of my wife.

She wasn't there. I called Milano's, but they hadn't seen her in days. She had no friends to go to. She was out alone in the city for the first time since we'd moved in. And I knew she was out looking for me. I joined the hunt.

The shelter. The Angelika. The vacant lot, a wedding garden turned into a swamp of weeds and trash and August rain. The rain came slow at first, like a sauna sweat, then in brigades, punishing the steaming night, ruining it, these clear bullets from the sky. Up to Rockefeller Center, standing alone in the attack, waiting for her to turn the corner. The steps of Saint Thomas and she wasn't there.

The Central Park rock where we'd hidden beneath the witch. West Village, escaping under scaffolding on Sixth and Tenth and only umbrellas bumped by, faces hidden beneath their defense. The Hat, where we'd eaten Mexican and danced to Tito Puente, crowded with junkies and bad actors. No Emma. I imagined her standing on an East Village corner letting her mouth fill with rain till the water spelled something, then swallowing the sentence, saving it for a sunny day. I saw the fluid beauty of her concentration, searching just as hard for me. I willed a rendezvous.

My cast was soaked through as I boarded the E to Queens. I threw away my pain pills, my hand beating like a second heart. Mahmed wasn't home. Eight months after I'd reminded him to quit, he'd added an hour to his schedule. You never know, he had said with a grim smile. His face had turned thin, skin fading to the color of a windshield. I left his cousin laughing at the weather report as if he'd won a long-forgotten bet.

Velcro was asleep. I knew from outside the door because it was so quiet. "I was making you a sweater," Maria said, knitting needles in hand. "For Christmas. I only have half a sleeve to go."

"I might only need one," I said, showing off my injury. She dried my hair, I dried the rest. She gave me leftover men's clothing, too big but dry. Inside my cast, rain slid down my stitches.

"I steal them," she said, showing off a small but impressive collection of sweatshirts and boxer shorts. "Like a tattoo. Proof."

"And if you don't spend the night, you get a sweater," I joked, her fist leaving a memory on my good shoulder.

"You haven't been here in so long you're not allowed. Trevor starts college next year," she exaggerated. "You're missing so much."

"I have my own family," I said too harshly. Then, withdrawing, "I'm sorry. That was lousy."

"No, you're right. I'm alone tonight. Grouchy."

"I'm in trouble, Maria."

"I know."

"I can't explain." I didn't know why I'd come. A kiss? To pretend? Maria didn't owe me anything, didn't know what to do. Maybe I just needed a face.

"Tell me what you can. The hand." It was her face. The firm lines, its solid shape. It was strong enough to absorb my mania.

"I hit a man. A doctor." My arm lifted on its own, proud.

"Did he deserve it?"

"Yes."

"Good," no smile, scooting forward on the couch. "What else?"

"I ran," my feet quickly reminded me. I took off my shoes to find blood and retired skin. "Far." Trevor sent a loud noise from his bed, then fell silent. "I broke windows. Many windows, and went to the hospital." I paused, so much compressed into words, the impossibility of conveying the secret life of the mind. There was no language for where I'd visited. "I can't."

"I don't mind," hand on my knee.

"The words are no good. This isn't what happened."

Maria understood. "Be quiet. I'll work on the sweater. You can stay or leave." She kissed my forehead, a gift.

"I have to go!" I shouted, bolt upright. It scared us both.

"Daniel. Sit down." I slowly fell into a chair. "No one takes care of you," she said.

"I don't need anyone to . . ."

"Stay or leave. But no more words." She made me tea, held my hand, offered to clean and bandage my feet. I refused. We sat for an hour or so, strangers buoyed by an imaginary friendship.

"I shouldn't have come," as I rose to my exit.

Maria kept knitting. "But you did. And that makes me happy."

"There's no one else," I realized.

"There never is."

❦ ❦ ❦

Far away from home. The subway ride was full of strange stares and unsolicited attention. Everyone knew something I didn't. I bowed my head and waited to arrive.

Emma came from the bathroom naked. She greeted me with a kiss inside the apartment, pointed out food left over from dinner. She took her time dressing, skirted around a seduction, was stronger than the patient I'd left behind. "Where were you?"

"Hmmm," she answered, looking up from her cat curl on the couch.

"I was all over. Thought you were . . . Did you take your medication?"

"Yes, Doctor." She smiled, stealing the malice from her tone.

"It was raining and I ran, I called." My jaw dropped first, then me to my knees, tears smearing sentences. Emma came close, but not enough. "I have so much to tell you." No hand on my shoulder. I gathered myself, almost embarrassed.

"Don't cry," she said flatly. "I went out."

"Where?"

"Like you. Out." Sorrow spun into an unfamiliar anger. I didn't know who either of us was. "I can't stay in here with you forever." The voice was loud and clear. A news report. "Why are you dry? What is that sweater? Where were you?" We sat there, total strangers, blocked by tranquilizers, consumed by the past.

"Are you pretending?" I asked.

"Of course." Just behind the eyes, dull lightning. A tiny flare.

"Why?"

"For you. For us."

"Don't," her face cold as bones in my grasp.

"You broke your hand. I can be whatever," she said, not breaking stride. "I've been learning. There is a way." The automation had returned. I shook her gently, hoping the record would skip. "To be here," she finished smoothly. "To be okay."

"Emma. Emma, listen to me." She was at my fingertips, but

already gone. There was no message that could reach her. She was away. "Emma, I love you."

"Yes."

I said the next phrase, believing it could save us, a prayer to bring back the dead. "I saw you waving," the words like poison on my tongue. "I saw the yellow dress."

"When some things tear, there is a clear line for repair. The thing itself tells you. It is its own map. For others, the rip only ruins. It is not that there is nothing to fix. It is simply beyond saving. All you can do is throw it away." Nina had told me that one day to the steady chug of her sewing machine. It was two weeks after Warren's funeral, and she was still working on her prom dress. It was cloud blue, with small white stars embedded in the fabric. As she explained this rule of thumb, she sewed the neck closed. When she finished, she looked at me with a victor's smile. I remember feeling a certain horror at this act, my blood reversing itself for a moment, choking my heart. When she left the room, I ripped the threads out, letting the dress breathe. Two days later I found the dress on Nina's bed, shoes and stockings laid out, and the neck sewed shut again. The only time in my life I tasted total fear.

Emma tore. In my hands, like wet paper, she split into a thousand pieces that no eye could match. She was at the door before I could stand, and I knew Nina had been right. Some things were beyond salvation.

51. There is a song in his head. He hears it through an open-eyed night. It has no melody, is made of the slightest notes. There is a song in his head, which only he can hear and only just before he falls asleep. Then it wakes him up. There is a song in Detective's head. Six A.M. The late-fall morning won't let the sun break in. Detective expects to see Emma's outline in the door frame of the kitchen. By the window, perched on the sill. Closing in on him, Sophie just beyond golden and singing.

He gets up and waits for the call. There is another body waiting for him. He knows he is already too late. Detective does pushups. Shoulders pop like corn, elbows full of jigsaw pieces. He is coming apart. From the inside. To quiet the growl, he opens a can of lima beans, eats them cold. It is the first can he's opened since his shopping spree. They are basement-damp and he doesn't stop till the can is only silver. Emma, call me. Talk to me, he thinks. Who's next? He sniffs the empty can for poison, checks his belly, rising like yeast.

On the street, citizens curse the early snow, ruining the wrong shoes, jumping puddles to land in slush. It is a skaters' day. Taxis shimmy fare to fare. Buses bully uptown, hoping for contact. That's her in the window, pulling the emergency brake. No. The steam rising from the manhole cover. No. He is hungry for her form, needs her solid before him.

At the precinct, he is ready to take the cage himself, let Emma and her spectral child float away on their own gust. He will take the fall to let them soar. But first he needs to find them. Discover the method, learn the disease. Breathe till he is sick with it, so that punishment feels like healing. He has to do more than confess, he must commit. Detective knows the next body should be his own.

He longs to be ill, drunk with fever, swollen with famine. He wants the hard push of needle, the poison hidden in the blood, the damage gorgeous, a beautiful decay. He will absolve her. Take credit for the crime, take his place among the dead, let her raise her daughter like wheat, for a harvest of laughter and song. He will do for Sophie what he never managed for his son. Listen. Then yield. She will be his child, the daughter of his dreams.

"I did it," Detective tells Captain. Captain is sweating again, November's descent no defense for his panic. His wife is at her sister's. He has no one to call.

"We're early," he says, reminding them they have nowhere else to be.

"I did it," Bell repeats.

"Your twitching little ME called. Asked if you wanted to watch him cut the cake."

Detective feels the tug of blade as Mahmed is unzipped. "Captain."

"Got that goddamn Rookie full of juice. How close are you?" clammy hands on fat neck. "Fix the heat," he yells.

"I did it."

"Did what, Detective? You're a fuckin' screwball."

"Telephone call, Detective," a small cop says, peering in.

"Is this a meeting?" Captain growls. "Did you just jump on my trampoline?"

Small cop doesn't mind. "Woman. Says it's urgent. That's all." He shuts the door, hearing Detective's question through the glass. He answers with a shout that stops all the phones from ringing. "Emma Clough. Like dough. Line seven."

"What did you do?" Captain yells as Bell slips by him. The door swings closed.

"Meet me," Emma says. In the background, Sophie sings her scattered notes. He doesn't have to ask where.

There is a lot, a vacant lot, with grass as tall as a woman. Trash meets in separate congregations across the field. Across the street, bakers on break watch a forty-four-year-old bearded man in jeans and a bottle-blue shirt climb over the fence. For a flash, they consider calling the cops.

Emma is visible in the back corner, near a rip in the fence where the cats get in. Detective can see the hint of curls, just above the grass line. He moves to her like a lover, rolling his ankle on an empty container, pulling sheaves apart to reach his intention. "Stop." They are too close, the snow camouflaging her perfect skin, only hair giving her away. Detective can hear Sophie humming, the notes new. She is clinging to her mother's neck, escaping Bell's vision.

"I've missed you."

"Every time," she says. "I was married here."

"I know," he tells her, remembering her beauty on that day. Her relief! And the face of the groom. His eager fatigue. "I was here."

"There is so much." It snows louder, putting space between her words. Sophie bundles closer, her music avalanched. Detective can't bear the wait, interrupts.

"I did it," he says, smiling.

"No." The word is an arrow that fits in his heel.

"I mean . . ."

"Don't. Daniel. Don't." She will not allow his imagination, his confession. She needs something else.

"But Sophie," he tries. "You should go. I have nothing."

Without steps, Emma is closer. "You have everything. Everything that remains."

"Why?"

Sophie tells him with lyrics he cannot fathom. Then Emma, "I came to say I am sorry." The sentence is from another language, and though he understands, the switch makes him disbelieve. "I took his life."

"What about me?" he asks, needing guidance on how to arrest her. How to pluck the child from her wing. Needing strength even to stand.

"There is one more body," she reminds him. "I just wanted you to know it was me."

"Where?" Detective stutters. "Who?" She is further, near a corner he cannot reach. "I can let you get away!" He speaks it as a revelation. She knows it isn't true.

Sophie's song reprises. Its current humming in Detective's bones. "Ask for help," she advises. "One more, then I am yours. I'll meet you there."

"Why?" Again, hungry, faint. "He loved you."

"Do you love me?" she says, knowing. It is his warning and his amnesty.

"I could do this for you." His hands powerless, his heart in defeat.

"This time," Emma whispers, "I am the gift."

He is alone in a field, beneath a relentless sky. There is a killer he cannot catch. A murderer he cannot free. She is made of spirit and light, and she will not fit in his hands.

At the precinct, Rookie is waiting. He has a corpse Detective Daniel Rowan Bell will be interested in. Rookie is shivering with news. His feet percussion on the dull cop floor. There is a third body, and it waits for Detective. Patiently. Knowing he will come.

52. I didn't find her for a week. Slow to follow, I had watched her taxi's taillights blink into the New York night. She'd gotten away, my mind too blind with hurry to capture the cab's license number.

I decided not to look that night. She would come home, I lied to myself. There would be the sound of keys, a door quietly opening, the scuff of sheets and skin, a warm body ready to tell stories. I fell asleep with this dumb hope and woke with a hangover.

I had broken the law. At Serendipity, over frozen hot chocolates, years before, I had made a vow, and in my desperate digging, my manic search for a cure, had been unfaithful. It was more than a tortured memory that sent Emma anonymously into the night. It was a betrayal.

At 9 A.M., New York's hot August stink rising between the tenements like tear gas, I sweated into an old pair of boots, fresh bandages on my feet. The sun was low, lazy: I bought sunglasses to see Emma better against all the yellow light. I visited the same old places, our sheltered existence making it easy to exhaust the list. I didn't call Maria. Checked every cab for Mahmed's focused eye. Told Paul he was right and that I might not be in for a few days. He bought me a drink and promised to hold my job. "Family," he said. I didn't know what he meant.

I had no energy and no idea where to go. I wanted to get drunk. To be a ship inside a bottle of Bushmill's and sail my way out, mouth open. To put my lips on a Guinness tap and let the foam run over my face, hiding my identity. To forget I was married, responsible, a man, and that I was so goddamned guilty.

The weight of dropping another angel from my shoulders was too ugly to bear. I had never warned Emma about how weak my hands were. She had been my opportunity to prove I had learned how to hang on. And when she broke open on the pavement, I brought a yellow dress to stop the bleeding. What she needed I didn't know how to provide.

I decided once I did find her I would let her go. That I would admit my poverty and release her to the riches she deserved. She needed a strong grip, a perfect love, my cast and ache proof I was not the one. I had no idea how I would survive without Emma, but I hadn't earned her presence. It was time for her to ascend and for me to disappear.

"Mom?" My mother opened the door, older than expected. The land beneath her face had shifted, sinking her cheeks, softening the nose. There were age spots making shy entrances, and her hair was the color of stone. She left the door open a minute, looking me over, expecting someone else.

"Come in." The house was uncharacteristically messy, kitchen chairs at the dining-room table. Glasses scattered, the formaldehyde smell of cognac. "Your father's away," she said shuffling into the kitchen, returning with a carton of milk, a Coke, and a six-pack perched in her arms. "Take your pick."

I tore a beer free and entered the den. It looked like a man who'd lost his front teeth. The TV was missing. "Hey, Mom." We were pretending I was a neighbor, that years had not gone by.

"I look terrible," she said, leaning on the couch arm. "I should have sent a picture. Just in case."

"In case of what?"

"In case you came by." She was drinking out of a tumbler that had a graph of the 1928 stock-market crash. "Your father's away," she repeated, lifting her glass. A toast. An excuse for an afternoon nip.

"I'll be staying," I announced, knowing that this was the perfect place to vanish.

"Bed's made." Mom swayed into a chair across from me. It was new, and the leather took her in with a puff. "Nina called. Hasn't heard from you." I think she laughed. "She's on Martha's Vineyard with some architect she can't stand." Then she did laugh, toasting me again. There was something antiseptic about our conversation, protecting us from the absurdity of it all. "How long?"

"A while," I answered. "Dad know about the TV?"

"He will next Wednesday." Another laugh, this one victorious.

"He'll get another one."

"If I'm lucky he'll go to the Hilton. They have HBO." Her face shut down after the sentence, apologizing for the candor. I was hearing a conversation she was having with herself. Eavesdropping. "How long?" again. "Maybe just till your father gets back. He shouldn't see Emma."

"I'm alone."

"Oh. Another drink?" She rose to mix herself one. She returned uncurious, and stared at the gap. "Pretty goddamn funny." She used the curse as a balance, to make it through the sentence. It was not yet five and my mother was at the good-bye end of an all-day cocktail party.

"I'm going to lie down," my beer doing its sedative best.

"First room on the left."

My room. The trophies hurt first. They were ancient, from my early teens, but the thick sweater of dust the miniature ball players wore made the place feel haunted. The bed was made, but the sheets were cool with summer's sweat. The bedspread was musty, the pillows stiff beneath. Under the bed were posters of Joe Namath, Earl Monroe, a signed photograph of Dean Meminger.

Bending down, I looked in the mirror on the dresser. The last reflection I'd ever seen in that mirror was of an eighteen-year-old boy eager to look cute for a girl on a train. My face that afternoon hadn't aged as much as it had given in. There was a gray exhaustion around the eyes, grief pulling at the mouth. A face the shape of regret. I needed a shave.

In my parents' bathroom, I heated the water and lathered up. That same sink had once been sacred, its waters holy as I shaved with razorless cartridges next to my dad. He taught me where to shave up and where to shave down. I had envied the scratch and tug of blade against whiskers, sometimes making the sound in my mouth as my smooth skin came clean. Dad had been an expert at shaving, rarely cutting himself, and he always left the bathroom smelling good enough to wrestle. I would wait for him in closets or under the bed, make him late for work, wanting to smell that good. He'd pin me between lacing wingtips and a Windsor knot, leave me laughing on the bed, wishing I could go to his office instead of school.

That was so long ago it seemed like something I'd read. Back when he could look at his first son and see something other than blame. "What's wrong with your hand?" Mother said without knocking. It was hard enough shaving left-handed, but her sudden entrance left a slice down my chin.

"Broke it."

"Sorry," less about the break than the cut. Because she had seen it. "You look good."

"I think I'm hungry."

"You and Emma . . . ?" and a flat gesture with her hand.

"Yes."

"I'll make you dinner." Something cleared and she bopped

down the steps, maybe whistling. I looked again at the mirror, the blood stuck in the white, too tired to spill anymore.

"Your eyes are yellow," Mom said, digging into the Chinese she'd ordered.

"Yours, too."

"I've been thirsty." Her hands shook almost imperceptibly as they dug for cashews with chopsticks.

"When did you quit talking to Dad?"

"Oh," she waved me off.

"There isn't enough room in Warren's coffin for all of us, Mom." She bit her tongue, but didn't feel it. The velvet rush of VSOP providing protection from her dead son's name. "One of us," I finished, "is going to have to survive." She had her shoulders hunched like the people at the shelter. She stayed focused on her dinner, offering no hole in her defense. "Mom, I love you." I said it to shock her, counting on its being the verbal equivalent of ten thousand volts. She looked up, but only to find her drink.

"Took you a while to lose that girl."

"Yes."

"We knew you'd come around." As if there'd been late-night family meetings. Strategies, formulas, plans of attack; she the weary general who'd finally won the war.

"I'm going to find her." Her spine pulled straight, drawing her shoulders into line. "And then I'm going to let her go." Confused, but relieved, Mom relaxed, her chicken once again the source of fascination. "Why do you hate her?"

"No one hates anyone."

"You, Nina, Dad."

"Your father has never met Emma. Thank God, never will. Your sister and I," she tried to use a facial expression, hoping I wouldn't demand words. She ended up looking like a drunk. She was a drunk. "Daniel, there are certain people . . . That's all I can say."

"She's a certain person," I fought.

"You don't fall in love with . . . that type of girl."

"I was in the hospital, too, Mom."

"That's not what I mean."

"Well, for the first time in your life, tell me what you mean!"

"Don't yell, Daniel," she mumbled, holding her head.

"Don't worry, Mom. There's enough booze here to make you forget you've even got a head. Or a son. Anyway, that happened a long time ago."

She had let me shove enough. She pushed her plate away, squared to me, took me in, took me on. "She got pregnant. At fifteen. For your information, little Miss Emma lived down the street from us. Your middle sister went out on a date with one of the brothers. Animals. That family was made up entirely of animals." I poured her next drink to keep her on line. "The father, when he was around, was a raging alcoholic. They were thieves, those boys stealing bicycles. A car once." Her face was purple, bruised by the memory of such an atrocity as the Cloughs. Her indignation swelled till it stuck in her liquored throat and had to be coughed out. Like us, I thought. She poured a third drink, each one raising her voice, thinning her anger into needles and scalpels.

"Girls get pregnant."

"Not that way." She let the innuendo flutter and flare.

"Mom?"

"She wouldn't say who the father was. She didn't have a boyfriend. The little slut practically pretended it was an immaculate conception." Mother was livid. The story doing more damage in the telling than in the knowing.

"All conceptions are immaculate."

"All I know is something happened in that house."

"What?"

"Something. And she wouldn't do the honorable thing. Had to bring that suffering child into the world."

"She died." Mom froze for a moment. "The baby. It was a little girl." It stole her steam, sidelining the outrage. A baby had died.

"How do you . . . ? Of course."

"Emma never told me. I went to United." Mother couldn't quarrel with a dead infant. Her focus had strayed from Emma to this child, still as December. Never begun.

"Better that way," she decided. The latest drink stopped short of her thirst.

"You knew all this."

"Too late. You were in the city two years before I knew."

"How?"

Mom stood, sat, a little woozy, then stood again. She needed to be in motion. "We found out. Nina found out. I had her go to River Glen." She looked at me, refusing to take the fall. "Well, we couldn't have you marrying someone crazy. I mean, grand-children." I pictured Dr. Kleiner, one arm around Nina's waist, illuminating her on the finer points of Emma's psychosis. "Not just the baby, you know. The suicides, the anorexia. No wonder that child died. She killed her."

I rose to strike my mother. I had never hit nor threatened any woman, yet there I stood, the cast a heavy reminder of the blow I could deliver. I let it fall of its own weight, the throb starting again when it hit my thigh. Mother stood with a mix of shock and complicity. Her behavior had lit the match, her tone speeding the fuse. "I'm sorry," I said shyly.

"Yes, well."

"You never told me."

"We forgot," she said, not being funny. They had released me from their memory banks, drowned me in their sorrows. "I guess I always knew you'd come back."

"When the prodigal son comes home," I schooled her, remembering from Sunday school, "they throw him a party. Not a funeral." I left the house and my mother in disarray.

Five Larkspur, and no one was home. The Volvo and big brother's car were both gone, and a SOLD sign had been stabbed into the earth. The front windows were still broken, fragments of glass in patterns at my feet. I checked the front door, unlocked, and walked in.

It was black, with the same shaft of summer sun spotlighting the kitchen. I didn't know which way to move. Upstairs seemed easiest. I would spot Emma's room instantly. The aroma, the light. There was no place that surrendered her spirit. There would be proof, her soul prints. At the top of the steps was a sawhorse and a three-inch-thick metal chain, bannister to bannister. I stepped over. The floorboards gave an inch, the wood had rotted. On tiptoes, weightless as Emma, I sought out her space.

The first room was charred from a small fire. The flames had been contained, but scars lashed up and down the near wall. Next was the master bedroom. The walls had been covered with framed pictures, old nails the clue. The room was bare except for scattered papers and a few loose wires. There was a painful desolation, the windows blacked out, ceiling too low. It was a room to escape.

Across the wide hall was one door, the only one on that entire side of the second floor. No closets, no bathrooms, just this door. Emma's room. The wallpaper was intact. Silver blue with yellow streaks. The carpet had been ripped up, but a swatch in the corner said navy. One of the windows was open, banged shut by a sudden summer wind. I opened it again, looking outside at all the empty homes, lights on timers, families on vacation. Finally, the houses safe. In the bathroom, the mirror was missing. It had been a large one, sink to ceiling, and at least four feet across. The tub was also gone, having taken four tiles as shoes.

I sat down in the middle of the bedroom and listened for her voice. "Emma," I spoke. She had nothing to say. I stared at the wallpaper, hoping the streaks would dash me back to what had happened. Who had knocked down her walls, given her Sophie too soon. Only blur and blaze. No evidence, no sign that my magical wife had grown up here. They'd stripped every inch bare of her essence. This was the scene of the crime. A place fled, abandoned. A room, a house no one would remember. It should have been torn down, unable to retain even the slightest scent of the girl who lived here. It deserved to be buried, burned, dissolved. I returned to my mother's address and slept in the yard.

In the morning, grass scars on my face, I went shopping. The cupboards were bare, so I took Mom's cash and went on a spree. Twenty-one bags full. Mostly canned goods, nonperishables. Mom hadn't been doing much shopping, and she needed food that would last. I filled the pantry with the excess, made her breakfast, still stuck on small talk, and called Nina. It was ten-thirty in the morning and I woke her up. "Hello?"

"Thirty and still sleeping in."

"Who is this?" Her voice all cigarettes and too much rest.

"Brother Daniel. I have some news."

"Daniel?"

"I'm at Mom's."

"Are you all right?"

"I'm leaving."

"Emma?" as if she'd been expecting the call.

"Everyone."

"I just woke up. I don't understand."

"I'm leaving."

"I got that part."

"I'm getting out of the way, Nina. I know what you did. I know what I did. It's time to go."

"What the hell are you . . . You're scaring me. Put Mom on."

I handed Mom the phone. She put down her after-eggs martini and slipped into her daughter's panic.

I went back to my room for one final look. I took down the trophies and wrapped them in the sports-star posters like gifts. Set them in the middle of the bed and wrapped them in my musky bedsheets, tossing the pillows in for padding. A fine sweat broke out over my whole body as I dragged my bounty down the stairs. Mom waved to me as I exited the front door. Up Thistle and onto Larkspur I pulled my Santa bag of sheets and victories, bad memories too surprised to sneak out. Past the firebush and boxwood that surrounded their property and up onto the Clough's porch.

In Emma's room, I opened my package and on the bare floor laid out sheets, blanket, bedspread, tucking the pillows underneath. I took the trophies and washed their moldy heads and feet, getting the best shine against my pants. I set them up in a row at the foot of the bed. With a hammer I'd stolen from home, I pulled nails from the master-bedroom walls and nailed my hero posters up on Emma's wall. Namath. Seaver. Frazier. They were crinkled like me. Not as heroic as before, but familiar against the wallpaper heaven. "Emma," I said clear and clean. "I saw you wave. The girl in the yellow dress. We could have been friends. Should have been." So hot, breathing became wheezing. I cooled my face on Emma's sky. "I could have been here," I told her, my bed in place, my dreams so apparent. "We could have locked the door."

Five days later, I decided Dr. Kleiner deserved a visit. I had one good hand left and he no spare nose. I didn't care if I got arrested. I was leaving anyway. I'd get where I was going. There were still some things I knew how to do.

The grass was as green, shoes as squeaky, walls as conspiratorial as the day I'd gone hunting, but this time I arrived with blood in my eye. Our apartment on Tenth was almost completely empty. Just a few boxes of Emma's things to sort through and then my escape. I told Maria she could move in by the following weekend. Told her Mahmed would help her move. Said I might be tied up, meaning locked up. I heard sirens in my skull. Kleiner entered his office head down, reading the *Times,* grumbling to himself. He breathed through his mouth, his nose packed shut. "Morning," I said, sending electroshock through his body. "Don't worry, Doctor, it's good for you."

He knew the distance to the phone and my fist were not in his favor. He leaned back in his chair. "I didn't call the police."

"Thanks."

"If you bring the files back, I don't see why this whole thing can't go away." His face was bandaged badly, and I could see there'd be a large bump at the bridge as a reminder.

"How come doctors always get the worst care?"

"The files."

"Burned. Destroyed. No more."

"Not smart." He leaned toward the phone like a school principal about to call a parent. I stepped forward, ending his idea. "I see you paid the price as well."

"You've got a hard head, Doc. To go with your heart."

"I know why you're here, Daniel. I need you to stay calm."

I jumped onto his desk, kicking his chair against the wall. A diploma smashed onto a vase, which held its ground. Then down to his level, so I could squeeze his nose. It ran red, and he made several inaudible requests. "Who do you fix?" I shouted.

"Please, please."

"My sister reads Emma's résumé because you like her tight dress. Do you have any idea the damage you've done?" Kleiner looked amazed, not that I had found him out, but that he could have done something wrong. I squeezed his nose again because it felt so damn good. His legs kicked, banging his shin on a bottom drawer. "I've got one good hand left, and I'm going to break it on you."

"Daniel, Daniel, wait," his hands a vain protection for his

injury. "That's why you're here?" His voice was tiny and thin, a splinter in his throat. "To hurt me. Because of Nina?"

"You had to figure I'd find out."

"No, that's not what I mean." The pause threw me. I let him stand up. He even got near the door, my feet stuck in the plush.

"I want to hit you," I said. "I need to hit you."

"I know. I'm sorry. For whatever happened." His bandage was Bing cherry red, his eyes crazy with burst vessels. "I just need to know why you're here."

I moved toward him quickly, but he put up his fists. He looked comical, backhanding the air, circling. I was able to corner him again. "Doc, what are you doing?"

"Daniel! Stop!" he screamed, fists still in front. It was so unexpected that I did. I stopped. I looked at Dr. Kleiner the way I had the year I'd spent inside. A little dopy. Trusting. I waited for his next word. I needed to hear it. "Daniel, we have your wife."

What was left of her. Emma had come home, but not to J Ward. She was in S Ward, surveillance ward, with soft restraints, the way they'd greeted her at age sixteen. The white restraints like butterfly stitches, hemming her in at the extremes.

Dr. Kleiner offered a weak handshake and fell back into his regret. We were alone, Emma and I, the beeping of her heart and brain monitors sounding my arrival, drowning out her song. When I was close enough to touch she opened her eyes. "There you are." Her face was tan, the color of a dig. She'd spent too long in the sun, her hands just as dark. I'd never seen her transparency so clouded. She was in there, somewhere, behind the mud and the tubes, tiny as Warren, too thin to fight.

I had imagined finding her flush with disappointment. Strong enough to hear my farewell and laugh or huff. I expected gratitude to flash across her screen. Though lonely, she would realize she'd be stronger without me. An embrace would become a push toward better days. Standing there, I realized there would be no push. I was not the one who'd be saying good-bye.

"What happened?" admitting the surprise she'd felt at her position. "How did I wind up here?" It was a small joke, as if she were showing me a faulty map, where all the roads led to the same place. I looked at her chart. It listed her weight at eighty-nine pounds. She had shrunk back to fit the space they had for her at River Glen. She was their little girl.

"Are you afraid?" A cough ripped through her, lifting her off the bed a few inches. It seemed her shoulders would snap like wishbones. She landed, the sound of a feather. "We won't talk," I tried. She shook her head.

"I was waiting for you."

"No one called."

"I told them you'd arrive. I wanted to tell you." She had a deep scratch beside her left eye. From a tree branch or a piece of metal. It would scar if she let it. The bed was too high to kneel beside, and all the chairs had been removed. There were bars on the window, a sick morning light breaking in. I untied her hands, but she was too weak to lift them. I placed one across my mouth so she could feel what I was saying. "I love you," I whispered. "It isn't enough."

"They take things," she said, the music waning, her lungs struggling to find the chords. "And for a while you try to get them back, and then . . ."

"You haven't eaten," I told her, the drip of the IV bottle too slow for my taste.

"You decide you don't need those things. Anymore."

"New things," I hoped.

"Yes." The s, late air from a balloon. "You were my new thing, Daniel. My only thing. I was going to take care."

"I can't."

"You did."

I laid my head lightly on her belly. A womb. A tomb. They take things, I realized, that cannot be replaced. "Sophie," tears and loss shaking my head. Emma placed her hand on top, keeping me there. We were finally a family, our invisible child rising up and through us, entering our exhausted hearts, giving us her life. Her new limbs, fresh skin digging into our earth, sowing herself, rejuvenating us. Emma kept me there, my neck unable to lift, until all the magic and light had been absorbed.

"Do you have her?" Emma asked.

"Sophie Claire Rowan." I spoke into Emma's belly of beauty and life. She released me, and as I stood I realized Emma had given me her sustenance. Her medicine, oxygen, vitamins, and hope. She had given me her heart. The color fell from her face, the final veil removed. There on the bed, whiter than light, was my Emma. Pure identity. Child, woman, partner, Emma. "I came to say good-bye," I protested, unable to lose her.

"It's not your turn." Her lips straightened enough to suggest a smile. Paler still, she gave in to a shiver, a journey over bumpy road. Then her hand, stronger than mine, squeezing, holding on, letting go. Inside, blood made its final circle. "Daniel," nearly shouting, eyes wide open, seeing what was ahead. "Everything. You gave me," in spurts, something black in pursuit. "I didn't know what it was."

"Emma, I can't. I'm the one who is leaving." But like everyone else, she left me behind.

"Daniel," she called, looking through me, past me, within me. "The yellow dress. I can see you waving. Can you see me?" Her eyes all that hung on, staring, knowing. "Can you see me?"

She left without waiting for an answer. Because she knew. It wasn't a question for her, it was a reminder for me. That she wouldn't stop waving. That we would never be apart. "Dear God," I prayed, unable to go any further, hoping someone, somewhere, understood the beauty that had been lost.

By the door, the sound of feet rushing down the hall, I felt the first tug. The strength of a tiny head pulling up toward the surface. Sophie was climbing my ribs, newborn feet on bones. I left the doctors to their discovery and hurried down the hall. "Hang on, Sophie. Hang on."

53. Nothing to ID. No prints, no paperwork. Rookie hands him a death certificate. And a map. They take a ride. The cemetery is familiar to Rookie. He supervised an exhumation here. He smirks when he stands over Daniel's still-empty tomb, fifty yards away. "Close family."

"Not close enough."

EMMA LAUREN CLOUGH. NOVEMBER 3, 1966—AUGUST 21, 1993. IN LOVING MEMORY FROM HER HUSBAND, DANIEL ROWAN. Detective has his third body, just as Emma promised him. "This one better be empty, too," Rookie kids Detective. "Otherwise, you've been seeing ghosts." Bell knows it's not empty. Knows the dust beneath this hard earth. He heads to the caretaker's office, makes a deal. He will pay to have Emma's casket moved next to Daniel's plot. He understands the cost. The difficulty. Uses his badge to cajole, bully. "Husband and wife," Detective convinces, "should be together."

Detective allows Rookie to dig. Sift Emma's skeleton for dental records, proof. They finally have their suspect in hand and somehow she is still out of reach. He heads to Daniel's house. At the door is the mother. She has a glass of wine in her hand. She offers him a sip. "Nina," he asks.

"Back to Boston. She was expecting you."

"Tell her that her sister-in-law is dead." Mother doesn't blink. "Emma."

"I know."

"You know?"

"I'm not surprised. We haven't heard from her. Daniel's funeral. She was a sick girl."

"No," he tells her, ready to spill wine. He shows his NYPD shield, hoping he can intimidate her into respecting Emma. In her lubrication, mother thinks he's kidding.

"Hell of a way to sell cars," a muffled laugh. "Buy or go directly to jail. Do not pass go." She tries a smile that worked on men thirty years ago. "You're a promotional genius." He wants to arrest her. Throw her in a cage for being such a souse.

"You're drunk."

"I certainly hope so." Her face straightens for a second. "Sister-in-law?"

"Do you have any idea where Emma was from?" Detective is in a hurry. Wants to get to a place where Emma can find him. Is willing to catch a plane, a ship. Ready to travel and start over. He refuses the grief. He expects a visit.

"He married that . . ."

Detective's proximity stops the sentence. Mother sets down her glass, the better to protect herself. The California white ceases to sedate. She is on alert. "Tell me," Detective advises.

"Take a walk." What she means as directions he takes as lack of cooperation. What could he arrest her for? Murder?

"Mrs. Rowan."

"And who are you?"

He has to think for a minute, looks again at his badge. "No one believes me," he says.

"Why should they?" the mother now on the offensive, wine back in her grasp. She drinks greedily, defends her ground. "You should leave."

"Your son," he looks for a seat, a welcoming. "We have the same name."

"Daniel."

"Yes. I am Daniel." His voice is the first day of school. Mother takes his extended hand. "Your son was a good man." She doesn't know how to hear this. He is describing a stranger. She tilts her head to hear him better. "Emma," he starts.

"Don't want to hear," she combats.

Detective retreats to solid ground. "He was worth knowing."

"But you didn't," connecting Detective to the lies, the funeral, Binghamton.

"I found out," he says. "Too late."

"Believe me, Officer," wine sneaking over the rim. "Everything is too goddamn late." They stare at each other, one in a hurry, the other giving up. "Does Nina know?"

"I showed her."

"I mean about Daniel. What you say."

"No."

"It's not easy," Mother attempts. "Something is lost. There's a hole. And everything seems to fall in." Another glass of wine to soothe the truth. "I thought if I stopped looking, maybe it would disappear." But everything else has, and this woman is alone in a large house, unable to hold on to what remains. Detective can feel the pull, an ugly gravity, and he scouts his escape. "There's nothing there," she says, surprising him with the address. He has her repeat it slowly, a foreigner. "Daniel was my son." Loud and bold. It is all she can claim, but to such a hunger the words taste good.

"Mrs. Rowan. May I visit again?" She takes his broken hand as an answer, squeezes it the way mothers never forget how.

"I'll be here." She toasts his exit, swallows the rest.

There is nothing there. FOR SALE, the sign reads, a string of weeds around its neck. No house. Just dirt, splotched by a new snow. And in the yard, yesterday's toys. A doll, old soldiers. A tricycle missing two wheels. Detective kicks at the things, giving him something to do with his feet. Whatever happened here is forgotten, its roots deep in the soil, all memories sunken, treasure and poison. "Is this where?" Detective asks. Then he remembers he must wait for her. He is not allowed to search, to unearth. She keeps her promises, Bell knows, but he is afraid he has forgotten how to wait.

"Are you sad?" she asks him in the hallway outside Maria's apartment, the last place she lived. Sophie is wide awake. She stares at Detective. Loves him.

"You could have told me."

"You never would have followed." Emma is whiter now, clearer. He can see the bloodless veins still blue beneath the shine. The child sits on Emma's shoulder, balanced, not needing to be held. She looks ready to push off into Detective's arms.

"You confessed. I had you."

"Now, it's your turn." She glides to him, her lips finding his cheek, delivering more than a kiss. Sophie leans in as well, whispering a song into his ear. They stay like this, sealed, a triangle of light and dark, until the music is complete. Sophie gives a little-girl tug to his ear as they step away. There is a song in his head. The notes connect in gentle flurries, the melody brand new, familiar. By the fire escape, mother and child flicker, a final flame.

Who killed Daniel? he asks without speaking.

"All of us," the answer undamming rivers in his heart. I will drown, he tries to say, the words washed away, whirlpools forming, eddies and floods. Don't let me drown.

When he clears the water from his eyes, they are gone. No shadows, no shimmer. Detective is alone in the hallway on the fifth floor of a New York City apartment building. He does not know what to do, how to speak, how to move. But there is a kiss on his cheek, he realizes, something new rising within. He touches his ear. A child's fingerprints remain. There is a song in his head.

54. Dr. Kleiner said they'd call me in the morning with news of where and when to pick up the body. There was paperwork to fill out, tests on machines. There had been no warning. Emma was ill, but not unto death. She had finally decided to surrender the fight. After so many years of clenching her spirit, a release. Dr. Kleiner blamed technology, apologized, felt responsible, promised an investigation. I knew where Emma had gone. Into the space between molecules, the breath after the last, to hide in the sting of a kiss and come riding the snow. She was all around. And Sophie was within.

The apartment seemed huge. Emma's final boxes lonesome in the bedroom corner. There was a note under the door from Maria and Velcro. I didn't read it, knowing it was kind and confused. They'd be coming. The door would be unlocked.

I wasn't sure what I'd discover in Emma's collectibles. These were boxes I'd never examined, banned from touching them. They'd always had a special role as night stand. Covered with a tablecloth, holding up lamps, mail, the night's reading material. Removing the covering was like undressing a mummy. I wouldn't have been surprised by a pile of dust. Revealed, each box bore the simple exclamation: EMMA'S STUFF! STAY OUT! The writing was youthful but serious. Even with her silent permission, I felt like a thief.

Money. The only thing inside the first one was money. It was neatly stacked, twenties together, fives in a row, all the Abes facing up. Ones took up most of the space, the unmistakable whiff of dried booze wafting off the cash. "Clough, like dough." I laughed, recalling an old joke. Emma had opened a bank in our bedroom. Second box. Money. A slice of every night's tips for all the years at Milano's. It was enough money to raise a family, though not to raise the dead. The second cardboard vault contained more serious stacks of twenties, and even a few fifties hidden at the bottom. I decided to open box number three. On top of more of the same was an envelope with my name written on it. Inside, Emma had written: "IN CASE I'VE GONE AWAY—DANIEL, YOU ARE THE ONE. RAISE SOPHIE. TELL HER ABOUT ME. I SEND MYSELF FROM WHER-EVER I AM. EMMA." It was dated December 10, 1985. Emma had known long before I that her center could not hold.

At the bank, the Assistant Manager eyed me warily, looking over my shoulder to the pillar of security by the door. "Cash business?" he croaked. He had a way of counting without looking. Eyes on his fingertips.

"Bartender."

"Good week."

"Thanks." The tally was $45,000, plus $206, which I handed to the first homeless woman outside the bank. I walked until I saw a FOR RENT sign. Up Second Avenue, wet like it rained from the humidity. Cutting crosstown when the feeling was right, 45K in a gray gym bag. Most landlords weren't in, or didn't want to bother with a sweaty man and his raggedy gym bag. It wasn't until Gramercy, on Twentieth, that I found a home. It was an old building, with apartments in front and back. The stone was blood brown, the hallway carpets in need of replacement. The landlady was tired from the heat, keys slipping in and out of her grasp. She was irritated with everything, from her onrushing fiftieth birthday to the polyester cling of her blouse. "Do I look old?" she griped, turning the bolt.

A palace. Fifteen-foot-high ceilings. Room to fit both of our old apartments inside. And more. The kitchen was actually a kitchen, and the water hurried out of the faucets, ready to clean. "I know it's a mess," she said. "Cleaning company. Call 'em and call 'em. Echh!"

"I'll take it."

"You got references? I'll need a credit check. Sixty-five bucks. I'll need the last few places you rented. Addresses. Landlords. Rent's a thousand a month, rent control, so I'll need all this information right away."

"I'll take it," I repeated, $12,000 from my bag for the first year.

Her hands trembled, a trip to Atlantic City lighting her eyes. "Welcome home, sweetheart."

"Do you mind if I have friends over?"

"Did I tell you I'm only fifty?"

"Happy birthday, ma'am," and she handed me the keys.

I had the clothes on my back and $33,000. I returned to Milano's and got my day shift back. "Emma's retired," I told Paul. He said he hoped she'd still come around. From the bar pay phone I called Mahmed. Unbelievably, he was home. "What are you doing?"

"My friend," he said. "Day off."

"No."

"First time in one year. Least." There was a chirp in his voice, a small joy. I didn't want to ruin it.

"I need the cab."

"I take you. Where?"

"No. Mahmed. Keep your day off. I'll take the train."

"I know the sound," he said, clinking glasses and Sinatra giving me away. "Thirty minute."

Mahmed ambushed me at the bar. I bought him a round, avoiding the discussion. "You look no good," he said. Neither did he. His eyes were yellow, lips split from mouth breathing. And so thin. His skull was making a forward advance against his skin.

"You're not going to stop," I guessed, beer rushing smooth over my thirst. "You won't listen to your Dad."

"I do not have to," he proclaimed, standing up. "I remember." The door opened near us and the wind had its way with him. He took a seat. "My Father, you say Dad." He grinned, enjoying the slang. "Dad said there will be seven years of famine, but not what." He sipped his Guinness, a foam mustache thick on his face. "Food. Look. Everywhere is food."

"Yeah."

"So Dad mean another thing. Must mean. Look. Food." His exuberance couldn't hide the fact that he didn't believe himself. It was his excuse for not being able to stop working. He was an addict, convincing himself he wasn't really sick. "So day off. To celebrate." But he had come to drive me. And the next day he'd be behind the wheel, counting cash, driving just slowly enough to be caught from behind. "Everyone has enough. More. I can take day off, see a friend." His hand like paper as he slapped my back.

"You're sure?" was the best I could muster. I didn't know what his father had told him, what it meant. I did know I was with a starving man who had stopped looking in the mirror years before.

"Sure."

"Mahmed, go home." I couldn't break his heart. "The train."

"I am the train," he said, and he hooked me into his taxi.

Mahmed wept. He pulled over so he could cry, finally letting me take the wheel. He hadn't known Emma, but her death was the shape of a secret place in his heart, and he was unlocked. He waved his hands at me as if I were still talking, trying too late to block the news. At the hospital he wouldn't leave the passenger seat, his head pressed into the dashboard.

Kleiner met me, his calico face bowed, hand extended. No longer the scared boxer, he had become the penitent diplomat. "I wish I could explain."

"Shut up," I said by accident, meaning to comfort him.

"I called a funeral director. The hospital wants to handle the cost." We were walking fast to the room where Emma rested, as if she would get away. It was a ridiculous pace and I stopped dead, Kleiner five steps in front before he realized. "If you don't mind, I could arrange something at Saint Timothy's. We have a special relationship."

"Do you think it's good," I asked the doctor, "for a hospital and a cemetery to have a special relationship?"

"Daniel."

"You had your chance. Now she's with me."

The hospital morgue was freezing after summer's blanket. My teeth chattered as they led me to a back table. "We need you to ID your wife, Mr. Rowan," a sterile stranger said.

"I was there when she died." I should have stayed in the cab with Mahmed.

"It's the law, Mr. Rowan."

"Don't call me that," thinking of my father. "My name is Daniel." I lifted a sheet to end the argument. Emma's face was dull white, her curls stiff. The skin was the color of escape, of surprise, something left behind suddenly, the lips a shocking purple. The scratch by her eye was still scabbed, the only sign of healing.

"Say yes, Daniel," Dr. Kleiner urged. "Nod your head." He wanted to spare me, but the longer I looked, the easier it was. Knowing Emma was gone, that this was her earthly design, the body took on an extra fascination. A mannequin of my wife. A perfect likeness. An artist's rendering, devoid of spirit, of personality. I wanted to be alone with the form, take the geometry in one last time. Wanted to open the eyes to see what was missing, so I could define what I had known with Emma. But it was asking vapor to harden, water to freeze for drinking. I stared long enough to be certain all traces were gone. So I could bury this fragment of who she had been, I had to make sure Emma had gotten out alive. "Thank you," I said to the body and to the doctors.

"Is this Emma Lauren Clough?"

"Not anymore," I said, and they led me away.

I had already called Saint Mary's Cemetery from the city. The proprietor had remembered me, the Rowans, Warren. His condolences came out with a professional texture, smooth and rehearsed, painful in their redundancy. Mahmed wanted to wait in the cab, but I told him to walk the grounds. The director didn't like the sight of such dark skin among his soft-gray tombs. "Don't worry, he's just visiting. We're not going to bury him."

He didn't like my tone, my clothes, or anything except my cash. Which he liked very much. He offered to sell me two plots, right next to Warren's. The area had been blocked off for the entire family, but we kept dying in reverse. Though I wanted Emma's memory close to my little brother, I knew my mother and Nina would succeed in digging her up at their next visit. I opted for a small plot under a sycamore about fifty yards away. He promised me a grave in six days. A thousand-dollar tip cut it to later that afternoon. I took Mahmed for a drive.

"I should have taken the train."

"I do not cry," he protested, starting up again. "There are so many dead."

"You've never been to the suburbs. We die faster out here. We just don't make as much noise."

"Where are your tears?"

I pointed to his face, thankful someone else was doing the work. "Thank you, my friend. You would have loved Emma." The sobs started again, and he didn't hide his grief.

I drove him around the neighborhood. By my junior high

school, the gym windows broken, parking lot empty. Past the
adjacent high school, where soccer players ran through the heat
with the orange ease of youth. On the sideline a coach tugged at his
encroaching waistline, sweated continents, yelled at the boys.
Angry at their speed, the joy of their feet, the rhythm, the rush.

Mahmed rolled down the window to look at my house as we
snuck by. "No one is inside," he said, both my parents' cars in the
driveway.

"No one."

"Where is Emma growing up?" He hadn't wiped his face, salt
streaks chalk down his cheeks.

"Far away," I answered, making a U-turn in front of her
house.

The sun had begun to nestle as we returned to the cemetery.
The gravediggers' job was done, a heap of dirt visible in the
distance. I ordered the stone, gave the epitaph, and headed out with
Mahmed to say good-bye. The wooden casket had already been
swallowed by the titanium outer coffin that would delay the inevitable. Mahmed faced the sun, its dying light pawing him through a
swath of branches. He spoke a prayer in his native tongue, then
hurried to the car. I could hear him wailing as he ran.

"I hope you're not mad. I wanted a place to visit. It's pretty
here, but you know that. Thank you for the gift. I know exactly
what to do with it." I spoke as though reading a list. The shadows,
the earth ignorant around me. I wanted the tree to scoop low and
listen. Or birds. Something. I didn't want to do this for myself.
"Emma?"

There was no rush of wind, no rustling of leaves or an owl's
salute. It was just me and my awkward eulogy. But she was there.
She gave me permission to be silent. Let me stand there till the sun
gave up and the dirt blew in circles, refusing to fall in. Then she
sent me home to do what I had to. Ten feet from the taxi, Mahmed
asleep at the wheel, I turned, a tiny tug on my ear. The gravedigger

was earning overtime, his outline defying the dark. I listened. The syncopation of shovel and soil, but that wasn't it. I covered my ears and then I could hear it. There were no words, but a series of notes that rhymed. It was a lullaby and a march. An opera and a violin solo. Chords formed in great chains, pulling each other forward, an impossible tune. As I returned to New York for the rest of my life, there was a song in my head.

55. Maria comes over the hill. Velcro sprints stone to stone, touching each for luck, leaping over flowers and bows. Maggie and John arrive together, her size and grace dwarfing John, who takes two steps to her one. Paul wears black glasses, using bangs as extra protection. He wears the only tie he owns, and a thrift-store overcoat. Nina keeps her mother's balance with a tender hand on elbow. Mother wears fur against the snowless sky. It is so blue it aches. Clouds have fled. The color is permanent. Slowly, then, back early from Dallas, comes Mr. Rowan. He is lost, following a compass of emotion he broke years ago. Today it points true.

Rookie brings his girlfriend. She is in tight pants, thin socks. She keeps her knees together to stay warm. Rookie knows he won't marry her, is sorry she's along. He wants to chase the little boy across the manicured lawn. Play tag, see his breath, break a sweat under his itchy cop sweater and his brand-new shave.

The van is not alone. There are four, and Chef organizes the contents. Broderick comes out behind the last wheel, helping his coworker up the grade as she fixes her bun. There are children and one man with a walker. New faces, some just along for the ride, but others with a reason to appear. Gratitude in their dignity, hope in their wallets.

Detective arrives last. He has a Bible, though he will not read from it. He also has his son. The boy follows, then catches up with his father, Detective Daniel Rowan Bell, Ninth Precinct, Homicide Division. He is strangely proud of the way everyone looks to his father, how they wait for him. Son's right eye is purple and gold. He seems to be winking. There are cuts on his ungloved hands, but he feels weak and a little scared. He pockets one hand, takes his Dad's sleeve with the other. Lets his father lead him over the hill.

There are many nods, half-hugs, but no words. The greetings will come. Now is the time for farewells. November is worn out. December's strong arm pins it to the edges. Cold sun pinches strangers close together. Trevor shivers on his mother's leg. Detective's son looks at his father, is sorry. They stand there in the bitter breeze waiting for the words to fall like snow.

Beside them is a recent burial. There are more flowers around the headstone than ever before, now that it's out from beneath the sycamore, the date of death blocked by irises and baby's breath. "Lauren," Nina says to herself, never having known Emma's middle name. Mrs. Rowan's knees lock so they won't give in.

Detective wants to sing. Wants to open his mouth and have Sophie's symphony swirl out and around them. To see Chef dance with Nina, watch Broderick wrestle Trevor, be able to hug his own son. When he opens up, all that exits is steam. They are freezing. They are silent. And no one moves. They stand as one over a grave.

"Daniel."

"Daniel."

"Daniel."

"Daniel."

"Daniel."

"Daniel."

"Daniel."

"Daniel." One by one they say it, waiting their turn, yearning for the chance.

"Daniel."

"Daniel."

"Daniel." Even the strangers know to say it, imagining his face, his joy, feeling the surge of the chorus.

"Daniel."

"Daniel," Detective's son says.

"Daniel," from Chef.

Out from behind Maria's coat, Trevor shouts, "Daniel," and they catch their breath.

"Daniel," Maria manages.

"Daniel," Nina and her mother say in unison.

"Daniel Patrick Rowan," Mr. Rowan grumbles, drawing stares. He looks up with the face of a boy forgotten. "My son," he explains, an old sadness buckling his expression.

The circle continues till only Detective remains. It is his name he's been hearing, his past that hovers over the grave, hoping there's enough room. "Daniel," Detective manages.

"Emma!" John shouts, his silver top poking in from behind Paul. There is a pause, but only long enough to prepare.

"Emma," they all say in rough unison.

They leave before the casket is lowered. Strangers all following Mr. Rowan back to his house for something to stem their hunger. There are no words, just the clicking of doors, the brush of hugs, hot tears, fallen faces.

Detective has his son go on ahead with the people from the shelter. He is alone at the top of the hill. He can see far down either side. His vision is clear. He will be home tonight. So will his son. Above him, no snow. He is alone with a corpse on the top of a hill.

"Daniel. You're alive."

56. The money was gone. I'd spent the last of Emma's stipend on a canned ham and a bottle of Bushmill's. My tenants were gone. Said good-bye to the last one as she tucked the ham under her arm. She muttered a warning and left as if fleeing. Without the strength to pour and aim, I lay down on my bed and held the whiskey to my lips, a baby bottle. The apartment, which had been temporary home to more than seven hundred people in the previous three years, was empty. The feeding had been done. I had stopped Mahmed's famine.

I had found them at the shelter. The refugees, driven from their homes on Christie Street and East Broadway. Strong arms from 205th and waitresses from Jamaica, Queens. Brown and white faces, all their eyes the shape of hunger. Slowly they came at first, unsure of my address, the strange idea. But the banquet changed their minds. Chicken on Thursdays, rice and beans Tuesday night. Tuna casserole, a personal favorite, every Monday night. We laughed and drank, bedrolls filling the front bedroom, sudden slumber parties, swapping stories, mostly true. I told them about Emma when I got too drunk to give a dam to my memories. Emma's will and my Milano's tips supported the program. Money easily, gladly spent. I called Mahmed several times before they disconnected the phone. He refused to come by. He didn't believe

I'd found his famine. He swore his body was strong. Come and tell stories, I pleaded, but he had nothing he wanted to tell.

Maria and Trevor came by a few times, helping with dinner, playing with the other kids. She never asked me where my love was. Just gave me a new sweater each Christmas and a kiss on the cheek. Thanked me for the apartment on Tenth, said her legs were strong, her back, her heart.

My landlady eased into her fifties, letting her hair relax into gray, her face relaxing with it. Sometimes she'd give half the rent back for groceries, toys for a little girl and her brother. Mondays she'd often join us. She loved my casserole, too.

In the three years since I'd opened my door, I had discovered countless things. The way a father hides his fear, that a mother's pride is an extra muscle, and the gratitude on an infant's face when the milk is sweet and on time. I remembered all these things, cherished them, a collection of wisdom for the years to come. But there was one thing I had forgotten to do, something I'd never been very good at. I had forgotten to eat.

The calendar said November 2, 1996. It was Friday, time to go to the shelter and pick up the new guests. But there was no more money. The bedrolls were gone, too, donated to a family of five who had to leave the city. I was alone, and all I could smell was the Bushmill's on my breath. I had missed my thirtieth birthday the day before. I was no longer young, and as I rolled onto my back, I realized I'd slid not only into thirty, but past desire. There was no flavor I could imagine, no texture to chew. I cooked every night, but I couldn't remember the last taste I'd taken. A long heat bubbled up. I took off my shirt.

My belly was a globe, hideous and lovely at once, a map of all the countries, states, cities I'd fed. Just below the breastbone the swelling began puffing out more than ten inches, shielding my ribs from the bad news. The belly button had popped out. An alarm I had ignored.

"Daniel." It was Emma. She hadn't called my name in years, but I recognized the silken tone, the calm urgency. She was in the room.

"Hey." I let my eyes scan the ceiling for any form. I couldn't guess at her appearance, but I knew by the slowing of my pulse that she'd come back to get me. There was more to do, I protested, but nothing to do it with. Everything was spent. It was time to turn in. I finished the bottle to clear my vision, floaters dashing across my horizon, the white ceiling crowding with hallucinations and ghosts.

Then, inches from my skin came the invitation. It arrived as a hook in my heart, curving me up off the bed like an archer's bow. I couldn't lift my hands to greet her, elbows hard into the mattress, empty bottle loud to the floor. She was taking us both back, me and the daughter she'd loaned me. It was demanding all of her spirit strength. She held me there till the pain was eclipsed by the moon of her face.

"Daniel," she promised, and I slipped through my skin into Emma's blur, leaving the hard shell behind. Proof of a life. Wondering if anyone would notice.

57. The bell is broken. Detective does not have a key. Through the rectangular glass peer four eyes, wife and son. It is another house, this one on Garfield. A temporary stop on their way to Manhattan. They take their time opening the door. Wife still doesn't quite believe. Detective can see the colors are migrating across his son's face, the other eye blackening, but still a light.

Maddy leads him in, son Benjamin on the periphery, not sure how to behave, used to running, closing doors. He feels blown open inside his chest, aches like December's first day. He goes into the living room, leaving his parents in the kitchen. He is close enough to listen, but his eyes won't let him look.

Detective is holding two small plastic bags. He keeps them at his side. Protection. Maddy eyes him like a suspect. She cools her hands on the Formica, is ready to pounce. She smells the ashes on him, wants to ask. It is the last flare of a burn he committed in a trash can outside the precinct house on Fifth Street. A lighter held to the edge of each file did the job. The investigation into the death of Daniel Patrick Rowan went up in flames on the Lower East Side of Manhattan. There are no suspects, no suspicion. For the first time in his career, Detective Daniel Rowan Bell knows exactly what happened. Maddy wonders if her husband started smoking. Kisses him to find out. "Beard."

"Like it?"

"Yes." They stay this close, her arms around him, his still at his side. The plastic bags. "Why?" she asks, hungry for an explanation, not for his prior departure, but for his unexpected return. He has no words, tries to show her with his face. He softens his furrows, strengthens his chin. His eyes are lifted. She can't see that high.

"I brought dinner," he tells her, setting the bags on the counter, holding enough for the three of them. One meal. "I hope it's enough." They look at each other, their only child peering in, and Daniel knows that it will be. The things that they need.